THE
EDGE
OF THE
WOODS

CEINWEN LANGLEY

FEED THE WRITER
— PRESS —

This book was written on Whadjuk Noongar country.

The author would like to acknowledge the traditional custodians of this land, and to pay her respects to Elders past, present and emerging.

Sovereignty was never ceded.

Always was, always will be, Aboriginal land.

Paperback ISBN # 978-0-9924740-9-6
eBook ISBN # 978-0-9924740-0-3

Cover and internal art by Maria Nguyen
Cover design by Ceinwen Langley
Formatting by Polgarus Studio
Publisher logo by Liam Ashurst

First published in 2014 by Feed the Writer Press.
Second edition published in 2020

For Mum and Dad,
who gave me their love of stories
and supported me when it grew
into a need to tell my own.

I barely remember my father.

I'm told he was a good, respectable man and that he had many friends. I know he was kind to me and Mama. I know he wore thick oval glasses and that his fingers were constantly bandaged from pricking himself with his sewing needles. I know he died from a watery cough when I was four years old, and I know his death meant the end of any hope of a comfortable life for us.

○

We were moved from our apartment above the shop into a tiny one-room house on the edge of the village the week after his funeral. Most widows were allowed to stay in their husband's houses until their sons or sons-in-law inherited them, but shops and the apartments above them belong to the village. We were lucky, really, that there was an empty house for us at all.

Mama did her best to make the downgrade seem like an improvement. *Now we can sleep in the same room every night and whisper to each other until we fall asleep,* she said. *Now we'll always be warm, because our beds are in the same room as the kitchen. Now our window overlooks the meadow, so we'll have the nicest view in the village.*

It was a simple life, but we were happy. At least, Mama never let me see that she wasn't. We fixed up the house as best we could with cheerful curtains and bunting and jars of wildflowers. We baked and played games in the morning and she gave me lessons and read to me in the afternoons. Sometimes we would go visiting in the village and I would play with the other children while she drank tea and gossiped with the wives of Father's former friends.

On my fifth birthday, as a treat, Mama set out a picnic in the centre of the meadow. The meadow began right behind our house and ran all the way down the hill to the woods, and for most of the year it made a brilliant rainbow of wildflowers. I had picked them from the side of our house many times, but this was the first time I had ever been allowed to run into the thick of them. As Mama laid out a crisp white cloth for us to sit on, she stressed that I was never to do so without her.

Thinking back, I can remember a sadness in Mama's face that I didn't understand as a child. We had come to the end of father's money, and she had spent the last of it on my special picnic. From that point on, she would have to find a job and earn her own money – shameful for a woman in our village, and shameful on the man who hadn't been able to provide for her. Father, however talented he had been at his trade, had died too young to save enough for us to live on without him.

Our picnic was set up in the very centre of the meadow, where the hill plateaus for a good twenty feet before sloping down to the trees below. Poppies, buttercups, daisies, snowdrops, cowslips, cornflowers and more danced around us on all sides. It reminded me of an image of the ocean from a book Mama had read me not long before. I told her that we were like a small white boat on the high seas, and she laughed and launched at me, pretending to be one of the pirates from the story.

I squealed and ran, diving from the safety of the white cloth into the rainbow waves. Mama chased after me, shouting and laughing. But as I charged for the slope, her tone changed.

'Emma, stop!' she shouted, sharper than I'd ever heard her before.

But the slope was too steep. I couldn't have stopped my little legs even if I'd wanted to. I crashed to the bottom, landing in a thick carpet of bluebells. In front of me was a single white tree, completely bare, and a little further beyond loomed the frontline of the woods.

'Mama!' I called, delighted by the change in flowers. They ran all the way into the woods and beyond. 'These are even more like the sea!' I picked a handful and held them close, breathing in the smell. Fresh and clean, clearing my head like the best kind of winter's morning.

But Mama had lost all interest in playing. She grabbed me by the wrist, pulled me to my feet and slapped me sharply across the cheek. It wasn't painful, but the shock made my eyes well.

'You never, ever go near the trees,' she said. Her voice was high and tight and her eyes were glistening. What I saw on her face wasn't anger, but fear. 'Not for anything. No matter who you're with, or what you see. Do you understand me?'

I nodded, tears spilling over. 'I didn't mean to.'

Mama's face softened. She pulled me close and kissed me on both wet cheeks. 'I know you didn't,' she soothed me, her voice soft and gentle again. 'I'm sorry I hit you. You scared me, that's all. The woods are too dangerous to play near.'

'Why?' I sniffed as she lifted me into her arms and carried me back up the hill.

'People disappear in them,' she told me, serious. 'Young people. Not very much older than you.'

I looked back to where the hill sloped down. The tops of the trees swayed gently in the breeze. They didn't look threatening, but Mama's words had given them a new sense of power. 'Why?'

'Nobody knows. Sometimes the older children get too close to the trees, and then days or weeks later they vanish.' She looked down at me, holding me so tight her fingers dug into my arms. 'I couldn't bear it if you ever disappeared.'

A shiver ran down my spine. 'What happens to them?'

She set me down on the white cloth and wiped her eyes. 'It might be monsters,' she said. Her tone had shifted. It was lighter, less serious. She was trying to distract me.

'What do they do?' I asked, too captivated to notice Mama's hands creeping around my back.

'They gobble you up!' she yelled in a monstrous voice, wriggling her fingers against my sides.

I squealed with fright, and then with laughter. The tickle

war raged on until we were both on our backs, out of breath and giggling.

Mama reached for the picnic basket and looked at me with a sly smile. 'What do you think about starting with dessert? Just this once?'

I bolted up with excitement. 'Can we?'

She drew two slices of cake frosted with lavender cream from the basket and set the largest in front of me.

I wolfed it down, so thrilled at the thought of eating a meal backwards that I didn't even protest when it was followed with a plate of meat and vegetables. 'Now this is dessert!' I laughed, scooping up a spoonful of boiled carrot. Everything tastes better when you call it dessert.

When we were done, Mama poured herself a cup of wine and a juice for me, letting me clink my cup against hers like a real grown up.

'Blessed birthday, Emma,' she said with a smile.

'Blessed birthday, Mama,' I replied, solemn and incorrect as I did my best to emulate her. She laughed and took a long drink of her wine.

We lay on our backs, my head against her belly, and took turn finding pictures in the clouds. Soon enough, between the feast, the warm sun and the gentle hum of the bees attending the meadow, we were both lulled to sleep.

○

I woke to a cool breeze and sat up, blinking and shivering. The sun had disappeared behind a thick layer of grey cloud, casting the meadow in shadow.

As I reached over to shake Mama awake, a spark of light caught my eye from between a nearby tangle of long grass and flower stalks. Forgetting Mama, I carefully picked my way towards it, trying to creep up on whatever it was.

The spark bobbed up into the air the moment I pounced, though I got a better look at it as I crashed down on empty air. It was a firefly. Sometimes Mama and I caught glimpses of them in the trees after dark, but I'd never seen one so close before, or so early in the day. I crowed with delight and tried to clap my hands around it, but it evaded me again.

I chased it round and round the picnic, calling out to Mama to wake up and look, but she didn't stir. It wasn't unusual. I'd learned from sharing a room with her that only a sharp shove or two could wake her before she was ready.

The firefly broke out of our merry loop and bounced over to the top of the slope. I skidded to a halt, remembering Mama's slap, but it bounced up and down, as if it was waiting for me. As if it wanted me to follow.

I looked back. Mama still hadn't moved.

Promising myself I would only go to the very edge of the hill, I crept towards the firefly with my hands outstretched. It hovered in place until my finger was a hair away, then skipped out over the drop.

I stamped my foot. 'Come back!' I ordered, digging my shoes into the earth and reaching out further.

Another firefly sprung up from the flowers at my feet and flew in fevered circles around my head and shoulders.

Startled, I flinched away and overbalanced, tumbling down, down, down the hill until I came to a halt in the bluebells.

Afraid of what Mama would do if she found me here again, I tried to stand up and immediately stumbled back down to my hands and knees. The world spun, and my stomach spun with it. Giving in, I rolled onto my back and stared up at the rumbling sky until everything was still again.

The fireflies reappeared above me. I held out my hand and one landed on an outstretched finger, as if it was rewarding me for playing along. I laughed as its scratchy little legs tickled my skin, then sat up and blew gently, sending it back into the air to join the other one.

All at once, I heard a sound so faint I couldn't tell if it had only just begun or if I'd only just noticed it.

Music.

Craning my head to listen, I caught snatches of a simple, cheerful tune. Before I knew what I was doing, I was on my feet, following the sound to the white tree.

A thrill ran through me as I touched the cool, smooth bark. I was afraid to be so near the woods, afraid of Mama yelling at me, but for some reason I couldn't turn away.

The music was much louder here, and my feet itched to dance. The fireflies flew past me, swirling around the trunk to settle on a little shape sitting in the roots on the other side. I shrank back in alarm as the shape moved, but the happy tune continued, and with it in my ear it was hard to be afraid of anything.

Braver than I'd ever been before, I inched around the tree and peered down until the shape made sense. It was a boy, about my age, playing a wooden flute.

Relieved, I crept closer and put a hand on his smooth, naked shoulder. His skin was warm, almost hot to the touch. 'Are you a monster?' I asked, my gaze glued to the delicate velvet horns curling out of his temples.

The boy flinched and dropped his flute, staring up at me with bright, startled eyes.

Mama shook me awake. The picnic basket was over her arm, and the sky above her was angry and dark, growling as the first drops of rain spattered down. 'Emma, we have to get inside!'

Blinking hard, I let her pull me to my feet and lead me up the hill. I twisted around, searching for a sign of the boy and the fireflies, listening for the music.

There was nothing.

Mama stopped and scooped me up, wrapping the picnic cloth around me to shield me from the rain. We reached the top of the hill and made it inside the house just as the sky opened.

Breathless, Mama dropped me on my bed and dried me off. I could see that she was speaking to me, smiling and pointing at the window as the rain hammered against it. But my head felt woolly and all of her words were muffled, like she was talking to me from behind a pane of glass.

'Emma?' Mama asked with a frown. 'Are you all right?'

I wanted to tell her about the sweet tune and the boy who

had played it, and to assure her there were no monsters in the wood, but with every second my throat grew thicker.

Without waiting for me to answer, Mama touched a hand to my forehead and pulled it away with shock. 'Lord, Emma, you're burning up!'

With the speed only a worried parent can muster, she had me in my nightclothes and tucked up in bed, a compress on my head and a steaming mug of tea on the windowsill. She stood over me, wringing her hands as I drifted into a troubled dream of half-heard whispers and circling fireflies.

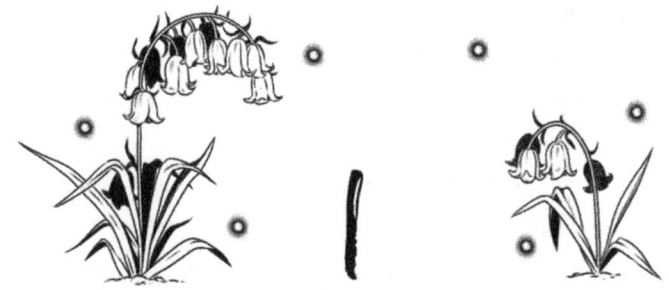

My eyes open half an hour before the roosters are due to crow.

I stretch and sit up, blinking in the morning light. Mama lies on her back on the other side of the room, mouth open and snoring. The sound is almost too loud to come from such a small person, but it doesn't bother me. That snorting, choking thunder is the sound of home.

Swinging my legs over the bed, I pad over to the pail beside the door. Mama has put the scrubbing brush on top of the soft cloth I prefer to clean myself with, probably hoping I'll finally give in and scrub myself raw like she does. Fat chance.

Bracing myself against the chill of the air and the water, I strip and wash myself quickly. I don't bother to keep quiet, letting the water swish and the bucket clang against the floorboards. Even if Mama could hear me over her snoring, it wouldn't wake her. She sleeps like the dead.

I'm pulling on my stockings when crowing fills the air. The snoring hiccups its way to a complete stop as Mama slowly wakes up – more from habit than anything the roosters could do.

It takes a few minutes for her to sit up, and another few to ease herself out of bed. She complains of the cold more often now, and grunts when she stands. I glance at her from the corner of my eye as I prepare breakfast. She's not old, but the years haven't been kind to her. The pretty face I remember has been hidden behind worry lines, her full cheeks worn away gaunt. She's lost too much weight, spent too much time on her knees scrubbing other people's floors.

'Breakfast, Mama,' I call when she's finished washing herself. She waves her hand at me, as she always does. She'll be ready when she's ready, the gesture says.

She eases herself down at the table, skin scoured to a bright, angry red, and we eat in a comfortable silence.

I finish my breakfast and scrub my teeth, leaving the plates for Mama to deal with. 'I'm going, Mama.' She stands and inspects me, same as she does every morning. My hair is neat, my clothes are spotless, my nails are bitten down to the quick. She nods her approval at everything but the latter, pursing her lips at my stubby nails but choosing not to say anything. Mama surrendered the war on my nail biting years ago.

'Speak to Andrew today,' she instructs me. 'Ask after his mother.'

'Yes, Mama,' I agree, trying not to sigh. Andrew seems about as interesting as dry toast.

She stands on her toes and kisses me on each cheek. I squat down to help her, trying not the let her notice that I'm doing it. I'm tall for a girl and she's short for a woman, and Mama doesn't like to be reminded of either.

'Blessed birthday, Emma,' she whispers.

'Thank you, Mama.'

'Seventeen,' she says with a shake of her head, more to herself than to me. She takes my face in her hands and pulls me down further to look at me, eyes searching every inch of my face. She does this every year, memorizing me at each stage of my life. I used to giggle and try to squirm away, but now I just pick a spot on the wall behind her head and stare awkwardly at it until she's done.

Mama finally releases me, the ritual over, and returns to the table.

'Be good,' she bids me, easing herself back into the chair.

○

The village has begun to stir to life as I walk down the high street. The air is thick with the smell of baking bread, masking the smell of the butcher further down the way. I wave to some of the shopkeepers through the window, receiving polite nods from the men and enthusiastic waves from their wives in return.

There are a few travelling traders in town, carts and stalls set up as normal around the village square. We see them often, peddling jewellery and spices and fabric, things we can't grow or make in the village. We usually see the same traders several times a year, with others passing through less often and some only once.

'A beautiful necklace for a beautiful neck,' one calls to me with an accent and a cheerful glint in his eye. I've never seen him before, but the necklaces on his stall are lovely. A silver chain dotted with glittering blue stones catches my eye.

'Will you charge less if it's my birthday?' I ask, baiting him. We both know he's only flattering me for the fun of it. The plain, rough cloth of my dress has already told him I can't afford anything he's selling.

'Of course, dear girl,' he jokes. 'Six for the price of five and a half.'

I laugh and keep moving, bidding him good morning.

'Joyous birthday,' he calls after me.

○

The schoolhouse is a long, simple building on the other side of the village. The yard is bare, a few wooden benches and a deteriorating rope swing hanging from a tree. Children don't go to school to play, the mayor tells us, but to learn to be adults.

The woods lie within distant sight of the schoolhouse, separated from it by the farms. Mostly the schoolyard smells like cow manure, but when the wind blows the right way, I sometimes get a hint of the crisp scent of bluebells and rich earth.

I'm usually the first person at school. The teachers are often late, tending to their families and helping their husbands before they head over. Our teachers are volunteers – or volunteered – from the ranks of the village wives. Other than a few solid instructions from the mayor regarding curriculum, they're not given any training. It's not an ideal system – most have no idea what they're doing, and even fewer have any interest in being there.

I let myself into the schoolhouse and begin preparing the room for class. The room is divided by screens: the girls take the left-hand side, and the boys the right. I ignore the boys' side of the room and arrange the girls' chairs in a large circle, setting out our books, cloth and thread.

'Emma, you're a treasure,' the teacher remarks as she and the other students begin to arrive. I smile modestly, ignoring a scowl from Nicole, another girl my age.

Behind her is a girl with hair bursting out of a half-braid. Mona. She good-naturedly rolls her eyes at me, then mouths '*Blessed birthday*,' from behind her book.

'*Thank you*,' I mouth back.

'Our Lord asks us to be gentle and patient,' the teacher begins. Her name is Eileen, but almost everyone refers to her as the butcher's wife, or 'Teacher,' if they're a student. Almost every adult in the village is referred to by their job, and for the women that means 'wife'.

Eileen the butcher's wife talks for a long while about what our Lord requires of us as future wives and mothers. We all know the speech by heart – she only has three approved of and supplied by the mayor. Today's is patience. Tomorrow's will be selflessness. The day after will be loyalty and purity. Then she'll start again. She delivers them in a dull monotone, bored by her own voice.

Staring out the window at the sad rope swing, I wonder idly what we'll be doing after the mandatory speech. As members of the older class, all of our lessons are skills we'll need to take care of our future husbands and children: cooking, cleaning, sewing, poise.

'Take up your cloth,' Eileen announces. 'We'll continue to work on our floral embroidery. Even the simplest gowns and aprons can be made more elegant with a good flower border.' I try not to notice the way she glances at my hem as she speaks.

'Not more carnations?' Mona says, exasperated. We're not supposed to speak up in class, but she doesn't pay as much attention to rules as the rest of us.

'Of course, Mona.' Eileen frowns. 'What other flowers could you want?'

'What about the wildflowers?' I suggest, hoping to take the focus off Mona. She gets into too much trouble already. 'The poppies are beautiful this time of year, and the bluebells have just come into bloom.'

Eileen's frown deepens. The other girls snap their heads towards me, mouths open.

I've definitely made them forget about Mona.

'We will be focusing on our carnations,' she says in a controlled voice.

I drop my gaze, nodding meekly and picking up my cloth.

○

'Were you trying to get yourself in trouble?' Mona asks, dropping onto the bench beside me and pulling an apple from her satchel. Today is our day to stay back and assist with the younger class. Every girl in her final year has to help in the

15

afternoons, though between the four of us we only have to do it every other day. On her days off, Mona works in the orchards just outside the village.

'Were you?' I retort, biting into a stale cheese sandwich.

She grins. 'Always.' She pulls a second apple from her satchel and hands it to me. I trade her the other half of my sandwich. It's a ritual so old we don't even acknowledge it.

'Do you think she'll tell the mayor?'

'No. She'll tell the tailor's wife and *she'll* tell the mayor.' The teachers are notorious gossips, and everyone knows they make weekly reports to the mayor. 'But you didn't say anything too bad. Your fondness for bluebells isn't exactly a well-kept secret.' She pulls something from her satchel and hands it to me. 'Here. Blessed birthday.'

'Oh!' I examine it. It's a little cloth bag with a blue and green thing embroidered on the front. 'What is it?'

Mona pretends to be insulted. 'It's a bluebell!'

I squint, and I can sort of make it out. 'Ah.' I smile at her, slipping the strap over my head. 'It's beautiful.'

She laughs. 'It's terrible. I'm sorry. But I made the bag as well.'

The bag is well made, with blue ribbon braided into the strap, but Mona's always had trouble with the more decorative stitches. Her satchel has three white and yellow blobs in the corner, which are meant to be daisies. 'Thanks, Mona. It's my favourite present.'

Well aware that it's my only present, she laughs again. 'No problem.' She flicks a stray curl of hair away from her face. 'I hope Eileen at least lets us branch out into stitching initials tomorrow. If I have to spend another morning bent over a carnation, I'm going to stick my needle in her eye.'

'Maybe we should let one of the other girls ask her.'

'Maybe.'

As if on cue, Eileen exits the schoolhouse. She nods at us politely. 'Good afternoon, girls,' she says, perfectly pleasant.

'Good afternoon, Teacher,' we echo.

'I bet she doesn't even know how to sew anything else,' Mona whispers when she's gone. 'The mayor's banned everything but carnations from her brain.'

I chuckle and look around warily out of habit. The mayor has the final say on everything in the village. Nobody knows what would happen if someone was caught speaking badly of him, and I don't want to be the one to find out.

The boys' class begins to filter out, laughing and shoving each other as they go. 'Oh no,' I groan. 'I'm supposed to talk to one of them today.'

'Which one? Andrew?'

'Mm.'

She rolls her eyes. 'Come on, then.' Putting aside my food, I follow her to stand beside the path from the schoolhouse door.

The oldest boys come last. There are only two of them our age, and though we all used to play together as children, we've barely spoken in the years since. They nod at us, and I half curtsey back at them. Mona only curtseys when adults are watching.

'Andrew,' Mona calls bluntly. 'Did you know it's Emma's birthday?'

Andrew clears his throat. 'Oh, um. No, I didn't. Blessed birthday.'

'Thank you.' I say, nervously eyeing the broad boy lingering beside him. Samuel. I hadn't expected him to stay. Having an audience throws me. 'How… how is your mother?'

Andrew toes the dirt, looking cornered. 'She's…' he searches for the word.

'Well?' suggests Samuel.

'Yes. She's well. Thank you.'

I smile politely. Obligation to Mama fulfilled, I can't think of a single other thing to say to him.

Andrew takes the opportunity to bow again and make his excuses. He all but runs away, leaving Mona and I alone with the mayor's son.

I look at Samuel expectantly, waiting for him to take his leave.

'Did your mother give you anything special?' he asks instead.

I study his face, trying to work out whether he's making fun of me. Everyone knows Mama and I are poor. 'Yes,' I lie curtly.

'So did I.' Mona takes the corner of my cloth back and holds it up. 'Don't you think it suits her?'

Samuel squints at the bag. 'What is that?'

'It's a flower,' I say defensively, even though I'd had the same reaction.

'Ah. So it is.'

'It's a bluebell, actually. They're her favourite,' Mona tells him, and I resist the urge to smack her.

'Unusual choice,' he remarks, glancing at the woods far behind us.

'I like the colour,' I mutter, embarrassed.

One of the younger girls arrives, pausing uncertainly at the sight of Samuel. Samuel notices her and gives her an apologetic bow. She giggles. He turns back to us and bows again. 'I'll let you finish your lunch. Blessed birthday, Emma.'

'Good afternoon,' Mona calls after him.

I shake my head at her as he leaves. 'What were you doing?'

'Helping.'

'With what?'

She snorts and bites into her apple. 'Nothing.'

○

Mona and I walk to the high street together after class, lingering in the square before we part ways. She lives on the other side of the village to me, on the Strangers Green – the only place strangers have been allowed to settle.

'Are you going to talk to Andrew again tomorrow?' she asks, teasing. 'You did so well at it today.'

I groan in response.

She snorts. 'You'll never get married with that attitude.'

'Can't I just marry you?' I ask. 'You can work in the orchard, and I can clean the shack and cook. Or you can move in with me and Mama.'

'How about this,' she says, straight-faced. 'If Andrew doesn't ask you, I will. And then we can both watch the mayor's head catch fire.'

I laugh and look at the rosy pink sky. 'I have to get my errands done,' I sigh. 'I'll see you in the morning.'

'I'll make a list of chores you can do once you move in,' she jokes.

I watch her cross the square alone, walking in a straight, resolute line as the other villagers give her a wide berth. They might not say it openly, but almost everyone in the village makes it clear how little they like or trust Strangers, even though the first Strangers arrived here long before Mama was born.

The fact that Mona is on course to finish her final year of school is a testament to her strength. She's put up with years of being targeted by teachers and ignored by the other girls, resisted a decade of being encouraged to give up. She's my hero, though she'd laugh if I ever told her so.

She looks back as she turns down a lane, raising her hand in a wave when she sees I'm still standing here. I return it and, tugging her wonderful, ugly bag further up my shoulder, I turn and make my way towards the butcher's shop.

●

The butcher has set aside a small chunk of salted beef for me, the baker a hard-crusted loaf. I thank them both, paying them with a few of the coins Mama left out for me. There's enough left over for a few vegetables, some crumbly cheese, a bottle of juice and a quarter of a chicken. It's not much, but we've had enough practice to know how to make it last.

Night has fully fallen by the time I get home. Mama is waiting for me and, despite her aching bones, she has a steaming cup of chocolate waiting for me on the table. She must have kept a little money to herself to surprise me with. It's too expensive to include in our weekly budget.

'Oh, Mama!' I kiss her in thanks and take a long sip. The cup stays in my hand as I prepare dinner, and it's finished all too soon.

'Did you have a nice birthday?' she asks as I set beef and toasted bread down in front of her.

I nod, lifting up my new bag for her to see. 'Mona made me this.'

Mama grimaces at the tangle of blue and green ribbon on the front. 'Well. You can always fix it.'

'I like it,' I say defensively.

'Did you speak to Andrew?' Mama asks as she tucks in.

'Yes, but I don't think I did very well. He ran away.'

Mama shrugs, unperturbed. 'Men always do that. Speak to him again tomorrow.'

'What about? We've already covered his mother. She's fine, by the way.'

'Emma,' Mama says with a weary sigh. 'The proposals will come in just a few months. You need to fight for one.'

'I know that,' I say. 'I just don't know how to talk to boys. It's so awkward.'

'It's the easiest thing in the world. You don't need to be clever or interesting. Just smile and let him talk about himself until he gets used to you.'

'Romantic.'

'That's marriage,' she says flatly. 'Or would you rather the alternative?'

'No,' I mumble. Unmarried women are as much of a horror story to the girls of the village as the woods are. Every girl has until the age of eighteen to find a husband. If she fails, she's cast out and left to fend for herself as a servant – or as a beggar, if there's no work to be found.

There aren't many unmarried women left in the village. Most choose to leave, either by the road to attempt to start a new life as a Stranger in another town or village, or they go into the woods and are never seen again. The few who remain here are shunned, walking through the village with their gazes fixed permanently to the ground.

'Andrew is a good boy,' Mama assures me. 'He'll inherit a modest house and a modest living. It's all we need. And you're much more agreeable than that awful Nicole. He'll have to choose you.'

I nod, resigning myself to trying again. I take a big bite of the beef and have to chew hard to get it to go down. If I marry Andrew, at least we'll be able to afford the better cuts. Maybe even get it fresh.

'Samuel asked after you today,' Mama says, almost as an afterthought, but I can see she's watching me closely.

I raise my eyebrows in surprise. 'What?'

'Pardon, Emma. Not what.'

'*Pardon*,' I correct myself.

'As I was leaving in the afternoon,' she says. Mama cleans

the mayor's house three times a week. Cleaning for widowers is where all of our money comes from. 'He asked if you were well.'

'But he'd only just seen me,' I say, confused.

Mama's mouth forms a line. 'You spoke to him?

'At lunchtime,' I explain. 'He stayed for a few minutes after Andrew left, but Mona did most of the talking.' Mama doesn't look impressed. I'm not sure why. 'He was just being polite.'

She leans back in her chair, chewing thoughtfully. 'He's never spoken to you before?'

'Only to say hello, just like everyone else does.'

Her face relaxes a little. 'Well, all right then.'

'What's wrong, Mama?'

'Nothing. But if he talks to you again, be polite and quiet and let Mona chase him off. The mayor's already decided to marry him to the doctor's daughter. The last thing you need is for him to start sniffing around you instead.'

I chuckle at the idea that the mayor's son would ever *sniff* around me. 'Yes, Mama.'

She pats my hand. 'Good girl.'

○

Mama is already fast asleep by the time I've cleaned the plates and tidied the kitchen. I cover a yawn, picking up the heavy pail of brown water and emptying it outside at the top of the meadow. I like the sound the water makes as it gushes down the hill, slowing to a trickle among the tangle of flower stalks.

After giving the pail a quick scrub, I head back into the village to make use of the well. A few of the younger boys from school do the same, and I keep my eyes downcast as I wait my turn. Collecting water is a man's job. That Mama and I have to do it for ourselves is just another mark of shame against us.

A happy little tune comes into my mind as I carry the heavy pail home, careful not to let the water slosh out. It makes me think of fireflies and blue skies and dancing barefoot in a field of bluebells.

Stopping outside the house, I leave the pail by the door and take the few steps to the top of the meadow.

It's hard to see them in the moonlight, but the tops of the trees stretch out below me, black and rustling. By day the woods look like they go forever, and maybe they do. Standing here, watching the faint twinkle of fireflies between the leaves, it's much easier to believe the stories about them.

A memory bubbles up of a dream I had once, a long time ago, of two fireflies bouncing in the sun.

Realising I've been humming the tune out loud, I shake my head and retreat indoors. Placing the pail in its spot by the stove, I change into my nightclothes and lay out a fresh dress for tomorrow.

But as I blow out the candle and climb into bed, my mind is on a strange little boy playing a wooden flute in a sweet sea of blue.

2

Nicole has begun seeking out Andrew. She hovers by the school gate after almost every class now, waiting to ambush him. It's forcing me to get creative.

'Lucky lad,' I overhear the baker chuckle to a customer on my way home from school. But Andrew doesn't act like he's lucky. He seems annoyed, as though Nicole and I fighting for a chance at a comfortable life is somehow taxing for him.

I don't let his attitude stop me, even though some of the adults – loudly and publicly – think I have an uphill battle ahead of me.

I disagree.

Nicole doesn't have that much more money than I do. Certainly not enough to make a difference. Neither of us is any prettier than the other, and even though I'm tall, gangly Andrew is still taller.

The only real advantage Nicole has over me is that she has a father to talk to his, though I'd be reckless to discount it. But I'm better than she is at everything we're taught in class. I have better manners, better posture, a better relationship with our teachers and all of the shopkeepers. That has to count for more than having a living father. It has to.

○

My attempts to engage Andrew in any sort of conversation haven't improved.

A few days after my birthday, I manage to corner him on the way to school.

'How is your father, Andrew?' I ask, pasting on my most enthusiastic face.

'He's the same,' he answers, as though he's confused by the question. 'He's always the same.'

Two days after that, I follow him into the sweet shop. 'How are your brother and sisters?' I ask, pretending to be able to afford peppermint humbugs.

His jaw tightens. Apparently it takes all of his patience to respond. 'Don't you see two of them every other afternoon?'

I feel my own jaw clench. Of course I do. That clearly isn't the point.

I bump into him the next day in the bakery, but he looks so irritated I let him go with nothing but a strained, 'Hello.' He's so relieved I wonder if I'd have better luck promising to leave him alone until after the wedding. Thinking back, he'd never been that friendly even when we were children.

'I'm not any good at this,' I complain to Mona, picking at my sandwich. 'He hates me.'

'That doesn't mean anything,' she says, ribbon between her teeth as she re-braids her hair. 'Andrew hates pretty much everyone.'

I look at Nicole waiting for him by the fence. Unaware anyone's watching her, her expression is somewhere between bored and annoyed. She clearly hasn't made any progress with Andrew either. 'I suppose that's true.'

'You've just got to keep trying,' she advises, smoothing her braid down. A curl has already bounced free to rest above her eyebrow. 'You'll wear him down eventually.'

'How? I've already run out of family members to ask about.'

She smirks at me. 'Just start back at his mother. It's been a week and a half. *Something* must have happened to her.'

○

I track Andrew down the following day, waiting for him in the square. 'Andrew!' I call, a little too desperately.

He approaches warily, too polite to ignore me but clearly unimpressed. 'My family is well,' he says quickly. 'All of them.' Someone else could have said it kindly, or playfully. Not Andrew.

'Oh, good.' He's on the very verge of saying good afternoon and leaving. I try a different tack, saying the first thing I think of. 'Are you working on the farms today?'

He nods, eyeing the high street behind me. Probably planning his escape.

Racking my brain for anything I know about the farms, I think of the paddocks behind the schoolhouse, dotted with miserable, moaning cows. 'Do you work with the cows?' I ask, cringing at myself.

He seems surprised by the question. 'I do. Do you like cows?'

I've never thought about a cow for longer than four seconds in my entire life. 'Of course,' I lie. 'They're lovely. What do you do with them?'

'Milking, mostly,' he shrugs. 'It's all they're really supposed to let us do until we come of age.' He brightens. 'But they birthed a calf the other week. I got to help.'

I'm not sure how to react to this. I immediately imagine Andrew up to his armpit in a cow's rear end. 'My goodness,' I say, hoping he'll mistake my expression for one of awe.

Thankfully, he does, and begins describing the birth of the calf in excruciating detail.

Behind him, Samuel passes with Dominick, a boy a year or so younger than us. I overhear Dominick saying something awful about one of the girls his age and notice that Samuel looks as trapped as I feel. He meets my eye and makes a face. I almost smile, but remember what Mama said and force my attention back to Andrew.

◉

Mama is thrilled with me when I tell her about the cow birthing conversation, which continued almost until he was due on the farm.

'We'll bake him something soon,' she decides, rubbing her hands together gleefully. 'You need to show his parents what a wonderful wife you'd make. That other girl hasn't done that yet, has she?'

Mama knows Nicole's name, but she's never been a good sport. 'Not that I know of.'

'Then we'll beat her to it.' She grabs my hand and pulls me into a silly little dance. 'Oh, Emma. You'll have such a nice life.' It's hard not to get swept up in her excitement, and we dance until she complains of her joints hurting again.

○

The good mood stays with me the next morning.

'What is that?' Mona asks me, settling in her seat as I lay out the books. She occasionally arrives early to sit with me, but never helps.

'What was what?' I ask.

She pushes a stray curl away from her face. 'That song. You were just humming it.'

'I didn't even notice.'

'It sounded happy. Did Andrew propose?'

I laugh. 'He talked about putting his hand inside a cow.'

She screws up her face. 'Lord. The boy needs even more help than you do.'

A voice makes us both jump. 'Good morning,' Samuel says, standing beside the room divider. I don't remember him ever being early for school before.

'Boys aren't supposed to come over this side,' Mona points out innocently. 'Did you need something?'

'Just wanted to be polite.'

'Anything else?'

Samuel glances at me. 'No. That was it.'

'Bye then,' she dismisses him, turning back to me and raising an eyebrow. I shrug and return to my seat as the other students begin to arrive. Andrew arrives last, peering over the divider and greeting me with a nod. I give him a brief smile in return. It's not much, but it's something.

Returning my attention to the class, I find Nicole glaring at me, knuckles white around her book. The fury in her face takes me aback. I swallow hard, not sure what to do.

The doctor's daughter, Roslyn, nudges her as Eileen finally arrives. Nicole drops her gaze, but I still feel the heat of it. I glance at Mona to see if she witnessed it, but she's doodling in her book of the Lord.

○

I don't try to speak to Andrew at lunch. I can't think of anything new to ask him about himself, and even if I could, I don't think I could smile and nod through another farming lecture.

As Mona and I trade our share of lunch, I wonder why he hasn't bothered asking me any questions about myself in return. He hasn't even asked after Mama. He's getting married too, shouldn't he put in *some* effort to get to know me or Nicole?

'Look out,' Mona says with a smirk as the boys' class is released. Andrew nods at me again and, maybe because I'm clearly leaving him alone today, rewards me with a 'Good Afternoon.'

Behind him, Samuel nods as well. 'Goodbye, Emma, Mona.' I'm glad that he includes Mona.

'Goodbye,' I allow. He smiles almost triumphantly, nods again and moves along.

Nicole waits predictably by the gate, and today Roslyn stands with her. She usually doesn't bother – nobody is challenging her for Samuel. He stops to talk to them both, but Andrew barely stays long enough to make his excuses.

'I wouldn't be surprised if that one decides not to marry either of you,' Mona remarks. 'I've heard that boys can.'

The thought hadn't even occurred to me. 'Of course they can,' I mutter darkly.

Samuel bows to Roslyn and Nicole and moves on. There's nothing else to look at in the bare schoolyard, so I watch them. It looks like the two girls are having an argument. 'What do you think that's about?'

Mona shrugs and focuses on her food, completely uninterested.

Whatever they're fighting about, Roslyn loses. Nicole turns and marches towards us. Roslyn throws her hands up and follows.

'Do you have any idea how ridiculous you look?' Nicole hisses at me.

'Pardon?' I ask, bewildered.

'Chasing Andrew all over the village! You're embarrassing yourself.'

Roslyn takes her arm, but Nicole shrugs her off.

'And you're not?' I raise my eyebrows, indicating the gate. 'You wait there every day and you still can't make him to

31

stand still long enough to talk to you.'

Nicole crosses her arms. 'That's different.'

'How?'

'Nicole,' Roslyn says warningly.

Nicole ignores her, her cheeks flushed with anger. 'Because he's not *for* you.'

'What's that supposed to mean?'

'You're practically unmarried already,' she spits. 'You've got no father, no brothers. You've never even lived in a real house. What sort of wife would you make?' She looks at Mona out the corner of her eye. 'Especially when you spend all your time with *them*.'

Perfect, prim Roslyn is mortified. 'Nicole!' she gasps.

'But at least *she* knows her place,' Nicole continues. 'You don't see *her* begging someone to marry her.'

'Well, you wouldn't,' Mona says dryly, somehow untroubled by Nicole's onslaught. 'I'm very subtle when I beg.'

But I'm not so noble. I stand up, livid. '*She* has a name,' I snap. 'Don't you dare look down at us. Having a father and a house with three rooms doesn't make you a better person than either of us. Everyone in the village likes me better than you, including Andrew. And I'll bet his parents will, too.'

Nicole looks as if she's been slapped, but she won't lose the chance to have the last word. 'People don't *like* you,' she snaps. 'They feel *sorry* for you. They've all been sniggering at your shrivelled up mother for years, and the only reason they're kind to you now is because they know you'll end up even worse than her.'

I open my mouth to retort, but my words catch painfully in my throat. Is it true? Do people laugh at Mama? Has everyone already written my future before I've even had the chance to fight for another path?

Nicole smiles coldly, knowing she's gotten under my skin. 'You might as well throw yourself into the woods and get it over with.'

My fists are clenched tight and trembling. I don't remember curling them. Mona covers one of them with her hand. 'I'd leave now if you don't want my foot up your backside,' she says to Nicole, her tone mild.

Nicole scowls at her, but wisely turns back to the gate. I glare at her as she goes.

Roslyn stays with us, good manners too deeply ingrained to just leave. 'I'm sorry,' she says. 'She's just... well. You know.'

'No,' I say flatly. 'I don't.'

Roslyn forces a smile and a curtsey. 'Anyway. Good afternoon.'

'Don't take it personally,' Mona assures me when she's gone. 'None of that was really about you.'

'What are you talking about?' I ask. 'How was that not personal?'

'She's just scared.'

'Are you actually taking Nicole's side? She insulted you too, you know.'

'Of course I'm not,' Mona says. 'I heard what she said. I've heard it more often than you.'

Chastened, I sit down and take a breath. 'What did you mean, then?' I ask once I've gathered my wits.

'Andrew paid attention to you today, in front of people, and then ignored her. That means she's losing, and you know what that means for her.'

'So?' I protest, still angry. 'You and I have nothing, and we've done all right. She's acting like living like us would be worse than dying.'

'Don't be stupid, Emma. Of course nobody wants to live like us. Not even you, or else you wouldn't be bothering with Andrew.'

'What about you, then?' I shoot back.

Her eyebrows furrow. 'I don't exactly have your options, do I?' she asks, a note of bitterness creeping into her voice.

The guilt hits me hard, and I regret saying anything. 'I'm sorry.'

She smiles, sweeping the hair from her face. The bitterness is gone, or maybe just hidden. 'Don't be.'

'I wish I didn't have to think about all this,' I sigh. 'Chasing boys and fighting other girls. Tell me what to do.'

'Practice your listening face,' she says sagely. 'You're not nearly as good a liar as you think you are.'

○

Nicole's words stay with me through the rest of the day, poisonous little barbs weaving through my every thought. Walking home through the square, I wonder how much of what she said was out of fear and how much was truth shared

34

in the heat of the moment. How many of the villagers I thought I was friendly with have been laughing at me behind my back? How much of their kindness has really been condescension?

I shouldn't be surprised. I know they do it to Mona and the other Strangers. I know the older wives gossip about Mama. But it's different, somehow, knowing it could be about me as well. I can feel angry for the others. Anger is useful. But I can only feel humiliated for myself.

Evening falls as I pass the meadow. On a whim, I stop and sit at the top of the hill. The poppies tickle my arms as I stare down over the flowers, gaze settling on the trees. The sound of rippling leaves and the gentle swaying of the treetops as they fade into the night calms me.

'Emma?' The front door creaks open and Mama sticks her head out. 'What are you doing out there?'

'Just thinking, Mama.'

She frowns at the meadow as I come inside but closes the door behind me without saying anything about it.

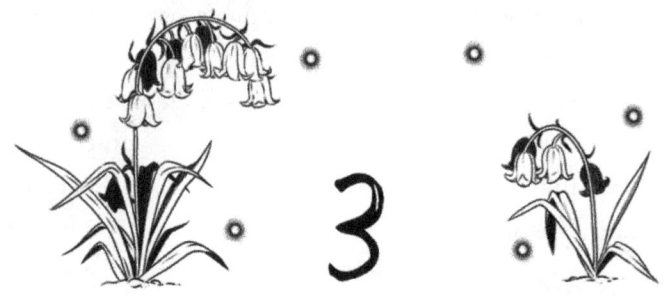

'We'll speak to Andrew after Deference,' Mama decides. 'You need to start putting yourself in front of his parents.'

'Mama?' I ask, opening the front door a crack to spy on the neighbours. They wander up the lane towards the high street dressed in their best Sunday whites. 'Don't you think...'

'Come away from there and get your stockings on,' she orders, pulling on her dress only to have it snag over her head. I move over to rescue her, tugging the thick wool over her shoulders. 'Hurry up,' she grumbles, without a word of thanks.

I always put my stockings on last, enjoying a few moments of having bare legs beneath my mustard coloured dress. Mama hates that I do it. Our Lord intended knees and ankles to be kept to ourselves, she insists. It's why He made them so ugly.

Picking a small bouquet of wildflowers from the top of the hill, we make our way to the high street and join the procession to the town hall. We stand out, as always. A speck of mustard and grey among the river of white dresses and crisp white trousers. There are some families with noticeably yellowed or faded whites, threads baring at the edges, but even they snicker at us. Old whites are better than none at all.

The seats in the hall are already filling up as we arrive. We lay our bouquet at the base of the podium and retreat to the back row of seats. We always sit here, making sure we're seen in attendance and then hiding ourselves from as many judgemental eyes as possible.

Deference isn't mandatory, but heavily encouraged. Anyone who isn't seen on any Sunday is the subject of gossip, every aspect of their lives suddenly under scrutiny in the light of their unfaithfulness. Only the Strangers are constant absentees, and as far as the others are concerned it proves everything everyone ever suspected about them.

Not that attending did them any favours, either. Mona and her grandmother came to every Deference until she was fifteen.

Beside me, Mama scans the hall for Andrew. Her roving squint is so obvious I'm glad nobody can see us.

'He's over there,' I mutter, indicating the middle of the hall. 'In front of Nicole.'

Mama grunts her disapproval. Nicole, seated between her younger sister and her mother in their dulling whites, has beaten us to it.

'I think we should wait for another day,' I whisper, tugging self-consciously at my dress. 'When we don't stand out so much. People will look…'

'Hisht,' Mama shushes me, as if she wasn't the one who started it. 'Pay attention.'

I sigh and look to the front of the hall, where Mayor Jones is taking the podium. It's hard to see the slight man from here, but when his honey voice fills every space in the hall without having to yell, it's easy to see why the village leans forward to hang on his every word.

Mayor Jones is the voice of the Lord in our village. He makes every major decision, every rule, and makes sure we live our lives according to our Lord's words.

He terrifies me. Even from the back of the hall, I feel as if he's staring straight at me as he lectures us on duty: a woman's duty to her husband and her father, a man's duty to his village. Everyone's duty to our Lord.

He's relentless and repetitive, threatening punishment and separation from our Lord if we fail. It feels like the whole hall holds its breath until, an hour later, he reaches a familiar conclusion: 'To turn our backs on even one of our Lord's teachings is to turn our back on our Lord. And they who fall into our Lord's shadow are lost.' Half the congregation murmurs it with him, the words rustling through the hall in hushed, fearful tones.

The mayor steps away from the podium and is replaced by Roslyn. Unaccompanied, she begins to sing in a high, clear voice. If some people are born blessed by our Lord, then Roslyn, it seems, is His favourite. The congregation relaxes under her song, a communal breath of release after the relentlessness of Mayor Jones' sermon.

A gentle babble fills the hall after Roslyn's voice fades as people stand and begin to mingle, chatting amiably with their friends and neighbours.

'Quickly, go,' Mama urges me, standing up.

'Thank you, Mama,' I breathe with relief, stepping into the aisle to leave. But Mama grips my sleeve and pulls me in the other direction, down the aisle to where Nicole's mother speaks to Andrew's. 'Mama, no,' I beg in a whisper. 'Please. Not while they're there. We'll look desperate.'

'This is your life, Emma,' Mama hisses back at me. 'Fight for it.'

I don't have time to retort before she nudges me forward, right between Andrew's mother and Nicole.

'Good afternoon, Elise,' Mama says brightly, completely ignoring Nicole and her family. Nicole's eyebrows shoot up so high I think they're going to disappear into her hair. 'Didn't the doctor's daughter sound wonderful today?'

'Yes,' Elise allows, not managing to cover her surprise. Mama hasn't approached anyone with pleasantries in years. 'She did. Sarah and I were just discussing that.'

'Hello, Grace,' Nicole's mother says shortly.

Mama barely looks at her. 'Sarah.'

I notice people glancing at us. Nicole sees them too, shooting me a superior look. At least Andrew has already wandered off to join his father and a group of men talking and laughing by the door.

'We're so sorry to bother you,' I jump in before Mama

can continue her small talk. She looks annoyed, but I keep going. 'I just wanted to ask you a question before we leave.'

'Yes?' Elise asks, recovering her composure. She even manages an encouraging smile. Nicole and her mother exchange a smug look. I'm being improper with my directness, and they expect it to get me nowhere.

I swallow my embarrassment and force a smile, eager to get this over with. 'I wondered if you'd like to have tea with Mama and I this week. Or whenever is most convenient for you.'

'Of course,' she agrees politely. Nicole and her mother exchange another look, and this one is more satisfying. 'Why don't I visit you at your house on Wednesday afternoon?' I hear Nicole snort at 'house'.

'That would be lovely,' I say with a curtsey. 'We'll leave you to your Sunday.'

I loop my arm through Mama's and practically drag her away. 'You were lucky,' she shakes her head at me. 'That's not how it's done.'

'People were looking,' I mutter. 'I'm sick of being laughed at.'

'Then get married,' she says. 'And pray he outlives you.'

◉

I spend every Sunday afternoon with Mona, meeting her in the square after Deference to look at beautiful things we can't afford on the traders' stalls. Today there's a leathery old woman selling roasted chestnuts, and I have just enough money to buy a small bag.

We follow the high street to the Strangers' Green. Taking a seat on a low stone wall near Mona's shack, we watch the only road out of the village, following it with our eyes to where it disappears into the woods. We keep hoping to catch sight of one of the traders coming or going, but we never do. They seem to leave only at dawn and arrive at dusk.

'Ezra told me about a tower that touches the sky,' Mona confesses dreamily, eyes on the road. 'It's made of rods of metal so thin it looks like it should fall over, but it never does.'

'He's lying,' I say decisively, holding a chestnut to my face and breathing in the rich smell. The old woman's used some sort of sweet herb on them. 'What would anyone use it for?'

'To see. He says there's a thousand steps to the top, and from there you can see the whole world.'

'Has he been to the top?'

'No,' she says with a chuckle. 'He says he's afraid of heights.'

On the other side of the road is a patch of land reserved for the traders to set up camp. Finished with their business for the day, they begin to light their cook fires. It's a signal to the Strangers, who drift across the road in family and friendship groups of twos and threes.

'He talked about the cities too,' she adds. 'Just like the silk maker and the piano tuner and that jewellery hawker with the funny beard. They must be real.'

I try to imagine a village a hundred times larger than ours, filled to the brim with people and sounds and smells. I shiver.

The imagined chaos is already too much for me. 'What do they do there?'

'They live. However they want to.'

I smile wistfully. 'Sounds nice.'

'Everyone who lives there comes from somewhere else,' Mona reports softly. 'So everyone's a Stranger, and everyone is friendly. There are houses for everyone, and jobs, and you can talk to anyone you like. And if you ever get tired of the city, you can just go back on the road.'

I feel a pang. She doesn't often sound so sad. 'Let's go, then.'

Mona scoffs. 'You'd never.'

'No,' I agree. 'But it does sound wonderful.'

A round of laughter erupts from the cook fires.

'Mona,' an older man with a long, greying braid calls out. 'There's meat tonight.'

Her eyes light up. 'Really?'

'You don't help cook; you don't help eat.'

'Coming, Papa!' Although they're not related, Papa Stone's been keeping a special eye on Mona since her grandmother's death.

The Strangers aren't allowed an official leader, but Papa Stone is practically it. He speaks to the farmers on behalf of the Strangers, trying for years to increase the quality of the food they're paid in, bargaining for a few extra coins per person for new clothes. Once he even went to the mayor's house to demand building supplies to fix up the shacks and build more. Though he's failed on every count, he never gives up.

'Wait a second,' Mona stops me as I stand up to leave. She disappears inside her shack for a moment and comes back with a small bag of raspberries.

'Mona!' I gasp as she hands them to me. Raspberries are expensive – there's no way she was given them. She holds a sly finger to her mouth, then waves as she runs across the road to join the others.

I leave the rest of the chestnuts on Mona's doorstep and turn for home, holding the bag of raspberries close.

○

'Mama,' I exclaim as I come through the door. 'Look!' I hold out the raspberries for her and her eyes crinkle with a wide smile.

'They're perfect,' she crows, taking the bag.

'Mona sent them over.'

'Bless that girl,' Mama holds one of the berries up to the light, giving it a gentle squeeze. 'We'll bake scones. You can take them to Andrew in the morning.'

My face drops. 'Andrew?'

'How often will we have this chance?' Mama asks impatiently. 'We won't impress his parents with a plain cake or an apple pie.'

'But we never get raspberries,' I complain.

'And neither do they. Quick, get to the bakery and beg me some soda before they close up.'

I reach for a raspberry but get my hand smacked away. 'They'll think we stole them,' I point out, but am ignored and directed firmly to the door.

The high street is almost deserted after nightfall. The bakery's windows are dark, the lights transferred upstairs to their apartment above the shop. I want to turn around and go home, but if I return empty handed I'll disappoint Mama. And Mama knows how to make her disappointment very loud.

I knock on the door, the sound echoing loudly around the empty street. It takes a long time for the baker to appear at the window. I think I see him sigh before he opens the door a crack.

'I'm sorry to bother you so late,' I say quickly, before he can shoo me away. 'Mama sent me for some soda. Just a little. It's an emergency.'

'A baking emergency?' he asks sceptically.

I nod lamely. 'And… and we can't pay,' I add, ashamed. The baker sighs again, but bids me to wait while he disappears back inside the shop.

He returns a moment later with a tiny pouch of baking soda. 'Tell your mother this is the last time,' he says, shaking his head.

'I will. Thank you.'

He bids me good evening and shuts the door. I wish his wife Caroline had come down instead. She teaches the boys in the afternoons, and she's always liked me. But women don't answer the door after dark.

I turn to head home, coming face to face with Samuel.

'What are you doing out so late?' he asks, before I have a

chance to. I hold up the pouch in answer. 'Strange time to be baking,' he observes.

I look behind him and see the downstairs light switch off in the tailors. 'Strange time for a fitting.'

He takes the lid off a long, thin box. Inside is a heavily embroidered scarf. 'Not for me.'

'Thank the Lord,' I say without thinking. The scarf is hideous.

He laughs and replaces the lid. It's a nice laugh, genuine and warm. I can't help but smile at it. 'Can I walk you home?'

I think of Mama's face if I turned up with any boy other than Andrew in tow. 'No, thank you.'

'You're not afraid to be out alone after dark?'

I shake my head. 'I have to do it all the time.'

'I suppose you would,' he acknowledges, then bows deeply. 'Well, I'll see you at school.'

This is where I'm supposed to curtsey, but instead I just nod. 'Good night, Samuel.'

'Walk safe, Emma,' he calls after me. And for some reason, it makes my cheeks feel warm.

○

Mama sends me out early the next morning with the scones carefully packed into a basket.

'Go straight to his house,' she instructs me at the door. 'Make sure you speak to his mother and tell her how much you're looking forward to tea. And then you thank Mona again.' She smiles, smug. 'There's no way they'll be able to match this.'

45

'Yes, Mama.'

She reaches up to kiss my cheeks, then hands me something. A raspberry. 'I couldn't resist,' she admits. I laugh and give her a hug goodbye, popping the raspberry in my mouth as she closes the door.

Wanting to make the best impression, I pick a handful of buttercups and daisies and bind them together with a long blade of grass, laying them across the top of the basket. The effect is quite pretty.

Andrew lives on my side of the village, and before I know it, I'm standing at his front door. Still, it takes me nearly a minute to force myself to knock.

His mother answers, thankfully, and smiles knowingly at the sight of me and my basket. 'Emma,' she says loudly. 'What a pleasant surprise.'

'Good morning, Elise,' I say formally, holding out the basket. It's easier to talk to her here, with nobody watching. 'Mama and I were baking yesterday, and we made too many.' It's a terrible lie, but Elise graciously plays along. 'They won't keep until our tea, so Mama thought you might like the extras.'

'Of course we would, thank you,' she takes the basket and peeks at the goods, her eyes widening. 'Lord, Emma, are those raspberries?'

'Yes, Ma'am.'

She takes a scone and smells it, sighing with happiness. 'I'm not even going to ask how you got these,' she laughs. 'Thank you.'

'It's no trouble,' I say with a curtsey. 'I should get to the schoolhouse. Mama and I are both looking forward to seeing you on Wednesday.'

'Wait a moment,' she says, holding up a hand to stop me. She looks back into the house, calling louder than she needs to. 'Andrew!' He appears after a moment, dressed but with his hair sticking out in all directions. 'Walk Emma to school, love.'

'But we'll be early,' he protests.

'You can stand to be early for once in your life,' she says pleasantly, but there's an underlying tone. She hands him a scone. 'Look what she's brought us.'

Andrew looks at the scone, then grudgingly gives in. 'Give me a second.'

'I'll wait out here,' I say, curtseying again at Elise. A triumphant little thrill runs up my spine.

Andrew reappears after a few minutes, hair tidied and munching on a scone. 'Come on, then,' he says, barely stopping for me. I trot a few steps to catch up and fall in beside him, but I don't bother speaking. The silence seems to throw him.

'Do you want to get married?' he asks, as we hit the square.

I'm surprised by the question, but it's clear it's not a proposal. 'To get married is to serve our Lord,' I say dutifully.

'But do you actually want to? To me?'

He seems genuine, though his eyes are fixed on the ground in front of him. I should lie, but somehow it seems different than pretending to care when he talks about the farms or forcing pleasantries.

'No,' I tell him. 'Not really.'

He rips the scone in half and offers me the end he hasn't chewed on. I want to snatch it and cram it into my mouth whole, but I resist and take it gracefully.

'What's this for?' I ask, trying to take dainty little bites.

He smiles, the first I've ever seen from him. 'I don't want to marry you, either.'

It should be funny, but the scone turns to sand in my mouth. 'Does that mean you want to marry Nicole?'

He makes a face. 'No.'

'But those are your options.'

'I know.'

'So what does that mean?' I ask unsteadily. 'You still have to choose one of us.'

He doesn't answer.

We arrive at the empty schoolhouse. I want to yell at him. But instead I keep my voice low. 'You know what happens to us if we don't marry,' I point out.

'I know,' he says. 'Don't worry, Father will choose one of you.'

His father. Which means however long he can stand to talk to me, however much his mother seems to like me, Nicole is still winning. Their fathers work on the farms together, drink at the pub together. All I have on my side are women, which might as well be nobody.

Nicole was right. Andrew was never meant for me.

'I just thought you should know that you don't have to waste your time on me,' Andrew says, as though he's doing me a favour. 'I'll go along with whatever he decides.'

'You're not even going to try?' I ask, furious. 'You're a *boy*. If you have a preference, he'll have to listen to you.'

'We should get in,' he says, ignoring me. 'Thanks for the scones.'

I chew on my lip, so angry I could scream. 'We expect the basket back when you're done with it,' I snap, parting ways with him at the room divider.

○

The day drags by. At lunch I escape and go to my favourite hiding place behind the schoolhouse. Nobody ever comes here. It's too close to the woods for most people, with nothing but a paddock and a couple of low-lying fences in the way. I stare at the trees and the rippling ocean of blue beneath them, but today even they don't calm me down.

Mona finds me after a few minutes. She sits beside me in the shade and waits for me to speak.

'Mama made me give the raspberries to Andrew's mother,' I tell her after a while.

'You're upset because of *that?*' she asks, dubious.

'Not entirely.' I bite my thumbnail and report what happened this morning, repeating my conversation with Andrew.

'Your mother was right, then,' Mona observes sensibly. 'You just have to focus on his father now, that's all. You'd have had to do it in the end anyway.'

'But he knows Nicole's father,' I remind her. 'They're friends.'

'But not *close* friends. You still have a chance,' Mona insists. 'He'll still eat the scones, and I can steal you some more good fruit. If Elise likes you, she'll talk about you to him. You think a man wants to live in a house where his wife and daughter-in-law don't get along? Just sew something nice for her until I can get near the blackberries, and then ask if he has any socks that need darning.'

'How do you know all this?' I ask with a grateful smile.

'You villagers are too predictable,' she says, rolling her eyes. 'You do the same things over and over again and act like you're the first people in the world to do it.'

'So how does this end, then?' I ask, playing along.

'He chooses you,' Mona says. 'And you have a good, boring life with a husband who never speaks to you.'

I laugh, but it sounds hollow even to my ears.

○

Walking home and running my errands, I try not to let myself give in to defeat. Mona's right, I would ultimately have had to win Andrew's father's approval in order to get a proposal anyway. I'd been counting on Andrew's endorsement, but that doesn't mean the fight is over. After all, he won't be putting Nicole's name forward either.

I just have to prove that I'm the better daughter-in-law. Starting with tea on Wednesday, where I'll need to get Elise to invite me over to dinner.

'Elise liked the scones,' I report, closing the door behind me. I decide not to tell Mama about what Andrew said. 'She let Andrew walk to school with me. People saw and everything.' I sort through my meagre bag of groceries. 'Do you want a cup of tea with dinner?'

Mama doesn't answer. Sitting solemnly at the table, staring at the wall, she hasn't heard a single word I've said.

'Mama?' I touch her shoulder. 'Is something wrong?'

'We've been invited to dinner,' she says dully. 'This Friday.'

I'm confused by her tone. 'Well, that's good, isn't it? The scones worked even better than you hoped.'

'Not by Elise and Bill,' she says. 'By the mayor.'

'What?' I ask, faint.

'Oh, Emma.' She sounds so tired. 'What have you done?'

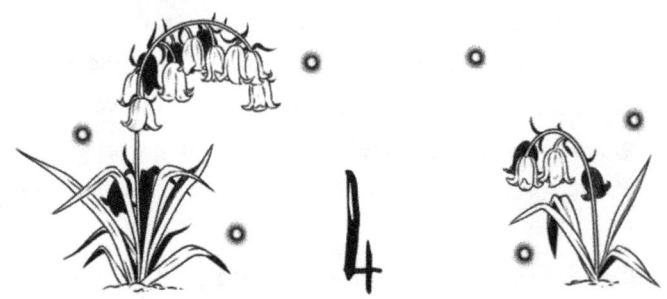

4

'Maybe there's a way to get him to take it back before anyone finds out,' Mama frets, wringing her hands. The floorboards creak underneath her as she circles the table for the hundredth time. 'But, no, one of those hateful women will still get wind of it and tell the whole village.'

'Can't we just say no?' I ask, watching Mama with concern. 'If you're so unhappy about going…'

'Don't be stupid, Emma,' Mama snaps, then looks sorry for it. 'The mayor asked me himself. What did you do to bring this on? Has Samuel spoken to you again?'

'Only last night. I bumped into him on the high street and he offered to walk me home. But I said no.'

'That'll do it,' she grumbles, shaking her head.

'Why are you so upset, Mama?' I ask. 'Isn't this a good thing? Samuel will be the next mayor. Their house is so big you could have a whole floor to yourself!'

'You can compete with that sour girl for an irrelevant labourer's boy, but you can't win the mayor's son from the doctor's daughter.'

'But the mayor agreed to dinner,' I point out.

Mama shakes her head again. 'He might be humouring Samuel for now, but he'll never approve of you, Emma. I'm sorry, but it's the way of things.' She sits down with a sigh. 'And I don't need a floor to myself. I just need to know you'll be taken care of.'

'Then I'll be so dull and rude they won't invite me again,' I suggest, wanting to make her feel better but not really sure how.

Mama looks at me like I've suggested running naked through the square. 'You can't,' she says sharply.

I throw up my hands. 'Tell me what you want me to do, then.'

She looks down at her hands for a long moment.

'Mama?' I ask, worried.

She lets out a long, slow breath. 'Forget Andrew,' she decides, her face setting with determination. 'We can't get out of this dinner unscathed. If you refuse, you'll offend the mayor, and Bill and Elise won't risk their son marrying someone who has done that. We'll go to this dinner, and we'll be perfect. If Samuel's taken a liking to you, you *might* have a chance.'

'But Elise is coming to tea on Wednesday.'

'We'll have to cancel.'

'Can't we just go to the dinner, give our apologies and go back to normal?'

Mama puts her hand on my cheek, smiling sadly. 'A girl in your situation doesn't get to court two boys. Like it or not, you're courting Samuel now.'

I frown. 'But he didn't even ask me.'

'They never do. Put the dinner on, we'll talk more after.'

I fill a pot with fresh water and set it on the stove. My hands are trembling so badly that it takes me three tries to light it. 'Mama?' I ask when I have the fire crackling.

'What is it?'

'Samuel seems like a nice person, doesn't he?'

Mama softens. 'Yes, Emma. He's a very nice young man. With very good taste.'

○

Mama has kept only a few of my father's things. Some for herself: his broken glasses, his shaving kit, a pair of his shoes that she keeps beside ours as though he's still coming home. Some for both of us: his book of the Lord, his sewing kit. And something for me: three reams of a lovely patterned blue-grey fabric I know she's saving for my wedding dress. But underneath it, which I haven't seen before, is a buttercup yellow fabric.

'Mama,' I protest as she pulls it from the chest beneath her bed. 'You could have sold this.'

'We sold enough to those people,' she says sourly. She has no real reason to dislike the current tailor and his wife, except that they're alive and in our old shop and father isn't. 'Besides, your father bought this especially for you.'

'Really?' I touch the corner. It feels beautiful, soft and light. The idea of him thinking of me so long ago makes me feel strange, and then guilty, when I think so rarely of him.

'It was his favourite colour,' Mama says quietly. I see her eyes shine with the threat of tears, but she blinks them away and holds the cloth up to my face. 'And it looks well with your skin tone. Come now, help me with it.' She unrolls the fabric and sets to work. 'If you want to be the next mayor's wife, you're going to have to prove you can look like one and sew like one. Even though you'll have every dress you'll ever own made by someone else, you'll still be expected to darn your husband and father-in-law's socks and embellish their handkerchiefs.'

'But you're doing most of the work,' I point out.

'Of course I am. I'm your mother.'

For all her aches and pains, she spends hours each night bent over it, carefully cutting and piecing it together. She makes all of my clothes and knows my measurements by heart, but for this dress she double checks everything.

'It has to be perfect,' she mutters to me as she pins the waist, making sure to flatter my figure while keeping almost every inch of it covered. The neck is high, the sleeves come down over my wrists, but the skirt doesn't quite reach the ground.

She looks up at me critically. 'Why are you so tall?' she asks, and I know she doesn't expect an answer. Thinking a moment, she shears a narrow strip from my wedding fabric and integrates it into the waist. The effect is pretty, and she decides to incorporate a little more into the sleeves.

The finished dress is the softest, sweetest thing I've ever

owned. But Mama isn't satisfied yet, and we stand together and stare at my reflection in the mirror.

'Something's missing,' she frets, staring me up and down. 'We can't overlook anything.'

I screw up my mouth and think of the mayor, and then it hits me. 'A carnation,' I suggest, gesturing to my heart. 'Right here.'

'Carnations!' She claps her hands around my neck and pulls me down to kiss my cheeks. 'Of course, you good, good girl.' She fishes a long piece of pink ribbon from the sewing kit as I slide out of the dress.

'Mama,' I ask, wanting to make an effort, 'can I do it?'

She's so pleased she kisses me again.

○

Word of my invitation spreads through the village quicker than even Mama anticipated. By Wednesday morning, it's clear the other students have heard the rumours, and when Samuel says good morning to me over the divider, they take it as confirmation. Andrew meets my eye across the schoolhouse with a surprisingly pleasant smile. At lunch, he makes a point of wishing me luck. I hadn't realised the thought of marrying me had been so undesirable, but it feels so genuine I find it hard to hold it against him and wish him the same.

Not everyone is so happy for me. I've made a point of sitting away from Roslyn and Nicole, afraid of another scene. While Roslyn has been unsettlingly calm, Nicole's glare has followed me everywhere.

I can't blame her. If all goes well and I marry Samuel, Nicole will be cast aside by Andrew's parents almost the second they realise that beautiful, talented Roslyn is available. It will be a huge step down for Roslyn, and a terrible life for Nicole.

I force myself not to care. I need this more than either of them.

○

Friday sees me too nervous to concentrate on anything. It feels like everyone in class is staring at me, though every time I check the only eyes on me are Mona's. She laughs at me as I accidentally stab my needle into my finger for the third time this morning.

At least someone's enjoying today.

The moment class ends, I grab her and drag her around the back of the schoolhouse before anyone has a chance to speak to me. I haven't been able to look at Samuel all day. If he speaks to me now, I might throw up on him.

'So you're excited for tonight, then,' Mona says wryly, rubbing her arm.

I lean against the schoolhouse, feeling ill. 'What am I going to do?'

'What do you mean?'

I stare across the paddock at the woods and put my aching finger to my lips. It's gone red from all the needle punctures. 'It's not going to work,' I say. My voice sounds small.

Mona looks like she's about to make a joke, but thinks

better of it and leans against the wall beside me. 'Yes it will,' she says encouragingly. 'It has to. You've spent enough time in that sad little house.'

'The mayor will hate me,' I insist, gnawing at my nail. 'He won't want me for a daughter-in-law.'

'He wouldn't have invited you if that was true. He has to at least be considering you, and that's all you need.'

'He'll know I'm scared of him.'

'He will if you keep sucking your finger like a baby,' she says, batting my finger from my mouth. 'For the rest of it, you know what to do. Just keep your eyes down and your back straight and make sure he knows you're willing to have at least a dozen children. You can cook and clean and sew, and you'll look beautiful in that dress. It'll be easy.'

'You think so?'

'Of course I do. He's just one man, Emma. What's scary about that?'

I venture a smile. She's right, as always.

'And once you've got Mayor Jones on your side,' she adds slyly, 'you can sneak off with Samuel and tell me how good he is at kissing.'

A mortified giggle escapes my lips. 'Mona!'

'What? If you're going to marry him, you'll have to kiss him *some* time. I think you should do it after dessert, so if it's terrible he'll still taste like cake.'

'Stop!' I laugh, clamping my hand over her mouth. She giggles through my palm and licks my hand.

'*Eurgh,*' I yelp, pulling my hand away and wiping the spit

on her neck. Soon we're squealing with laughter, licking our hands and trying to score hits on each other.

'Girls!' We've been so loud we've caught the attention of Mary, the tailor's wife.

We quickly wipe our hands on our skirts and stand straight, eyes lowered. 'Sorry, Teacher,' we mumble together as meekly as possible.

But Mary can't help herself. 'I expect this sort of thing from *you*,' she says to Mona, 'but dragging poor Emma into it.'

I see Mona stiffen. I feel terrible. I should have been more careful. 'Teacher, I was the one…' I begin, but Mona reaches out and pulls at the hair on my arm. The sharp pain sends me quiet.

'I'm sorry, Teacher,' she says submissively.

The tailor's wife only huffs. We follow her into the schoolhouse in silence.

○

'Good luck,' Mona whispers to me as we part ways at the high street. 'Tell me everything on Sunday.'

'I will. I promise.'

I head home, trying to focus on Mona's advice. Taking a deep breath, I slow down, gently fold my hands over my waist and fix my posture. Being taller than the other girls makes me slouch, and I can't slouch in front of the mayor.

As I practice looking calm and demure, I wonder what the inside of Samuel's house looks like. It's a two-storied, beautiful building standing behind a moat of pink and white carnations and immaculate green grass. I can't even fathom what two people could use all that space for. What I'd use it for.

My hands start to shake. I clench them tight around each other.

I can do this.

Mama practically pulls me through the door when I arrive, scrubbing brush in hand. 'Strip,' she orders.

'Mama,' I protest, backing away. 'I can't be bright red for dinner. I'll look strange.'

She purses her lips but doesn't drop the brush. To Mama, being scrubbed raw is the same as being beautiful. 'Nobody can laugh at you if you're clean,' she told me once, a long time ago. 'Nobody can judge you.'

'The mayor might think I have a bad constitution,' I try, desperate.

That strikes a note, and she grudgingly hands me the cloth. Nobody wants a sickly daughter-in-law. I sigh with relief and shed my clothes, pleasantly surprised to find that Mama has warmed up the water for me.

She helps me into the dress, buttoning me in and checking for any sign of imperfection: loose threads, a sliver of skin, an incomplete hem. But she's done my father proud. She stands on a chair behind me to braid my hair up demurely behind my head and then pinches my cheeks hard until they glow.

'Mama?' I ask as she checks herself over in our small mirror. She almost never bothers with it, but tonight she makes the effort for both our sakes.

'Yes?'

'Were you and my father happy together?'

She looks at me with surprise. I haven't asked her about him in years.

'Yes,' she says after a moment.

'Were you in love?'

She smiles, the ghost of a memory playing across her face. 'No,' she confesses. 'But we became good friends.' She takes my hands, still trembling, and strokes them. 'Emma,' she says seriously. 'Tonight has to go well. It *has* to.'

'I'm afraid of him,' I admit softly.

'I know,' she confesses. 'And you should be. But he's a man of principle, and your father was respected before he died. The mayor will remember that. If we follow his rules, agree with everything he says, he'll have no good reason to refuse you. Remember what you've been taught and leave the rest to me.'

I nod. She kisses me, for luck I think, and shepherds me out the door.

○

We're a novel sight for the other villagers. The dinner has already sent the gossips wild, and many of them just happen to be in the square when we pass through. I raise my chin as they whisper around us, assuring myself that we've given them no reason to criticise or pity us. I look nicer than I ever have before, and Mama has done her hair nicely and worn the few pieces of jewellery she kept for herself. She might be wearing the same grey dress she wears to Deference every week, but tonight she looks almost like the fine woman they all remember.

'Beautiful work,' Matthew the tailor says from his shop door, low enough that only Mama and I can hear. Mama doesn't give him the satisfaction of a response, but I see her glow with pride.

My stomach feels heavier with each step we take towards the mayor's house. I wish the walk were longer. I wish there wasn't so much pressure on my performance tonight. I wish I'd thought to ask Mona to come and see me in my dress. But before I can waste any more time on wishes, we reach the house and its cloying guard of carnations.

Mama only knocks twice before the white painted door swings open. I expect to see the mayor, or even Samuel, but that's naïve of me. A young woman opens the door, her eyes on our feet. She curtseys and steps aside, silently inviting us in.

Of course they have an unmarried woman to open their door for them.

●

They wait for us in the sitting room, and I have to force myself not to stare at the extravagance of the room. Everything is decorated in rich shades of burgundy and brown, with the occasional touch of a pale, dusty pink. There are paintings on every wall and trinkets on every available surface, but it's the sofa that catches my attention: fat and inviting, covered with squashy pink cushions. I've never seen anything in my life that looked so comfortable.

Afraid of giving myself away, I look discreetly to our host. This is the closest I've ever been to him.

Mayor Jones is shorter than I am, which makes me want to stoop. His moustache, peppered with a distinguished grey, is perfectly symmetrical. Everything about the mayor is polished, meticulously in place.

Glancing at him from beneath my eyelashes, I notice he's wearing the awful embroidered scarf Samuel showed me that night. I catch Samuel's eye over his father's shoulder, and he grins as if he knows exactly what I'm thinking. I look down to the floor, trying not to smile.

'Madam,' Mayor Jones politely greets Mama. 'And Miss Emma.' He bows to me, and I'm a little annoyed he didn't bow to Mama as well. 'What a lovely young lady you've grown into.'

'Thank you, sir,' I say softly, remembering to keep my eyes downcast and curtsey with my back straight. 'You have a beautiful home.' I don't think I was supposed to speak again, but complimenting the host's house is expected, and it would have been strange if Mama had said it. Of course she knows they have a beautiful home. She's the one who keeps it that way.

If he disapproves of my saying anything, he doesn't show it. 'Thank you. That's a very pretty dress. Your father made one very much like it for Samuel's mother, once, Lord keep her in His light.'

'Lord keep her in His light,' I repeat in chorus with Samuel and Mama. I look to Mama, not sure what else to say.

'She followed her father's pattern,' she says smoothly, giving me all of the credit. 'She worked very hard on it. She finished the carnation only last night.'

Mayor Jones looks impressed. 'Is that so?'

I nod modestly, hoping he's not going to make me prove it, though I don't even know what that would involve. I have a sudden, ridiculous image of me speed-darning socks at the dinner table.

'And do you like carnations?' he asks, glancing at the one on my chest. It's an innocent move, but enough to make me wish I'd put the carnation somewhere else. Like my shoulder. Or my forehead.

'I do, sir,' I lie. 'Very much.'

The mayor smirks, and I know I've been caught out. 'I've heard differently,' he says lightly.

I clasp my hands together tightly, resisting the urge to gnaw on my thumbnail. He's been asking about me. 'I also like bluebells,' I admit before he can trip me up. 'From afar, of course. They have the loveliest colour. I only wish the Lord had made blue carnations as well as pink and white.'

Mama hides an approving smile at my recovery. Mayor Jones nods thoughtfully and indicates for us to take a seat. 'Our Lord does work in mysterious ways,' he says.

Mama and I nod sagely as we sink into the plump sofa. It's every bit as comfortable as it looks. If my future didn't depend on making this marriage happen, this seat would be motivation enough.

'Samuel,' Mayor Jones says, looking to his son. He's been standing quietly out of the way. 'You may say hello.'

Samuel steps forward and kneels before me, taking my hand and kissing it. As he does, I feel him press something soft into my palm and close my fingers around it. 'Hello, Emma,' he says simply.

I hear myself gasp, surprised by the kiss and the mystery thing, and hope it makes me sound prim and proper. 'Hello, Samuel.'

'You avoided me at lunch today,' he observes. So, he did notice.

'Good,' Mayor Jones says before I can say anything. He pulls Samuel up and away from my hand. I return my closed fist to my lap. 'A man goes to school to learn, not to be distracted by pretty girls. I've often wondered if we shouldn't have a second schoolhouse, to keep the boys and girls apart more effectively.'

He launches into a diatribe about the value of keeping the sexes segregated and I begin to relax. The mayor is much less intimidating up close. More boring than scary. And Samuel…

The mayor turns his back to pour us some lemonade, giving me the opportunity to open my hand and look at the delicate thing inside.

A bluebell.

○

The young unmarried woman enters the room a short while later, calling us silently to dinner with a curtsey. I recognise her, though I haven't seen her around the village for some time. Jane, the tanner's daughter.

Samuel stands and offers me his elbow to escort me to the dining room. I glance at Mama and she nods. I can see the mayor is impressed by my level of obedience.

I awkwardly navigate my way out of the sofa and loop my arm through his, keeping the bluebell hidden inside my sleeve.

'Do you like it?' he whispers, careful not to let his father hear him as we walk through the house.

Too many questions rush to the front of my mind. Did he go into the woods to get it? When did he go? How did he do it with nobody seeing him? And, most importantly, *why?*

But I don't dare ask any of them with the mayor so close by. Instead, I meet his eyes and smile. My cheeks start to burn as he smiles back, just like they did the night I bumped into him in the high street. But this time, it doesn't feel strange at all.

●

Dinner consists of three courses, and I almost faint at the sight of each one. I've never seen so much food in my life – and all for only four people. It's a struggle to eat slowly and daintily when all I want to do is dig in with my hands. I wonder if Mama is having the same problem.

Mayor Jones speaks for most of the meal, with Samuel occasionally chiming in when prompted and Mama agreeing or complimenting him in the few moments he allows a silence to fall. I sneak a few glances at Samuel across the table, and he meets them each time with a shy, secret smile.

'Emma,' the mayor turns his attention to me as we wait for dessert. 'Do you have plans for next year?'

'I hope to continue on at the schoolhouse,' I say, which is true. 'The tailor says he'd like his wife to spend more time at home, so there may be a place for me.' Also true, though Mary is the one saying it, not the tailor. 'If selected by you, that is.'

Mayor Jones nods with approval. 'A fine position for a young woman. But of course, you must be married first.'

'Of course,' I smile bashfully, wanting to kick myself. Only married women can teach. 'There are many fine young men in the village.' Which we all know isn't true at all.

'Ah yes,' the mayor plays along. 'But Samuel must be the best candidate.'

I know I'm not supposed to answer that one. Instead, I lower my head and try to blush with embarrassment.

'Samuel is the finest young man we know,' Mama answers for me. 'Emma speaks very highly of him.'

'And he of her,' the mayor confides.

'Father!' Samuel protests. It's his turn to feign embarrassment. What fun we're having.

'I wonder if you would agree, Madam, to letting the two of them spend some time alone together. Chaperoned, of course.'

Mama doesn't even pretend to think about it. 'I'd be delighted. Emma, would you enjoy that?'

I smile gracefully in lieu of an answer.

Jane brings dessert out, a light cake heaped with

strawberries. I steal a glance at her. She's only a few years older than I am, but her face is already lined, her hands cracked and hard. If she ever looked me in the eye, I'm afraid of what I'd see.

Mayor Jones doesn't thank Jane as she sets a bowl in front of him, doesn't even deign to look at her. I bite the inside of my cheeks to keep myself from protesting. Is this how he treats Mama when she comes to work for him? Is this pleasant demeanor something he can switch on and off so easily?

'Then it's settled,' he announces after Jane has left the room again.

○

'There is one small matter that is yet to be discussed,' Mayor Jones says as we sit with cups of tea back in the sitting room.

Mama's eyes narrow minutely, a guarded look so subtle nobody but me would notice. I look questioningly to Samuel, but he's immersed in sugaring his tea.

'Yes, Mayor Jones?' Mama asks.

'To be a wife is a noble role, you yourself know this. But to be the wife of the mayor holds certain responsibilities. She has an image to maintain.'

I work to keep my expression carefully neutral, trying to anticipate what could possibly be wrong with my image other than my clothes or where I live.

'Quite,' Mama says without missing a beat. 'Your wife set such a wonderful example for us all, Lord keep her in His light.'

'Lord keep her in his light,' I mumble with Samuel and the mayor.

The mayor continues. 'To get to point of the matter, Madam, it has been noted that Emma keeps certain company.'

I look up, forgetting myself. 'What company?'

The mayor's lip twitches at my unsolicited question and answers Mama instead. 'She spends much of her time with… undesirable people.'

Mama looks at me nervously, urging me to keep quiet. She's understood something I haven't. 'You must forgive her, Mayor. She is young and sees the best in everyone.'

'An admirable trait,' the mayor says. 'And of course, we should all strive to be so patient. The Stranger girl is Emma's classmate, and I know they work together in the afternoons.' My jaw drops. He means Mona. Mama nudges her foot against my leg, warning me to stay silent. 'But to spend so much time together outside of the schoolhouse is unseemly, and she has been seen on numerous occasions at the Strangers' Green. Which, I remind you, is no place for decent folk, let alone a young woman.'

I'm furious. I grip the handle of my teacup so hard it shakes.

'Mona was born here,' Mama says cautiously. 'She has no family left. Emma has always felt a certain sympathy for her, given our own sad situation.'

'We're friends because we like each other, not because I feel sorry for her,' I say, unable to help myself.

The mayor speaks over me as if I'm not here. 'We know

this, and I can understand why Emma has forgotten herself. But there are other girls her age she'd be much better suited to spending time with. Roslyn the doctor's daughter is a *very* fine young woman.'

'She is,' Mama admits reluctantly. 'Very fine.'

I look at Samuel. His hands are tightly knit, his gaze firmly fixed on his right knee, which bounces up and down in quick, nervous succession.

'The fact is, dear Grace,' the Mayor continues, lowering his voice to a conspiratorial whisper, 'we don't know why these people came here, or what they want. They arrived and they built their little houses and had their children, and my father and grandfather let them because they were kind men. But we cannot keep allowing our kindness to be taken advantage of. No matter what we give them, they always want more. Our values and traditions are important, and the Strangers don't share them. We cannot allow them to corrupt our way of life.' It sounds like one of his Sunday sermons, only much less subtle. 'Don't you agree, Samuel?'

We all look at Samuel, startling him with the attention. I furrow my eyebrows, waiting for him to speak up in Mona's defense.

Samuel glances at me, then picks up his teacup. 'Yes, Father,' he says quietly, taking a tip.

My fist curls into an angry ball inside my sleeve, crushing the bluebell.

'You're right, of course,' Mama assures Mayor Jones. I'm so disgusted I can't look at her. 'Emma will limit the time she spends with Mona to the schoolhouse.'

The mayor smiles broadly. 'I knew we would come to an agreement.' He looks to me, eyes cold and triumphant. 'You're a very agreeable young woman, Emma.'

So this is the real Mayor Jones. The one Mama knew I'd never impress.

Well, the feeling's mutual.

○

I stay a few steps ahead of Mama as we walk home. Her joints always ache in the night air. I should be assisting her, but I'm too angry with her, too frustrated by the whole evening.

'Emma, wait,' she says finally.

Grudgingly, I stop and offer her my arm. 'Why did you say all that?' I ask. 'Why did you agree with him about Mona?'

'What else could I do?' she asks. 'Samuel's chosen you for the moment, but one word from his father and he's marrying Roslyn. You can't afford to displease him.'

'I can't give up Mona!' I insist. 'She's my best friend.'

'You'll make new friends.'

My mouth drops open. I can't believe she can be so cold. 'If I do what they want, she'll be all alone.'

'Better her than you,' Mama says, grim.

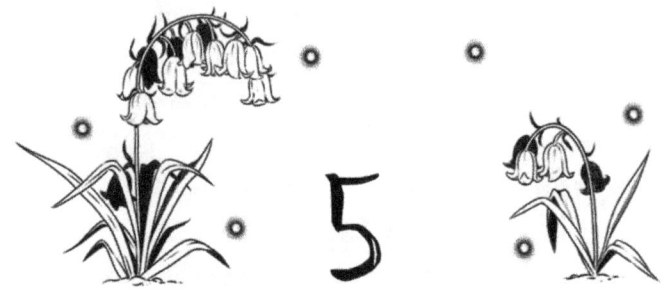

The sky is a deep velvet blue, filled with stars. I stand in the centre of the meadow, and even though it's been twelve years, I can almost see the outline of my birthday picnic in the long grass.

A light, summery breeze wraps around me, filling my nightdress and tangling my hair. I can hear the faintest whisper of a tune behind it. It's a beautiful melody, slow and sad. I cock my head and search for the source.

My feet seem to move of their own accord, taking me down the hill and into the bluebells. The music is louder here, leading me to the white tree. Fireflies drift sedately above the flowers, throwing long, flickering shadows up into its branches. The patterns are so mesmerizing it takes me a moment to see him, leaning against the trunk as if he were part of it.

A man.

No, a boy – almost a man – playing a wooden flute. His face is obscured by shadows, but in the moonlight I can see he's taller than anyone in the village and naked to the waist.

Though I blush with embarrassment to see a boy so undressed, he looks completely unbothered by it. His hair is as long as my own, tumbling freely over his shoulders. Something sprouts from either side of his head, branching and reaching for the sky. I stare at them, perplexed, and then it comes to me. This boy, this man, has horns.

The music stops, and his head turns towards me. I can't see his eyes, but I can feel them on me. Staring.

I take a nervous step backwards, suddenly acutely aware of all the stories and warnings about the woods.

'Are you a monster?' he asks.

○

I open my eyes. The house is dark, quiet but for Mama's snoring. I sit up and stare out the window. The heads of the wildflowers dance as the breeze whispers across them, leeched of all their colour in the bright moonlight. I search for a sign of the boy, but from here I can only see the edge of the plateau and the treetops stretching out below. There's not even any sign of the fireflies.

Settling back into bed and pulling the covers up to my chin, I give a disbelieving little laugh. It would appear that, for all these years, I've kept the strange little boy from my dream alive.

And now he's grown up.

○

Mama and I don't speak as we go about our Saturday chores. After I steadfastly ignored her every attempt to discuss dinner or Samuel or Mona, she finally gave up in a huff. Now she's ignoring me just as much as I am her.

She tends to our laundry with enough banging and muttering to let me know that she's annoyed by my attitude. The noise grates, but I refuse to let her get to me and focus on cleaning the house top to bottom.

I know that, to Mama, there's no question of what I should do: cut my ties with Mona and spend more time with Roslyn and the younger wives. Act more like a future mayor's wife would.

But I can't just give up a lifelong friendship for the chance to marry a boy I barely know. Surely she understands that. Surely Samuel does, too. He sought out a relationship with *me*. He knows Mona and I spend all our time together.

But he agreed with his father.

So what if he braved the woods to pick me a flower? So what if he has a beautiful house and more money and food than he knows what to do with? We haven't even really spoken yet, not properly. He might be dull. He might be cruel. He might have no sense of humour. Am I really supposed to abandon the only person who makes me laugh just so I'll never have to struggle?

Mama barks across the room at me, and I realise I've been scrubbing so viciously at the window the pane has started rattling.

I lower my arm, dropping the rag back in the pail and reach for a dry cloth. My eyes settle on the edge of the plateau. My thoughts turn to my dream. I smile, wondering if dreaming of the boy after so long means my mind is buckling under the pressure of Mayor Jones' demand. Maybe I'm going mad. I almost hope so.

Then I wouldn't have to decide anything.

○

Saturday slips into Sunday too quickly. I don't dream, I don't come to a decision. I *have* chewed two nails down to the quick, though, and received a sharp smack from Mama when she noticed.

We get ready for Deference in tense silence. Pulling on my stockings, I get the wild urge to throw them aside and run out the door barefoot. But Mama would have a heart attack, and the mayor certainly wouldn't want me then.

People whisper to each other as we make our way up the aisle to lay our flowers by the podium, though today it might not be about our coloured clothes. I'm eager to escape up the back and hide from them again, but Mama tugs on my arm before I can retreat and ushers me into a seat near the very front. She squeezes in beside me, letting me have the aisle.

I've never felt so exposed in my life.

The whispers finally die away, and all eyes turn away from me to the front as Mayor Jones takes the podium. I notice Samuel slipping into the aisle seat in the front row and wonder if he'll give long, passive aggressive sermons like his father when he takes his place as mayor.

Probably.

Mayor Jones begins. Today his topic is the importance of

tradition. It sounds like what he said after dinner, only worse, and somehow I feel it's for my benefit. Our traditions don't just involve keeping the Strangers as far out of our lives as possible, but reminding women of our place, our duties. He hints at penalties for defying tradition, describing the lives of unmarried women and Strangers without ever mentioning them by name.

He hasn't so much as glanced at me once during the entire sermon, but I feel as if he's warning me.

'To defy our Lord is to live separately to Him and all who follow Him,' the mayor cautions. 'There is no coincidence in the types of people who are punished. The righteous need not fear, for we only lose the wicked.'

I snort softly. According to the mayor, unmarried women and Strangers have brought their misfortunes on themselves.

'To turn our backs on even one of our Lord's teachings is to turn our back on our Lord,' I hear the mayor announce, bringing the sermon to a close.

Mama joins in with the chorus this time: 'And they who fall into our Lord's shadow are lost.'

Roslyn doesn't sing for us this time, and the congregation breaks up in heavy silence.

I see Samuel turn around to look at me as we stand. Mama nudges me. 'Be good,' she mutters, almost pleading. She tries to smooth my hair, but I flinch away.

'Emma!' Samuel catches up with us and bows to me, and then again to Mama. 'Madam. It's nice to see you again.'

'And you, Samuel,' she replies formally, but warmly. I

can't tell how much of the warmth is real. 'Have you been enjoying this blessed weather?'

'Not as much as I'd like,' he says. 'I was hoping you and Emma would permit me to walk you home so I can enjoy a little more of it.'

'That's very kind of you. We'd be delighted for the company.'

It takes all I have not to scowl. 'I can't,' I remind her pointedly. 'I'm not going home.'

'I'd be happy to walk you wherever you're headed,' Samuel changes tack smoothly. I have the sudden urge to kick him. How can he act so casual after what his rotten father asked? Maybe it's not such a difficult decision after all.

'Emma,' Mama says warningly.

'Fine,' I shrug. 'You can walk us to the square. You can escort Mama home from there, if you like.'

Samuel's thrown for a moment but recovers with a wide smile and offers me his arm. 'I'll take what I can get.' It's the same smile he gave me the night I saw him on the high street, but it's at its full strength in the daylight: wide and open, making his freckles dance across his cheeks and crinkling the corners of his eyes. It's hard to resist smiling back, but I manage.

I stay quiet as we walk up the street, letting him and Mama talk to each other instead. People watch us out the corner of their eyes, and the whispering starts again. I try to look like it doesn't bother me, but I feel awkward, like some sort of exhibit. Do they really have nothing better to do?

'What's waiting for you in the square?' Samuel asks me, pulling me back into the conversation.

'I like to look at the stalls,' I say, challenging him. 'Mona and I go every Sunday.'

Mama purses her lips into a long, deep line.

Samuel looks concerned. 'Are you going alone today?'

'No,' I say shortly.

Samuel stops, and being attached to his arm I stop with him. Mama keeps a respectful distance, but her eyes send me a silent message: *don't ruin this*.

'Emma,' Samuel says quietly. 'You can't. Not today. Father will hear about it, if he doesn't see you first.'

'I don't care,' I whisper back, angry. 'I haven't seen her since Friday. I can't just leave her waiting.'

'Can we at least talk first?' he asks, his tone serious but a smile gracing his lips. It's a different smile, more for the benefit of the people around us than for me. It doesn't reach his eyes at all.

'About what?' I hiss. 'I know what you want from me, but you can't seriously expect me to give up my best friend without speaking to her first.' Mama's face is pale. I'm insulting him, and that's not good for my prospects.

'Please,' he glances at the people who've given up on subtlety and have started staring. 'Just walk with me for a few minutes.'

'No,' I say, pulling my arm away from his. 'I didn't ask you to court me. But if you've got any interest in continuing, you can tell your father that I'm following our Lord's teachings and keeping a promise to a friend while I still have one.'

'Emma, wait!' Samuel reaches out, but I pull away.

'I'll tell her,' I say, my voice a harsh whisper. 'Just... give me the time to do it properly.'

He steps back with a look of defeat and lets me go. I don't look back as I march to the square. I don't want to see the look on Mama's face.

Mona waits for me by the well, as always. 'So,' she says with a cheeky smile. 'How was dinner? Tell me everything.'

I bite my lip, knowing I can't tell her what really happened. 'Fine,' I say, trying to sound nonchalant.

Mona frowns. 'That doesn't sound good. What happened?'

'Nothing,' I say with a shrug. 'We went, we ate, I behaved.'

'Have you been invited back again?'

'We don't know yet,' I say vaguely. 'It was implied, but... I suppose it depends.'

'On what?'

Behind her, my eyes fall on Mayor Jones. Samuel isn't with him, and I wonder if he really did escort Mama back to the house.

The mayor looks our way, his gaze lingering on us for less than a second. It might be the distance, but I don't see anything that looks like disappointment or anger. He looks almost... pleased.

He must think I'm telling her. But does he really expect me to do it here, with people all around us?

'I don't really feel like looking at the stalls today,' I say, changing the subject.

She gives me a strange look, but accepts that I don't want to talk about it. 'Come on, then. I've got something to show you.'

○

We sit outside Mona's house, a small shape wriggling in my lap.

'Joseph's dog gave birth a few weeks ago,' Mona explains. 'He was going to drown the littlest ones.'

The jet-black puppy rolls over, tiny teeth gnawing gently at one of my fingers. 'So, you stole her?'

'No, me and some of the others asked if we could keep them instead. Joseph said he didn't care, so long as we didn't let them run wild.' She rolls her eyes as she says it. I get the feeling Joseph didn't put it so politely.

The puppy's pink tongue snakes out at the palm of my hand, tickling me. I smile and hand her back to Mona. 'What are you going to call her?'

'Stranger,' she says, matter of fact, and we both laugh.

We sit in comfortable silence for a while, playing with Stranger and cooing over her clumsy run and the way her entire body moves from side to side with every wag of her tail.

I should tell Mona now. Telling her what the mayor asked doesn't have to mean I've made a decision. We can just talk about it. She could help me, even.

But as I open my mouth, I think of how her face will look when I say it. How do you tell someone your future rests on never speaking to them again? How can anyone I'm supposed to respect ask me to do it?

'I had a dream the other night,' I say, unable to go through with it. 'About the meadow. There was a boy.'

Mona raises an eyebrow. 'What kind of boy?'

'A naked boy,' I chuckle, expecting her to laugh with me. 'At least, half naked. He was standing by that white tree at the bottom of our hill. Near the woods.'

She shakes her head and laughs. 'You dreamed about a naked boy the night you had dinner with Samuel? Did he look anything like him?'

'I couldn't see his face, but I don't think so,' I admit, deciding not to mention the horns. 'He had long hair.'

'Like Papa Stone?' She asks with a smirk. 'No wonder you're always hanging around here.'

I elbow her in the ribs, giggling. 'Shut up.'

Stranger yawns in her lap and snuggles close. Mona strokes her head, contemplatively. 'You didn't go in though, did you?' she asks after a while.

'Where?'

'The woods, in your dream.'

'No, I was in the bluebells.'

'Try not to, if you dream about him again. You don't know what will happen.'

'You sound just like your grandmother,' I joke. 'She always listened to too many stories.'

'All stories have something true in them,' she says. 'None of us really know why all those girls went into the woods.'

'The prospect of rotten husbands?' I suggest with a tight smile. 'Or none at all.'

'Or extremely handsome naked boys,' Mona says.

I smile. 'I didn't say he was handsome.'

'I highly doubt you're dreaming about an unattractive naked boy.'

'Fine,' I say with a snort. 'If I dream about him again, I won't go in.'

'Good,' she says, giving a satisfied nod. 'Now describe him to me properly. In detail.'

○

Walking home, I stop by the meadow to gather some buttercups for Mama, hoping it'll soften her anger long enough to let me apologise.

Mama's already in her nightclothes, sitting in bed with Father's favourite book. A candle burns on the table beside her. She doesn't look up when I come in, staring instead at the page in an unnerving silence.

'Good evening, Mama,' I say tentatively, waiting for her to yell at me.

She turns a page.

I hold out the meagre bouquet. 'I got these for you. Buttercups.'

She doesn't move. I take a jar from the shelf and dip it in the water pail, putting the flowers inside.

'I'll just leave them on the table for you.'

Another page turns, too loud in the quiet of the house.

'I know I was too rude to Samuel, Mama,' I say nervously. 'I'm sorry. I'll apologise to him tomorrow before school. I'll explain that I'll tell Mona what his father wants me to do before our next dinner, but that I just need time to do it the right way. He'll understand. I'm sure he will.'

Mama snaps the book shut loudly.

'There will be no more dinners, Emma,' she says coldly.

I falter. 'What do you mean?'

'There was a letter, sent this evening. Written and signed by Mayor Jones himself. Can you guess what it said?'

'But… I saw him today in the square earlier. He didn't look angry.'

'No,' Mama says. 'I'm sure he was quite happy to find a reason not to let his son marry a penniless, fatherless girl.'

'Then…' I say, searching for a solution. 'Then what about Andrew? We can make his mother something nice out of my dress. We can reschedule tea, get a dinner invitation. I'll be better at it now that I've had practice.'

Mama is frustrated with me. 'Use your head, Emma! You deliberately ignored Mayor Jones. He won't speak well of you now, not to anybody. Do you think Andrew's parents will let their son marry a girl the mayor disapproves of?'

'I…' I begin, then fall silent. I'm out of ideas. Out of options.

'I *told* you, Emma,' Mama goes on, swinging her legs out of bed. 'Once Samuel took an interest in you, he became your only chance. Andrew won't have you now that you've been refused. And you *have* been refused. Your display today made sure of that.'

Tears burn threateningly behind my eyes. 'But that's unfair!'

'What gave you the idea that anything about this would be fair?'

'Well, we don't need them then!' I say, desperate. 'We've been all right, all these years. We can just stay like this.'

'How, Emma? When Samuel marries Roslyn they'll only need one servant, and Jane is younger than I am. The other widowers can't pay me enough to feed us both. And what will you do? Between the Strangers and the other unmarried women and widows, there's no work for you. You'll have to beg, and you know how often anyone pays attention to beggars in this town. And after I'm dead, what then?'

I step back against the door, unable to answer.

'It's my own fault,' she shakes her head bitterly. 'I indulged you, tried to protect you from our life. And now you don't understand how anything works.'

'I do,' I croak defensively, my throat tight.

'Then why did you do it, Emma? You could have had a real life.'

'Mona's my friend,' I whisper. 'I didn't want to hurt her.'

Mama gives me a level look. 'I hope she's worth ruining our lives over.'

Biting my lip to keep the tears from spilling over, I fumble for the doorknob and flee outside. I round the corner of the house and sit beneath my window, pulling my knees to my chest and burying my face in my skirt.

I hear Mama come outside after a while. She sounds worried as she calls my name, and maybe even sorry. But I stay where I am. Eventually, she goes back in.

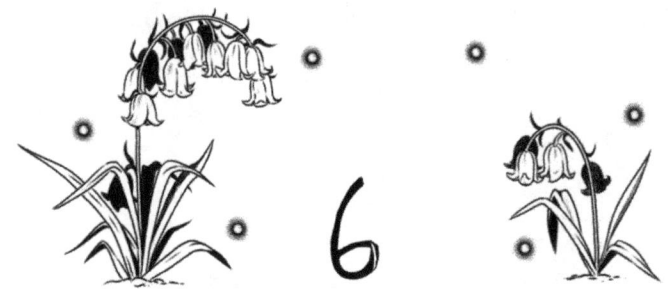

I arrive at the schoolhouse early on Monday morning, but I make no effort to set up for class. I take my seat and slump over the desk, stiff and sore from falling asleep outside.

'I thought you'd be here.' Samuel's voice comes from the doorway.

His footsteps approach, but I don't bother looking at him. 'You're not allowed over here.'

'I'm the mayor's son,' he reminds me. 'I can get away with a few things.'

'Lucky you.'

'I wanted to apologise for dinner. I didn't ask if you wanted me to court you. I just thought... well, you didn't ever seem very enthusiastic about Andrew. Not in a real way.'

'I didn't have to be enthusiastic,' I point out, annoyed. 'I had a chance.'

'You still can. I could talk to him for you.'

'Your father's already done enough talking,' I say bitterly, looking up at him. 'Andrew will marry who his father tells him to, and after insulting the mayor, it won't be me.'

'Well…' he looks uncomfortable at that. 'I did try to warn you.'

'Pardon?' I ask darkly.

'Yesterday. You wouldn't listen.'

'What was the point? I knew what you were going to say.'

'No, you didn't.' He pulls a chair beside my table, sitting close. 'I don't care who you're friends with, Emma. We could have worked something out. I could have gone to Mona myself and explained everything or given someone a note to pass on. But you just ran off.'

I blink at him. 'Why didn't you warn me sooner, then?' I ask. 'You had all week to tell me what he was going to ask.'

'I thought you'd see it coming,' he says, defensive. 'He's never been shy about how much he dislikes the Strangers. What did you think he was going to say? What did you think would happen with you and Mona when you came of age?'

'I didn't,' I admit grudgingly.

He sighs, sounding truly unhappy. 'I really am sorry,' he says.

'Why?' I ask faintly.

'Because I think things aren't going to be very easy for you from now on, and it's my fault. And,' he says, his cheeks turning pink, 'because I really did like the idea of marrying you.'

'But we've barely spoken to each other.'

'Not true. We used to speak all the time.'

I'm surprised he even remembers. 'That was years ago. We

were children. We could be completely different people now.'

'I'm not,' he says. 'And I don't think you are, either. I see the faces you and Mona make at each other behind the adults' backs. I see you smiling to yourself all the time when you walk around town. Sometimes I see you rolling your eyes at Deference. You're the same bright, stubborn girl who used to make me laugh until my stomach hurt.'

My heartbeat quickens, though I'm not sure why. 'You seem to see me a lot.'

'I do,' he says. 'I always hoped you'd see me, too.'

'I see you,' I say softly.

He gives a slight smile. 'That's nice to know.' He stands up, walk out of my side of the school and out of my life. It stings more than I thought it would.

Footsteps approach the door. Roslyn surveys the bare room in surprise. 'You didn't set up the room today,' she says.

'I wasn't in the mood,' I say softly.

'It's all right, we're happy to do it for a change. You always make us look so lazy.' She doesn't say it meanly, but Nicole grins. She must have heard about the mayor's rejection of me. Lord, everyone must have by now.

I press my forehead back to the desk as they begin arranging the chairs around me, thinking of Samuel. I wish I'd seen this side of him earlier.

But maybe I had.

Maybe that's what the bluebell was supposed to mean. Maybe it was more than a sweet gesture. He could only have gotten it from the edge of the woods, after all. His father would never approve of him going so close to the trees alone.

Lord, I'm a fool. It *was* a message, and I'd missed it. And now it's too late.

○

Mona and I sit beside the well that Friday evening, watching Roslyn and her parents making the short walk across the square to Samuel's house. They're the perfect family: her mother dressed in flattering, modest blue, the doctor in a top hat with his trademark silver cane, their three youngest children clean, well-mannered and dressed in their Sunday best. And Roslyn, stunning in a pink gown embroidered all over in white carnations, with her hair braided back from her temples to fall down her back in loose curls. Who could ever want Mama and I over them?

'Well this is all horribly predictable,' Mona says, stretching her arms. Stranger sniffs at the ground by our feet, searching for crumbs.

'They suit each other,' I say darkly, unprepared for how much the sight of Roslyn's beautiful, happy family annoys me.

Mona looks to me, surprised. 'What really happened at dinner?'

I bite my thumbnail. 'What do you mean?'

'You said everything went fine, and now he's having dinner with the competition.'

I shrug.

'And you're jealous about it.'

'I'm am not.'

'Which means you like Samuel.'

'I *don't*.'

'Which means something must have happened with the mayor.'

I frown. She presses on, reasoning it out. 'He can't have disapproved of you. Nobody decent in the village will say a bad thing about you, even if you are poor. Even *Mary* likes you, and that's saying something.'

I'm too busy trying to think of an excuse to be flattered by her assessment. 'Mona,' I say, hoping something will come to me. But it doesn't.

'It can't be your mother,' she goes on. 'I know people are awful to her now that she's *debased* herself with work, but she *was* married. She's never had to stoop to begging, and she's never let either of you miss Deference. She hasn't done anything he can disapprove of. Not by the law *nor* the Lord.'

'Nothing happened,' I insist. 'Samuel just likes Roslyn better than me. And who can blame him. Look at her dress. Lord, look at her face. I can't compete with her.'

'Horseshit,' Mona swears. 'He's been looking at you all week, and you've been acting strangely ever since I said goodbye to you on Sunday.'

'All right, fine,' I pretend to give in. 'I didn't impress the mayor. Maybe I talked too much. Or didn't curtsey enough.'

'Maybe? You don't know?'

I shrug weakly, and her eyes widen with realisation. 'So… it had to do with me, then.'

'No,' I protest, but it's not convincing enough. The moment I've been dreading plays out on her face. I've never seen her so hurt. But the worst part is that she doesn't look even a little bit surprised.

'Oh,' she says softly.

'They wanted me to stop seeing you outside of the school,' I reveal hesitantly. 'The mayor did, anyway. He said I shouldn't be anything more than polite to you.'

'Polite,' she murmurs. 'That's nice of him.'

I stay quiet. What can I possibly say?

Eventually Mona lets out a loud breath of air. 'But you didn't do it. You went against the mayor and gave up all hope of a good future because of me.'

I shrug again, and she manages a sad smile. 'That was stupid, Emma.'

'It was worth it,' I say firmly. 'We can live together on the edge of town and scare all the children. The mad old unmarried woman and the terrible Stranger. And their fearsome, adorable dog.'

She lets out a laugh and my hand finds hers. We sit together quietly until night falls fully.

○

Monday brings a clear, warm morning. I take a lingering look over the meadow as I walk to school, feeling the urge to skive off and spend the day laying in the middle of the plateau. After all, what good will sitting inside and sewing or cooking or reciting passages from the book of the Lord do me now? I won't ever be a wife or mother, and what can they teach me about finding work?

I force myself to move on. Skipping school would affect nobody, but Mama would be unhappy, and things are already tense enough between us.

'Emma,' Mary the tailor's wife calls out to me from her shop. *Our shop*, Mama would say. 'I can't make the girls' lesson this afternoon. Matthew's had that many orders. Are you able to take the class alone?'

'Of course,' I say, even though it's the last thing I feel like doing today. It's not as though I haven't done it before. Mary finds a reason to plead out at least once every month or so. 'I'd be happy to.'

'You're a good girl, Emma,' she says with a grateful smile. 'It's such a shame that…' she trails off, thinking better of finishing the sentence. She gives me a pitying look and shuts the door.

An idea strikes me, and I hurry to the bakery, asking the baker if I can speak to his wife.

Caroline appears from out the back, flour in her hair as usual. She teaches the younger boys. 'Emma. Is there something wrong?'

'I wondered if you'd let me borrow Mona this afternoon to help with the girls. Mary can't attend, and I'm feeling a little under the weather myself…'

'Of course you can,' she assures me, the same pity in her eyes as the tailor's wife. 'I think I can manage my scallywags alone for one day.'

I thank her and hurry along to the schoolhouse. For once,

I'm one of the last girls there. I try to catch Mona's eye as I take my seat, but she's lost in her own thoughts and doesn't notice me. She didn't meet me in the square yesterday either, and when I went to her house she told me she wasn't feeling well.

Now I wonder if she was telling the truth.

❂

Mona disappears for lunch before I can catch up. Confused by her odd behaviour, I sit down on the bench alone and take out a cold beef sandwich. The bread was only bought yesterday, and is so soft I wolf it down in barely a minute. There's a silver lining to all this pity: the baker slipped me better bread than we can afford.

I notice Roslyn and Nicole waiting outside the schoolhouse door for Andrew and Samuel. Andrew ignores Nicole as usual, but she no longer looks discouraged by it. She shoots me a triumphant look, and I feel myself hoping he *does* choose not to marry anyone. It would serve her right.

My heart sinks a little as I see Samuel stop to say a few words to Roslyn. I can't hear what they're saying, but they're both wearing polite smiles and standing a respectful distance from each other.

He offers his arm to her. She takes it elegantly, her fingers barely even brushing his sleeve. They walk past me, his eyes meeting mine for a brief moment. My cheeks flush and I drop my gaze immediately, embarrassed at myself for staring.

❂

Mona reappears just before class begins, and is surprised when Caroline sends her up to my end of the room. I hand the girls their books while we wait for the last few to turn up. This year there are fifteen girls in the afternoon class, all aged ten to twelve. With a small pang, I realise that this is another door closed to me. Unmarried women can't teach.

'I'll be your teacher this afternoon,' I announce when the group is full. 'Mona will assist me.' The girls blink at us. A change in teacher doesn't mean much to them. 'However, today we'll be doing something a little different. We'll take our lesson outside, in the beautiful day our Lord has sent us.' My voice is loud enough for Caroline to hear. She looks startled, but nods her approval across the divider.

The girls buzz with excitement and leap to their feet. It's not against the rules, but the teachers almost never take them outside. 'This is still a lesson,' I caution. 'Please form two lines and take the hand of your partner.'

Taking the head of the column, I lead them out into the yard. We really should stay close and have the lesson right here, but it's bare and boring. I don't want to stare at cows for the afternoon, and neither do the girls. Instead, I lead them up the lane, turning into the square and making for my house.

Adults stop to look at us curiously as we head down the high street. The girls wave excitedly to their mothers or fathers and anyone else they know well enough. I recite a passage from the book of the Lord loudly enough for everyone near enough to us to hear, and they echo me in solidarity. I see Mona hide a smile at the back of the group, holding the hand of the odd girl out.

In minutes, we're on my lane. The girls stop at the sight of the meadow, the breeze making ripples in the flowers. For many of the girls who live in the better parts of the village, the sight of the meadow is a pure novelty. The only people who have reason to pass it are the people who live here – daughters of farm labourers and woodsmen.

'We're having class here?' Bridget, one of the youngest and smallest girls asks.

I nod. She squeals, taking off at a run down the hill. Most of the other girls follow her, but the oldest girl hangs back. Nicole's sister, Louise, a serious but good natured twelve-year-old.

'Go on,' I urge her. 'Nobody will yell.' A slow smile spreads across her face. She drops her books and tears after the younger girls. 'But not too far!'

Mona and I watch them as a game of chase breaks out. The girls laugh and scream as they run in circles around each other.

'We should probably pretend to teach them something,' Mona says.

'In a minute,' I say. 'Let them play.'

○

We seat the girls in a circle in the middle of the plateau. They sit with their books in their laps, looking more relaxed and happy to be in class than I've ever seen them.

I have them take turns reading out loud, helping the

younger girls slowly sound out the letters. Louise builds a chain of poppies as she waits her turn. Handing the chain to me, I help her loop it and put it on her head. Naturally, the other girls want one as soon as they see it, and soon every girl is linking flowers together while they wait for their turn to read.

'I want some blue ones!' Bridget exclaims, holding up a haphazard rainbow chain of poppies, buttercups and white daisies.

'Shh!' an older girl smacks her leg, a little too hard. Bridget's eyes brim as she rubs at it.

'Fiona,' I caution sternly. 'We don't hit.'

'I'm sorry, Teacher. But she shouldn't talk about the blue ones.' We all look down the hill towards the carpet of bluebells. 'They're too close.'

'She's right,' Mona gently tells Bridget. 'You can't ever go near the woods.'

'Why not?'

'You'll get lost,' I say sensibly, but I'm drowned out by a cacophony of suggestions from the other girls.

'Monsters!'

'Demons!'

'You'll get eaten!'

'You'll turn into one of them!'

'Mayor Jones says the woods only attract the wicked,' Louise whispers. 'Good people don't want to go there.'

'That's not what he meant,' I begin to explain, but the other girls speak over me again.

'My mother says the woods try to steal girls before they get married,' Rhonda, another older girl offers.

'Father said that if you kiss a boy before you're married, the demons will take you away.'

'I heard they drag you away in the night if you don't go to Deference. And once you're inside, you can't ever escape.'

'Should we be sitting here?' Louise asks, eyeing the woods nervously.

'We're safe in the meadow, and anywhere on the edge of the village, like the schoolhouse,' Mona assures them. 'The bluebells act as a warning, set there by our Lord to protect us from the creatures.'

The girls nod sagely, taking in every word. It was cleverly done. They'd all go home praising our Lord and afraid of the woods and we wouldn't get in trouble for taking them so close.

'Who wants to make a bouquet for their mother?' I ask, attempting to diffuse the tension. I don't want the littler ones to be so scared they can't sleep.

The girls only take a moment to adjust, the youngest jumping to their feet. 'Only pick the red, yellow, or white ones,' I set the rules, though after their little sharing session, there's no way they'll go anywhere near the bluebells. 'And see if you can tell me what each flower is called.'

The girls rush off, but stay close. Louise and Fiona are a little slower, sneaking fearful glances at the trees.

'You've been avoiding me,' I accuse Mona when the children are out of earshot.

'I had to check on Stranger,' she says nonchalantly. She's a much better liar than I am.

'Not just at lunch. You wouldn't even look at me in class this morning, and you fobbed me off completely yesterday.'

She sighs, giving up. 'All right. I was.'

I gnaw at my thumbnail. 'Did I do something? Was it what I said the other night?'

'No. I've been thinking, that's all.'

'And you didn't want to talk to me about it?'

'I wasn't sure how.'

I'm worried. 'Can you tell me now?' I ask.

Mona takes a moment. 'I think you should do what the mayor wants and forget about me,' she says at last.

I feel like someone's thrown cold water over me. 'Why?' My voice comes out small.

'Because it'll be better. You might still have a chance with Samuel if you apologise. I mean, *really* apologise. And if not, Andrew's still there.'

'But why?' I demand.

Mona looks uncomfortable. 'Because I don't want you to be alone.'

'I won't be alone, I'll have you.'

'But you won't. I won't be here.'

She's lost me. 'Where are you going?'

Mona takes a deep breath and looks away. 'I'm leaving.'

I don't understand. 'What do you mean?'

'I'm going to take the road.'

'What's on the road?' I ask angrily, even though all the

98

wonderful whispers and gossip she's shared from the traders and other Strangers fills my head.

There's a fire in her eyes when she looks back at me. 'The whole world, Emma,' she says. 'I can't stay here. I've lived here my whole life and I'm still a Stranger to them. They'll never let me be anything else.'

'But…'

'I want to work for money, not just scraps. I want to sleep in a dry house that doesn't let the wind whistle through it. I want to find a city and know what it's like to belong somewhere. I want to meet and fall in love with people who treat me like a real person.' She looks at me, and I know I look as wounded as I feel. 'I've been thinking about it for a long time. I should have told you sooner. I wish I had.'

Biting my lip, I want to beg her to reconsider. But how can I, when what she's saying is everything I want too. At least I have the opportunity, however slim, to get some of them here.

'I love you, Emma,' she goes on. 'You're more than my best friend, you're my sister. What you did, going against the mayor for me… it was incredible. But I can't stay here and waste my life. Not even for you. Not even after that.'

I feel sick. 'When will you leave?' I ask weakly.

'I'm not sure yet. When I'm old enough. When I'm brave enough.'

My eyes find the woods. I concentrate on them to keep myself from crying.

'We can still be friends, can't we?' I ask finally. 'Until you go?'

She looks away, and my heart sinks. 'I think it would be better if we tried to get used to not having each other. I think it would it make things easier, in the long run.'

It's hard to form the words. 'Will you at least come and say goodbye?'

One of the girls screams. Rhonda. She's dropped her bouquet and is chasing Fiona.

Mona looks at me, eyes glistening, and squeezes my hand before going to see what the trouble is. I blink hard against the prickling behind my eyes and walk to the edge of the plateau, staring down at the sea of bluebells.

Adulthood isn't looking at all like I thought it would. I wish I could go back, to be like the girls romping through the flowers. To be five years old and without a care in the world.

A sudden spark of light catches my attention. I snap my head towards it, staring at the trees.

There.

A small point of light flashes between the tree trunks on the very edge of the woods, and is gone. I keep looking, searching for what must have been a firefly, but the spark doesn't come again.

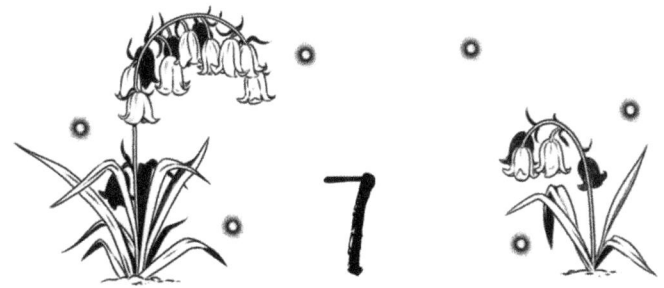

7

I'm exhausted by the time I return the girls to the schoolhouse and head home. Nicole returns to collect Louise, and they walk home a little way ahead of me. I hear Louise asking Nicole a stream of questions about the woods until she's awarded with a sharp 'Shut it.'

Mama doesn't greet me when I arrive home. We're still barely speaking. Sometimes she looks at me with sad eyes and I think she's about to apologise, but she never does.

But then, I do the same to her, the words dying on my lips before I can tell her how sorry I am for ruining the rest of her life along with mine. She must have been looking forward to spending the next few years in comfort, allowing her bent back and creaking knees the time to heal.

'I heard you took the girls to the meadow today,' she says eventually, finishing her dinner.

'Yes,' I murmur.

And that's all we say for the rest of the night.

After tidying the house and collecting fresh water, I fall

into bed. I had expected Mama to be asleep already but, though she says nothing, it takes what feels like an hour or so for the tell-tale snoring to fill the house.

Only then, when I'm really alone, do I let myself cry.

○

A firefly lands on the bridge of my nose, waking me with its soft glow. It crawls up and over my forehead, its scratchy little feet trekking a path of tears as it goes. Strange. I didn't think people could cry in dreams.

Sitting up, I find myself nestled amongst the bluebells beneath the white tree. 'Why are you sad?' a voice asks from the shadows. I look up. The shape of the boy is just visible beside the tree's smooth trunk. 'Does growing up hurt that much?'

I nod slowly. Heavy tears slide down my cheeks.

He crouches down, anchoring himself to the tree with one hand and reaches out the other to wipe a tear from my cheek. His fingers are warm against the cool air. 'What's wrong?' he asks.

'I've ruined everything,' I admit, the words bubbling up with the tears in heaving bursts. I let them come. If I can't be honest with myself in a dream, then when? 'I was stupid, and now my best friend is leaving, and my mother is angry at me, and Samuel and Andrew will marry Roslyn and Nicole and I'll end up old and alone. If I even live that long because I won't have any food or money.'

The boy settles his back against the trunk of the tree, sitting in the embrace of a looping root. 'Your kind worries too much,' he says rather unhelpfully. Several fireflies land on his shoulders, casting strange upward shadows on his face and horns. 'If things are bad, make them better or forget them. It's not so hard.'

'For you, maybe,' I point out. 'You don't exist.'

'I exist. I'm right here.' He stretches, the fireflies illuminating his naked chest. I avert my eyes, embarrassed. He laughs, a lovely musical sound.

'What's your name?' I ask, wiping my wet cheeks on my sleeve.

'Don't have one.'

'Everyone has a name,' I protest.

'Give me one, then, if it means so much.'

The word pops into my head and escapes before I even know it's there: 'Lonesome.'

A firefly lands in his hair, illuminating the bottom half of his face. He gives a lopsided smile. 'Why?' he asks.

'Because that's when I think about you.'

'Are you lonesome now?'

'I think so.'

He cocks his head. The glow falls on the far-left side of his face. I see the sharp line of a cheekbone and long hair tucked behind an inhuman ear. 'You could run away,' he suggests. 'I could help. I could show you somewhere beautiful. Somewhere nobody has ever been alone or sad.'

'There's no place like that.'

'There is,' he insists. 'I live there.'

'Where?' I ask. 'In the woods?'

He nods. 'It's wonderful there. Nobody's angry. Nobody starves. Nobody leaves.'

'Then why are you here?'

'For you.' He moves into a crouch and holds out his hand. 'I can take you now. We just have to follow the fireflies.'

Smiling though my tears, I shake my head. 'I don't think I should, dream boy.'

'I thought you said my name was Lonesome?'

'You like it, then?'

The firefly in his hair flutters away, momentarily shedding golden light on his whole face. My breath catches. He's beautiful. All sharp lines and large, bright eyes. 'I like that you gave it to me,' he says, the crooked smile fading a little. There's something in his face, for all his talk of this wonderful place he comes from. He looks as lonely as I am. And then his face is cloaked in shadows once more.

'I'm glad.'

He drops his arm, standing and pulling something from his pocket. The flute. 'Dance with me then, if you won't run away with me.' His back never leaving the tree, he begins to play the cheerful tune. The one I heard when I was just a child.

I stay on the ground and listen, but it's too infectious to resist. Before I know it, I'm on my feet, cheeks dry and a smile warming my face. The fireflies flock to the music and surround us, casting so much light that our tiny circle it feels like a golden afternoon. Lonesome taps his feet to the music, his bright eyes never leaving my face. I hear myself laugh as I begin to dance.

○

I open my eyes to the steely grey of early morning, hair glued to my face from all the crying.

I sit up and gaze restlessly out the window. A thick layer of clouds is gathering, a contrast to the starry sky in my dream.

Triggered by the thought, images of the dream swirl through my mind. The firefly landing on my face, Lonesome's outstretched hand, his offer to take me away.

So this is where my life has brought me. Dreaming of running away with a boy I've invented.

Filled with the urge to check if the fireflies are still out this late, I slip quietly out the door and run down the hill and across the plateau. I shiver in my thin nightdress. The morning is colder than I'd anticipated, much colder than in the dream.

I step onto the hill and slip in the dewy grass. I squawk, gathering speed as I go. Too late, I come to my senses and realise what a terrible plan this is. I slide down the hill, flailing my arms for balance until I come to a stop in the bluebells.

The fresh smell greets me, making me drop to my knees. The scent was missing from the dream, I realise now. I pick a bunch and hold them to my face, enjoying being this close to them again for real. If only I could take them home with me.

Eventually, my eyes are drawn to the white tree. I walk to it, seeing it up close with adult eyes for the first time. It's not like any of the other trees in the woods, which are thick and brown and leafy. It's tall and spindly, bare but not dead. Its pale branches look uncannily like Lonesome's velvet horns.

The nearby woods look so peaceful and quiet, with shafts of light breaking through the canopy to fall on the carpet of bluebells running deep inside. Seeing them this closely, it's not hard to believe how many unhappy young people have been drawn inside. Even in this grim light, the colours are warm and inviting. But there are no fireflies. No signs of life.

'Hello?' I whisper, feeling completely foolish. As expected, there's no answer.

I don't know what I was hoping for.

○

Dragging my heels on my way to the schoolhouse, I look back and see Andrew turning into the high street behind me. I stop and wait.

He looks at me strangely as I fall in step with him. 'Um, what are you doing?' he asks, forgoing any politeness.

'Walking to school with you,' I shrug. 'Is there a rule against it?'

'It's not normal. People will talk.'

'So what?' I ask. 'We're both going to the same place.'

He scratches his chin. 'I suppose.'

Readjusting my bag strap, I look at him out the corner of my eye. He looks uncomfortable. 'Did the mayor say something to your father about me?'

'It's not really my business.'

'So, he did. He told your father not to let you marry me.'

'He didn't say that,' Andrew says. A small surge of hope rushes through me, only to be snuffed out immediately. 'He just said that not having a father has made you disobedient, and my father said that's what happens when women raise children alone.'

'He won't even consider me, then?' I ask, gritting my teeth. 'He won't even meet me to decide for himself?'

He shakes his head, sealing my fate. 'Father's decided on Nicole. Sorry.'

'Are you?' I snort.

'Look, for what it's worth, I wanted things to work out with you and Samuel.' He gives a proud grin. 'For a couple of days, I got to court the doctor's daughter.'

He's actually blushing. I'd laugh if everything wasn't crashing down around me. Another thought occurs to me: 'Andrew, if your father had chosen me, would he have asked me to stop seeing Mona?'

Andrew seems confused that I'd even ask. 'No, he would have told you to. And if he hadn't, I would.'

The next few weeks give me a taste of the future. I walk to the schoolhouse alone, I spend lunch alone, I shop for our food without saying a word. Eileen gives up calling on me to lead the class in our readings or hold up my needlework as an example. Mary and even Caroline grow impatient with me in the afternoon classes. I don't talk to anyone, I don't look at anyone.

I might as well get used to it.

'Just tell them all what you think of them,' Lonesome recommends, spinning his flute around his fingers. At first, I dreamed about him once or twice a week, then every few days. Now I'm in the meadow nightly. It's all I have left to look forward to.

'I couldn't. I don't even know what would happen.'

'So do it and see,' he shrugs. 'If it's not good, come find me.'

I shake my head at him. 'Life's not as easy as you make it sound. You can't just do whatever you want and hope it works out.'

The corner of his mouth gives an amused twitch. 'It *is* that easy. So what if Grumpy, Selfish, Stupid and Moustache don't want to hear the truth? They deserve it.'

I raise an eyebrow. 'Who?'

'The people you always talk about. Mama, Mona, Stupid Samuel, that little man with the...' he holds his finger under his nose, simulating a moustache. 'James?'

'Jones,' I say with a snort. I can't deny his assessment of Mama, but... 'Samuel isn't stupid. And Mona isn't selfish.' She's been avoiding me at school, hanging back after class so we don't accidentally walk up to the square together. I see her on the weekends, sometimes, with the other Stranger women. Anytime our eyes met, she smiles sadly and politely, then looks away.

I hate it. It feels so strange to miss her so badly when she's right in front of me. So strange to be so angry at one of the people I love most in the world. In my darkest, loneliest moments, I wonder if she'll even bother to say goodbye when the time comes, or if she'll just let an empty seat and an empty shack speak for her. And why? Because it'll make leaving easier? Because it certainly isn't for my benefit.

Maybe I do think she's being selfish.

Lonesome raises his eyebrows triumphantly, as if he knows what I'm thinking.

'They've already got names, anyway,' I say. 'They don't need new ones.'

'You gave me a name when I didn't need one,' he reminds me. 'These are the ones I've given them.'

I smile. 'What name have you given me, then?'

He leans over and pulls a firefly out of my hair. Trapped gently between his fingers, it bathes us both in golden light. 'I like the one you already have,' he says with his crooked smile. 'Emma.'

○

At home, Mama teaches me how to clean a house properly, insisting that knowing how to clean our own bare wooden house is nothing compared to one with trinkets and carpets and wallpaper. I should be happy that she's speaking to me again, but it's only ever about cleaning, cooking, money and my ruined future. Before, at least, there was time for laughter and news. Before, I could talk to her without feeling like my every word and action was a disappointment. Now, it's just easier to nod and silently agree with everything she says.

She's already worked out a plan for the moment I come of age, wanting me take over her cleaning duties while she offers a laundry service to the wealthier wives.

'And maybe,' she muses, 'Our Lord will smile on you at last and make a new widower to look after.'

○

'That's what I have to look forward to,' I tell Lonesome, laying on my back and staring up at the stars. 'Waiting for some poor woman to die so I can clean her house and cook for her husband.'

'So leave,' he says again, for what must be the hundredth time. 'Come away with me.'

I reach my hand up, stretching towards the stars, but all I touch is the belly of a firefly zipping through the air. I let my arm drop back down, crushing some bluebells beneath it. 'I can't.'

Lonesome rolls onto his side, resting his cheek against his palm. There's at least two feet of space between us, each of us lying on either side of the invisible line marked by the white tree. 'Why not?'

A memory of Mona stirs. I hear her voice warning me to stay away from the trees. I hear the whispers about the woods, the stories about the missing girls, Mama's warnings all those years.

But this is just a dream.

'I don't know,' I say.

○

It feels like Samuel is everywhere.

Neither of our routines seem to have changed, so he must always have been there. But now I notice him. Without meaning to, my eyes find him across the schoolhouse, in the crowds on the high street, at Deference, crossing the square. Even though I look away every time I catch myself doing it, I've learned so much more about Samuel by watching from afar than I did when he was standing in front of me.

This is what I know: He always stops to speak to the older

members of the village, listening to their stories and complaints and helping them to run their errands in the afternoons. If they falter, he offers his arm without hesitation, fanfare or condescension. He blushes when they thank him, waving their praise away.

He plays in the square with the village children too young to go to school, letting the smallest ride on his shoulders. He walks unmarried Jane home some nights after she's finished at his house, even though she walks several feet away from him and keeps her eyes on the ground. He smiles easily and often, but when his father preaches sermons on fear and obedience his smile turns false and wooden.

I wish I'd paid attention earlier, before he turned his attention to Roslyn. She's been to dinner at his house three times now, and he and the mayor have been to hers twice, with another planned next week.

'She's a much better match for him than the old tailor's daughter,' the money lender's wife says to the blacksmith's wife as they stand in line at the bakery.

'Mm,' agrees the blacksmith's wife. 'A girl shouldn't be as tall as her husband.'

I wonder if they don't notice that I'm behind them, or if they don't care. They don't look at me as they take their bags of bread and buns and leave, and neither does the baker. He takes the coin I give him and hands me a small, hard loaf without a word.

I turn to the door and stop, finding myself face to face with Samuel. My lips part, stomach churning and heart fluttering. I should say something. Smile, at the very least. But before I can, he drops his gaze to the floor and steps out of the way to let me pass.

Lord, it hurts.

○

I'm exhausted from all the work Mama has me doing at home. The house has never been so clean, nor my hands so blistered and chapped. The only part of the day I look forward to is blowing out the candle and curling up in bed, waiting for Lonesome to meet me in my dreams.

Never judging and always glad to see me, he creates shadow creatures on the trunk of the white tree to make me laugh and plays music so heartbreakingly lovely to help me forget. Every night, he offers to take me away, and every night I hesitate longer before turning him down.

○

Waking up is the hardest. The loneliness has seeped into my bones, cold and heavy, and I have to fight just to sit up and put my feet on the ground, and then again to bathe, again to eat, again to braid my hair and dress and walk out the door.

The days blend together in a quiet, grey blur. I walk to school. I stare at the wall. I follow the teacher's instruction without question or comment. I walk home. I run errands. I clean. I cook. I clean again. I fetch the water. I blow out the candle.

'Emma,' Mama says as I let my hair down and begin to strip for bed. Her voice has been gentler these past few weeks, not that it matters. 'The water.'

The pail sits beside the door, filled with today's old brown water. Nodding in her direction, I button my dress back up and fetch my cloak.

I slosh the dirty water down the top of the meadow, but don't linger to listen to it flow down through the flowers or search for fireflies. I walk on, letting the pail bang loudly against my leg.

The square is empty, but the sound of deep, mannish laughter comes from the pub. I ignore it, attaching the pail to the rope and letting it fall into the dark. I wait for the rope to go taut, then crank the handle to bring it back up. Usually I can do it one handed – which has resulted in one arm being distinctly thicker than the other – but tonight I struggle and have to use two. By the time I get the pail to the top, I'm out of breath.

Did I eat today? Tonight?

I don't remember.

A door opens somewhere in the square, but I don't look up. I reach for the pail, wrapping my fingers around the thin handle and lifting it from the hook.

The pail drops back onto the hook, too heavy for my weak fingers, and careens back down to the water.

Something inside me breaks. I sit down, not caring who sees me, and wrap my arms tight around my legs and bury my dry face in my knees.

I can't do this. I can't live like this.

'Emma?'

I don't recognise the voice. I stay as I am, waiting them to leave me alone. No such luck. I hear the sound of skirts rustling in front of me, of a tired sigh as overworked muscles ease down to the ground.

A hand touches mine, and the voice repeats my name. I reluctantly raise my head. Unmarried Jane sits opposite me, a plain cloth bag hooked over her shoulder, her face framed with dark flyaway hairs after a day of work. Her gaze is fixed on the cobblestones between us.

'Are you all right?' she asks, her voice so soft and quiet that I almost think I've imagined it. It's the first time I've heard her speak since she was in school.

I ought to ignore her. I ought to stand, turn my back on her and walk home. It's what the mayor would want me to do.

'No,' I say. I haven't heard my voice in a while, either. At least, not here in the waking world. I expected it to sound small and weak, but it's loud and cold and dull, devoid of anything that sounds like myself. 'I'm not.'

Jane nods. If she's surprised by my honesty, she doesn't show it. She puts her bag down and stands up. Stepping around me, she takes hold of the handle and retrieves the full pail with ease. 'Up you get,' she says, then, without waiting for me, sets off with the pail in the direction of my house.

I blink in surprise, then snatch up her bag and scurry after her. I want to ask why she's helping me, but I don't seem to have the energy to form the words. She makes no effort to speak to me either, so I let the silence stand.

Jane looks down to the woods as we approach my house, coming to a sudden stop. 'You're so close,' she murmurs, looking out at the rustling expanse of the trees.

'Yes,' I agree. She holds out the pail. I reach for it and draw in a surprised hiss of air as her hand clamps on my wrist. I'm about to wrench my hand away when her eyes meet mine. Even in the moonlight, I can see the fire in them.

'Don't give in,' she warns me in a voice so low I have to lean close to hear her. 'There's always a reason to stay.' She lets go of my hand, and the pail drops heavily to my side.

'What's yours?' I ask, but the moment is already over. She takes her bag and retreats back the way we came. I watch her go, noticing for the first time how square her shoulders are, how tall she walks even with her head bowed.

Lugging the water inside, I find Mama already asleep, mouth open and snoring. A candle burns on the kitchen table, and as I take it up to carry to my bedside, I catch a glimpse of a stranger in the mirror.

I almost drop the candle in shock. Gripping it, I look behind me. The house is empty, just as it should be. I hold the candle high and step close to the mirror. The stranger steps with me, her eyes trained on mine. She's a pathetic creature, her skin ashen, her eyes dull and lifeless. Her hair falls over her shoulders in a lank, greasy sheet.

She looks like a monster. She looks like me.

I turn my back on the mirror, the candle shaking in my fist. Before I know what I'm doing, I'm outside and running down the hill of the meadow like the mayor himself is chasing me.

Wax drips down the side of the candle, stinging my fingers. The pain brings me to a halt at the end of the plateau, just as I'm about to plunge down into the bluebells and the woods beyond.

I drop the candle. The flame flutters and goes out. Bringing my throbbing red fingers to my lips, I sink to my knees and try to breathe.

What am I doing here?

What am I *doing?*

My face is a mess of tears, my vision so blurred I can only just see the fireflies drifting sedately through the trees below.

Lonesome said that if I follow the fireflies, I'd find a place without fear. Without loneliness. But Lonesome isn't real. The only thing I'll find at the end of the firefly road is the same thing that came to every other girl who went missing in the woods: an accident in the dark.

I wipe my cheeks and nose on my sleeve and stand on shaking legs. Taking my time, I walk back across the plateau, letting my hands trail through the grass.

A haunting tune tugs at my mind, so strong it almost sounds as if I'm hearing it with my ears instead of in a memory. It calls to me, begs me to come back and escape while I still can. My feet stop of their own accord, itching to turn back. To see. To hope. To run.

But I think of Mama, and the tune falters. She's been so hard on me. She's hurt my feelings, pushed me to be someone I don't care to be. But not because she wanted to. Everything she's ever done has been to protect me, to give me the best chance at a comfortable, secure life.

The music fades, taking the itch in my feet with it. I walk

back up the hill and slip silently inside, closing the door behind me.

Moonlight spills through the open window, casting the house in a strange, low light. I can just make out Mama's face as she sleeps in her narrow, uncomfortable bed. She looks so old. So different from the elegant woman I knew as a child. Being poor and friendless has hardened her, but she's never given up. Never stopped trying, stopped working, stopped living. And neither will I.

I've moped around for long enough. I won't let this village break me.

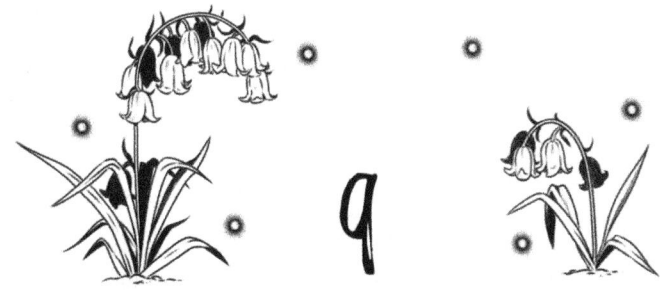

I rise early and set out Mama's breakfast, then pour some water into a bowl and carry it outside. I lean over it in the wan light of dawn, taking the time to thoroughly clean my long hair from root to tip. The sun is up by the time I've combed out every wet snare, the air pleasantly warm as spring draws closer to summer.

'You're in a good mood,' Mama observes cautiously at the table. I check myself in the mirror. I haven't managed to fix myself much. There are still bags under my eyes, my skin still looks ashen. But there's a subtle difference in my face from the night before. At least now I recognise myself.

'I am,' I answer her, leaning down to kiss her cheek and wrap my arms around her shoulders. She stiffens in surprise, but relaxes into it after a moment.

'You're leaving already?' she asks as I pull away and sit down to put on my shoes.

'I want to get to the schoolhouse early,' I tell her.

A surprised smile sends her wrinkles dancing. 'Really?'

'Really. I'll see you tonight.'

Walking up the high street, I make a point of looking at people and wishing them good morning. They're confused at my sudden turn, but politeness requires them to echo it back to me. I won't come of age for months and months yet, and I'm going to make sure they see me before I do.

And then I'm going to keep doing it anyway.

The schoolhouse is empty when I arrive. For the first time since that awful dinner with the mayor, I set up the girls' side of the room. And then, realising just how early I am, I set up the boys' side for something to do and return to my seat.

I frown at myself. The boys in this village have enough done for them. They can stand to organise one thing on their own, surely.

Screwing up my mouth, I listen at the door for anyone coming and walk past the divider.

'You're not supposed to be on this side,' Samuel says, an eyebrow raised as he watches me drag the last desk back to the corner.

My heart races, though I'm not sure if it's because I've been caught, or because I've been caught by him.

'Oh, I exist now?' I ask archly, refusing to let him have the upper hand.

'I beg your pardon?' Samuel asks, his eyebrows diving into a frown.

'You wouldn't even look at me at the bakery the other day,' I say. 'Or at Deference. Or anywhere.'

'I didn't think you wanted me to look at you.'

'I never said that,' I say softly. 'Or, if I did, I didn't mean it.'

Samuel's face softens, and then he frowns again.

I hear voices outside. 'I should go,' I say.

Samuel doesn't move as I walk past him to get back to the girls' side. Our arms touch.

'Emma,' he says quietly, turning to follow me. Before he can say anything else, two of the younger girls arrive, and I hear the voice of Eileen behind them. 'Ah,' Samuel says, faltering, then recovers with a deep bow at all three of us. 'Good morning.'

The girls exchange a confused glance and return his bow with a curtsey. 'Good morning,' they echo.

His eyes linger on me as he steps behind the divider. It's enough to make me wonder.

By the end of the day, I think I have the beginning of a plan.

○

Lonesome paces around the white tree, fingers trailing over the bark. Hundreds of fireflies have settled in its branches, making it look like a tree made of stars.

Lonesome hasn't seen me yet. Smiling, I touch his shoulder to get his attention. The heat from his skin shoots up my arm like a bolt of fire. It doesn't hurt, but it surprises me. I pull my hand away.

'This is it, isn't it?' he asks, turning to look at me with a wide, crooked grin. 'You're finally ready to come away. I knew you'd make up your mind eventually.'

'But I haven't,' I say.

'You have. You came last night. I saw you. You were awake and you came looking for me.'

For a moment I wonder how he could have known that, and then I remember that he's a product of my own imagination. Everything I know, he knows. 'But I didn't,' I remind him. 'I stopped myself. I went home to Mama.'

His smile fades in the golden light, but only a little. 'You got scared. But I can help you.' He takes my hand, and the spark of fire rushes through me again. This time it reaches my head, sending everything spinning. 'We can go together.'

'I'm sorry,' I say, stepping away from the tree. He doesn't step with me. Our hands part, and the world stands still again. 'I was upset, that's all. I gave up on myself, but I'm better now.'

His smile falls completely. He looks different when he's not smiling. Harder. Colder. 'You're always upset,' he says, his voice as stony as his face.

I shiver. It's not like him to be annoyed with me. 'I don't think I feel like talking tonight,' I say, taking another step back.

'Then dance with me,' he says, his eyes hidden in shadow. 'If that's what you need.'

He raises his flute to his lips before I can answer. The tune is new, uncharacteristically dark and moody. I don't feel like dancing either, but my feet move without me, and I can do nothing but follow.

●

Waiting out the front of the schoolhouse, I nervously twist my fingers in the strap of my ugly bluebell bag.

Mona arrives a few minutes early, as I'd hoped. She gives me a questioning look as she passes, but with Roslyn and Nicole only a few feet behind her, she doesn't stop. I thrust a note into her hand, and she conceals it immediately.

Roslyn and Nicole exchange a bewildered look as I linger. Nobody lurks around the front of the schoolhouse unless they're waiting for someone, and as far as they're concerned, the only person I'd have any reason to wait for just went inside.

'Roslyn,' I smile politely. 'Nicole.'

'Emma,' they nod back in unison. Nicole hardly bothers to gloat at me now that I don't present a threat to her. It's been the one silver lining to this whole situation.

'Why are you out here in the sun?' Roslyn asks, too polite not to at least attempt small talk. 'You'll freckle.'

'I was waiting for you, actually,' I say earnestly. 'I need to ask a favour.'

Her lovely face doesn't betray any surprise. 'Go on, then.'

'I was hoping you'd be willing to give me singing lessons.'

Nicole scoffs. 'What could you possibly want to sing for? Scraps?'

I lower my voice. 'It's for Mama,' I say, hoping I sound genuine, and am rewarded by Nicole looking guiltily at her feet. 'It's getting harder for her to read by candlelight. I don't know if I have the voice for it, but if I do I think it would make her evenings a little better. She's always so happy when you sing at Deference.'

Roslyn puts a hand to her heart. 'How can I say no to that?' she asks. 'Would you like to start this evening?'

'Tomorrow would be better,' I suggest, pleased with myself.

'Tomorrow it is.'

Nicole shivers and wraps her arms around herself. 'Can we get inside? The trees are staring and it turns my blood cold.'

Roslyn and I glance across the paddock to the woods. As superstitious as Nicole sounds, her words ring oddly true. It does feel like they're watching us.

I follow Roslyn and Nicole inside and glance at Mona as I pull my seat into place. She meets my eye and gives me the briefest shadow of a smile. She's read my note. I let the corner of my mouth twitch in gratitude, savouring the brief moment of contact between us, then open my book and wait for Eileen.

For once, I hope we're practicing our carnations.

○

Ignoring the woods, I lean against the wall of the schoolhouse and stare at a lone cow chewing a mouthful of grass. The rest of its herd is on the other side of the paddock. I wonder why it's decided to strike out on its own.

'Is lurking a new hobby of yours?' Samuel asks, making me jump as he rounds the side of the schoolhouse.

'Practicing for next year,' I joke weakly, nervous now that he's actually here.

The joke doesn't go over well. He looks away guiltily and

clears his throat. 'Mona says you wanted to see me?' he asks.

'Yes,' I say, but I'm not sure how to explain why I've asked him here. It suddenly feels presumptuous and vain and more than a little bit desperate. Not to mention terrifying.

'And?' he prompts, looking at me. If he'd looked bored or annoyed, or even polite, I'd make an excuse and run. But he looks nervous, too. And excited.

'I like you,' I say. It doesn't come out as confidently as I'd hoped it would. 'I... I think I might have misjudged you.'

'Really?' he asks, a tiny line forming between his eyebrows.

It's not quite the reaction I was hoping for, but at least he hasn't laughed in my face. 'Yes.'

'Why now?' he asks, looking at the lonely cow.

'I never really paid much attention to you before,' I admit. 'There was never any point. You're the mayor's son. You were always going to marry someone else, and we were never going to be allowed to be friends. But lately I can't seem to stop myself from looking at you. And it's not because I think you're handsome, though I do like your face very much...' He smiles at that, rubbing his chin and looking at me sidelong. I take it as encouragement. 'And it's definitely not because you're the mayor's son. I just... I like the way you treat people. I think you might be the best man in the village. I just wish I'd noticed that sooner.'

Samuel's smile fades, then returns shyly. 'Me too. That you'd noticed me, I mean. Not that I think I'm wonderful. And handsome. And charming.'

I laugh, a little breathless with relief. 'I never said charming.'

'It felt implied.'

I laugh and look down. 'What about Roslyn?' I ask, not really wanting to hear the answer. 'Do you like her, too?'

Samuel shrugs awkwardly. 'I don't *dis*like her,' he says. 'She's very, very… nice.'

'Is that what you want?'

'Life with her won't be terribly interesting, but it won't be awful either. I could do worse.' He glances at me. 'I probably could have done better.'

'So if there was a way…' I begin tentatively.

'Father wants me to marry Roslyn,' he says, shaking his head. 'She's exactly what he wants in a wife.'

My heart sinks. 'What about what you want?'

'The only time my father listens to me is when I'm agreeing with him,' he says, leaning back against the schoolhouse wall. 'What I want doesn't matter.'

I take his hand and weave my fingers through his. They're clammy and damp with sweat, but they feel good locked with mine. He smiles at me, gently pulling me closer until our shoulders are pressed together.

'I don't want to defend your father,' I tell him. 'But he did listen to you at least once. Maybe we can still reason with him.'

'We?'

'I have an idea. I think I can get him to change his mind about me.'

Samuel looks dubious. 'Father doesn't change his mind about anything.'

'I can do it,' I say, determined. 'But only with your help. And only if you still want me.'

'Of course I do,' he says simply. 'But what if it doesn't work?'

I shrug helplessly. 'It has to.'

He releases my hand and puts his arm around me, pulling me into a hug. The butterflies in my stomach go wild as I wrap my arms around his shoulders, but in the most pleasant, giddy way.

'So,' he says softly, lips moving against my jaw as he speaks. 'Tell me your plan.'

○

Caroline is happy to let me leave the afternoon class early. I walk briskly, skipping over gaps in the cobblestones. I've only given myself a few minutes head start on the tailor's wife, but hopefully it's enough. I only need a moment alone with her husband.

The bell tinkles as I open the door.

'Just a second,' the voice comes from the back. I stand quietly, looking at an elegant grey coat on display. It's beautiful work.

'Emma,' Matthew sounds surprised as he emerges from the back, pins sticking out of his sleeve. He nods to the coat. 'For the doctor. I only finished it yesterday.'

'It's very handsome.'

'It's your father's pattern,' he says, as if it's meant to be a compliment. 'What can I do for you? More thread?'

I take a breath and speak before I lose my courage. 'Actually, I came to beg some of your offcuts.'

Matthew looks like he doesn't know what to say. 'I don't just give those away, Emma,' he says after a moment. 'Some of them come from very expensive cloth.'

'Please, Matthew,' I say, kissing my dignity goodbye. 'Mama and I have never asked you for anything before, not for free, and I wouldn't be doing it now if I had any other choice.'

His face clouds over. I'm afraid he's going to throw me out, but he just sighs. 'Wait here.'

I place a coin on the counter. 'And thread, and pink and green ribbon please.'

He returns after a few minutes with a small sack and my ribbon and thread. 'This is all I can spare,' he warns. 'Be sure to bring back whatever you don't use.'

'I will,' I say, relief making me sound every bit as grateful as I am. 'Lord bless you, Matthew. Truly.' I hurry out of the store, neatly avoiding having to run into his wife.

Turning for home, I peer into the sack, eager to see what I have to work with.

○

Mama is sceptical of my plan. What I'm attempting to do breaks tradition, and we all know how the mayor feels about that. But, accepting that I can hardly make matters worse for myself, she agrees to help me.

We take our dinner on the floor and pour over the pile of scraps. Most are too small to do anything with, and some are of questionable colour or low-quality cloth, but we salvage a small, attractive pile of whites, greys and blues.

Mama squints in the candlelight, winnowing the pile again to four large pieces of navy and light blue silk and several long strips of white and grey cotton. 'These,' she says. 'Anything else and we'll be making patchwork.'

She sits with me long into the night, patiently teaching me how to sew a row of tiny perfect stitches in fine fabric. As I work on the squares, she begins joining the strips together, organizing them so that the colours appear to fade into each other, dark to light, like smoke. We fall into an exhausted sleep sometime after midnight, leaving our dinner dishes unclean and forgotten on the floor. And we still have so much to do.

○

Lonesome isn't waiting for me by the tree. I cover a yawn and look across the field of bluebells. The woods and meadow are darker than I'm used to dreaming about. The moon and stars are hidden behind a layer of cloud, and only a handful of fireflies drift through the air.

'Lonesome?' I call into the gloom.

His voice drifts down from somewhere above me. 'You look happy.'

'I am,' I say, looking up. I can just make out his silhouette against the sky, perched on a high white branch. 'I had a good day.'

'With Stupid. I know.'

I blink, and the silhouette is gone. I step forward, trying to find him again. 'Don't call him that.'

'Maybe I should name *you* Stupid, then,' he says, his voice sounding further away.

'Well, that's rude,' I say, crossing my arms.

'It's fitting if you honestly believe he's not going to upset you again.'

'He won't. I'm going to fix things with his father, and then everything will be all right again.'

A snort of laughter comes from my right. I look for him there, but it's too dark too see anything, and getting darker.

'What was that for?' I ask, hurt.

'You,' he said, his voice growing even fainter. Is he going back to the trees? 'You're not going to fix anything. They'll never let you. All you'll ever be is disappointed and alone.'

'You don't know that!'

There's no answer. At least, none that I can hear. I rest one hand on the white tree and step past it, cocking my head to listen. I hear nothing.

'Lonesome?' I call.

Nothing.

'Why aren't you happy for me?' I ask the darkness. 'I thought you were my friend!'

One by one, the fireflies wink out.

○

I meet Roslyn outside the schoolhouse after her afternoon class. Her two younger brothers race ahead as Nicole and Louise join us. Louise walks beside me, chatting cheerfully as Roslyn and Nicole whisper behind us. I try not to imagine what they're saying, though with Nicole doing most of the whispering I can easily imagine.

We part ways in the square. Louise gives me a little wave, which I return before Nicole takes her hand and pulls her away.

'Well?' Roslyn asks with a pleasant smile. 'Shall we?'

I smile tersely and nod. I've never been alone with Roslyn before. I'm afraid it'll be like spending the afternoon with one of the tailor's mannequins, but she's an important part of the plan. I need to be a respectable girl, and for that I need to spend time with other respectable girls.

I'm surprised when Roslyn links her arm through mine and leads me across the square, and I'm not the only one. People glance at us as we walk together, intrigued by the latest development in the drama of my existence. At least it means there'll be plenty of gossip to travel back to the mayor.

Roslyn's two-story house is every bit as beautiful and well-kept as she is. Her father's surgery and consultation rooms are attached to the house, all concealed behind a high stone wall covered in peach coloured roses.

A change comes over Roslyn as she shuts the gate behind us. Her posture slumps and her shuttered face comes alive. 'Come on,' she says, tugging my arm towards the door. 'I'm starving.'

Roslyn's mother, Charlotte, greets us in the cosy kitchen with a pot of tea and a tray of still-warm biscuits she assures us she baked herself. My stomach rumbles at the sight of them, but I force myself to take a small, polite bite at a time. 'Delicious,' I tell Charlotte, meaning it with every fibre of my being. 'But I wouldn't had judged you for buying them.'

Charlotte gives a long-suffering smile and hoists her youngest daughter, Lily, onto her hip. 'You'd be the only one,' she says, nodding tolerantly as Lily babbles emphatically at the three of us, only a third of which seems to be in a language we can recognise. 'Yes, darling, I know.' A heavy thud and a peal of boyish laughter comes from upstairs. Charlotte doesn't even wince.

'The tailor's wife saw Mummy buying a cake from the bakery three years ago,' Roslyn says, unbothered by the thunder of her siblings as she dips her biscuit in her tea. 'And she's *still* telling people that Mummy thinks she's too good to have to act like a real wife.'

'I had a newborn and two very active little boys to deal with,' Charlotte said. 'Lord forbid I *buy* my eldest daughter a birthday cake.'

I bite back a laugh. I hadn't expected Roslyn's home to be so chaotic or so comfortable. 'That sounds like Mary,' I say, erring on the side of diplomacy.

'How's your mother, Emma?' Charlotte asks, handing Lily a biscuit and releasing her back to the floor.

'She's well,' I say, taking a sip of my tea.

Charlotte smiles fondly. 'It's been far too long since I've spoken with her. We used to be quite friendly when we were younger, but… Well.' Her smile fades. She looks away.

'Shall I tell her you say hello?' I ask.

'Oh, please do.'

'Come on,' Roslyn says, picking up her tea and taking a handful of biscuits. 'I'll teach you something to surprise her with.'

I pick up my cup and follow Roslyn into an intimate sitting room arranged around an upright piano. There are only a few of them in the village, as they have to be specially and brought in pieces to be assembled on site. The tuner only visits once a year.

Roslyn sets her teacup beside a vase of cut roses and hands me two more biscuits. 'Eat,' she urges me. 'No one's looking.' I hesitate for a moment, then cram a full biscuit into my mouth. Roslyn grins and takes a seat at the piano, hands poised. 'Do you sing often?'

I swallow hard before I answer. 'Not in front of anyone,' I say, suddenly nervous at the prospect of doing it now. 'I don't even know if I can.'

'Do you know the Dedication to Our Lord?'

I bite my thumbnail. 'Most of it.'

She bats my hand away from my mouth as easily as Mama or Mona would. 'Do you know any song all the way through?'

'Not really.'

Roslyn laughs and shakes her head. 'That's all right. Just try to match the note with me. Ready?'

Roslyn spends the next hour making me sing the note she strikes on the piano. Her voice is high and sweet, and mine struggles to follow her. 'It just means you have a lower register,' she assures me. 'Not that you're awful.' I find it hard to believe her, but the further we move down the keys, the better I manage. When she's satisfied with what she hears, she teaches me a simple song about a bluebird in the rain.

'It's strange we haven't really spoken since we started

morning school, don't you think?' she asks when we finish. 'When we see each other every day.'

'Not that strange,' I say. 'You and Nicole always used to tease Mona.'

'I know,' she says. 'We shouldn't have. She always nice to us.'

'Why did you?'

'We heard the teacher say something about her and her grandmother one day. I suppose we thought it was funny to repeat it.'

'It wasn't.'

'No,' she agrees. She hesitates, then says, 'We used to make fun of you, too. Behind your back.'

It stings to hear her admit to it, though I'm not exactly surprised. 'I assumed you still did,' I say.

'No, not for years. Mummy caught me doing it and gave me such a whacking I didn't dare.'

I blink in surprise. 'Why would she care if you made fun of me?'

'She said that what happened to you and your mother could happen to any of us,' she says, playing a scale. 'That you deserve kindness, not cruelty.'

'Oh,' I say, taken aback. 'That's nice to hear.'

Roslyn looks at me sidelong and strikes a note, high and optimistic. 'I know what you're up to, you know.'

My heart races. 'What do you mean?' I ask, trying to sound guiltless. She gives a low laugh, and I know I haven't succeeded.

'I've seen you and Samuel looking at each other,' she says. She sounds oddly unbothered. 'It's obvious he'd rather be courting you than me.'

I watch her, frowning. 'Doesn't that upset you?'

'No,' she says, hitting another note.

I can't tell where she's going with this. 'Are you going to stop me?'

She shakes her head. 'It doesn't make much difference to me. If you fail, I'll marry Samuel. If you don't, I'll marry Andrew.'

'But Andrew's got no money,' I point out. 'It's a huge difference.'

'Daddy and the farm doctor know each other quite well. If I marry Andrew, he'll recommend him for an apprenticeship. It's good money.'

My eyebrows shoot up. 'You've already talked about it?'

'The night you went to the mayor's house for dinner. Daddy's a practical man. The only real difference is that I won't get to be the mayor's wife, and I don't think I mind much about that.'

'But what about Nicole?' I ask. 'You're her best friend. She and Andrew are practically engaged now.'

Roslyn closes the piano and looks at me. 'Nicole's no match for me,' she says plainly. 'I'm not saying it to be cruel, or because I think I'm better than she is. It's just how things are. I'm rich, and Andrew's family isn't. If you can get the mayor to consider you again, and I don't blame you for trying, then Andrew's father will call on mine within the hour. I'll marry Andrew, you'll marry Samuel, and Nicole will be unmarried.'

I stare at her, aghast. 'Will you shun her?'

Roslyn shakes her head at me, as though she's disappointed. 'I don't want to, Emma, but there are rules. You tried to ignore them and look where that got you.'

I feel a hollow pit in my stomach. 'They're bad rules.'

'I know,' she says with a resigned sigh. 'But once they're on your side, you'll hardly notice they were ever there.'

That night, although I call and call, the meadow is empty.

10

I take a deep breath, check the bundle under my arm for the thousandth time, and approach Mayor Jones' house.

It's taken me over a week to finish my gifts. Mama poured over each item this morning, studying them outside in the daylight to make sure every stitch is perfect. Finally, she returned them to me and kissed my cheeks to commend me on my work.

I expel the air in a long, nervous stream and raise my trembling hand to the door. I knock twice, then step back and bow my head. Luckily, although a thin layer of grey cloud has gathered overhead, there's no sign of rain. Nothing can possibly ruin the bundle unless I drop it, which, given the state of my sweat-slicked hands, is a real possibility.

The door opens so silently I barely have time to pull myself together. I don't know why I'm surprised. Rich people's doors don't groan when they open. Jane stands in the doorway, dressed in plain brown.

'I'd like to speak with the mayor,' I say without curtseying.

Today I'm doing nothing wrong, and that means treating Jane like a piece of furniture.

Jane glances up at me through her eyelashes, intrigued. She curtseys and steps back, silently inviting me inside. Escorting me to the sitting room, she holds out a hand and bids me to wait.

I don't sit or stare at the gold and silver trinkets or the amazingly soft sofa this time. I stand in the centre of the room and face the entrance, eyes lowered, bundle clasped gently in my hands. My hair is perfectly smooth and braided tightly around my head. I'm wearing my Sunday clothes even though it's a Saturday. Every inch of me is scrubbed so clean I think I'm missing a layer of skin. But it's worked. My cheeks are pink with health and eyes bright and clear. I look like my old self again. I might even look like a perfect woman, if I could just get my hands to stop shaking.

Mayor Jones enters after a minute or so with Samuel close behind him. I wish I could look at their faces, see if Mayor Jones is surprised or angry to see me, but I don't let myself give in to the temptation.

'That will be all, Samuel,' Mayor Jones says. It's a clear order.

'Yes, Father,' Samuel says. 'Good afternoon, Emma.'

I don't respond with anything but a slight curtsey. His footsteps are quiet as he leaves the room.

'Miss Emma,' the mayor says, waiting until Samuel is well out of the way before he even acknowledges I'm here. 'This is… unusual.'

'Good afternoon, Mayor Jones,' I say and curtsey again. This time I go as low as I can, keeping my spine straight and my eyes on his feet. It's a textbook curtsey, and it hurts my knees. 'I apologise for calling on you like this, but such business is ordinarily done by fathers and, as you know, I don't have the privilege of a living one. By rights my mother should serve in his stead, but my mother is in your employment and it would be out of order for her to approach you like this.' I try to keep my voice soft, but steady. 'So without a father, or brothers, or a mother of means, it only leaves me to speak with you.'

I want to look up and gauge his reaction, but I don't dare.

'Please, sit with me,' he says. I see his hand indicate the wonderful sofa. I curtsey again and take the very edge of it, not letting myself sink into the cushions. Proper young women probably aren't supposed to look too comfortable.

'I assume this is in regard to my withdrawing consent for Samuel to court you,' he says. 'Emma, you must understand my reasoning.'

'I do,' I force myself to agree, hoping I sound convincing. 'However, I'd like to explain myself and my decision to see the Stranger girl that day, against your wishes.'

I pause and wait for his permission. Rushing to talk over him won't win me any favours here.

'Go on,' he says.

'It was due to a promise,' I explain. 'To meet with her after Deference. I made it before our dinner, and I had no opportunity to see her the day after.' I swallow hard, hating the taste of the words. 'I wrestled with myself over it, wondering if it would be best to just leave her waiting. But I remembered what you said that night, about how we should do our best to be polite to everyone. And I considered the words of our Lord, that we can never trust one who breaks a vow, however small, for a vow is also a pact with our Lord to be truthful.' I've stared at that passage in class enough to be able to reel it off from memory. 'I worried, sir, that breaking my promise would endanger my standing with our Lord which, begging your pardon, is more important to me than my standing with any mortal man, even ones so esteemed as you and your son.' I leave it there, afraid of saying too much.

'And you told the Stranger girl of your decision that day?'

'No,' I admit, aware he would have been told about us seeing each other after that by *some*one, if not half the village. If he caught me in a lie now, I'd have no hope. 'I told her the following week, after you had the doctor's family over to dinner.'

'Why the delay?' He's looking for any hole in my story. But I've prepared for it.

'She was upset, sir. Seeing everyone return from Deference makes her feel different.'

'She is different.'

'And she knows it,' I say. 'But as much as I knew I had to break contact with her, for my own good, I couldn't bring myself to tell her on that day. It would not have been kind.'

'And the following days?'

'*I* was upset. You had already sent my mother the letter withdrawing Samuel's interest. It took several days recover from the disappointment of losing his company. But I did tell her, sir. Our friendship has been over for some time now, and I feel the better for it.'

The mayor falls quiet, thinking it over.

Taking the opportunity, I unwrap my bundle and hold it out: four perfectly square handkerchiefs and one grey and white cravat. Each immaculately hemmed and embroidered, the handkerchiefs with pink buds and the cravat a chain of blooming pink and white carnations.

'I made you a gift,' I say, stating the obvious. 'I have much to offer as a wife. And as one who cannot remember a father, it would be an honour to care for you as one in his stead.' This is where I hope Mona is wrong, and I'm not as bad a liar as she says.

The mayor takes the gifts and opens out the cravat, taking a long time to look it over completely. 'You made this? Yourself?' he asks finally.

I nod. 'Mama taught me some of the stitches, but everything was done by my own hand. We have very little, and this was all we could afford. But if you like them, I'd be happy to make you more, or anything else you wanted.'

'I have heard positive things about you since we last spoke,' the mayor concedes. 'You haven't spoken with the Stranger girl since you said. You've been seen with the doctor's daughter. And the parents have been talking about your lesson in the meadow. The children are more wary of the woods than ever, and it pleases all of us.' I can't tell if he's been specifically checking up on me, or if the adults have nothing better to talk about. 'It would seem that you've been making an effort.'

I'm cautiously optimistic, but I sense I'm still on dangerous ground. 'Yes, Mayor Jones.'

'But you must see how good a match Roslyn is for Samuel,' he continues. 'They have seen each other many times now. Would you have me tell the doctor that his daughter is being rejected for the daughter of my cleaning woman? Who, until very recently, was only ever seen in the company of a Stranger girl, and is now using his daughter and his home to get into my good graces? Who spends Deference rolling her eyes and looking at my son rather than focusing on our Lord, however well she thinks she can recite the words?'

Struck by what he's saying, I glance up and meet his eyes accidentally. They're cold, almost triumphant.

I've lost.

'This is the problem with young women who fancy themselves as being intelligent,' he says, standing up. He takes the rare opportunity to tower over me, smug as he moves to a crystal decanter and pours himself a drink. He doesn't even pretend to offer me one. 'You look too high above your own station. You could have been perfectly content with the farm labourer's boy, had he chosen you, but no. Samuel's position and wealth were much more appealing.'

My mouth drops open. 'Samuel courted *me*,' I say. 'Not the other way around.'

'But after what encouragement from you? After what coaching from your mother?'

My hands ball into fists, no longer trembling from fear but fury. I want to shout at him, to grab him by his perfectly tailored lapels and tell him that Mama and I never wanted his son's attention in the first place. To demand to know how favouring Roslyn and all her money and prestige is any better than what he's accusing me of. But I'm speechless. So many words and thoughts rush into my mouth that they jam together and create an impasse on my lips.

'Just as I thought,' he takes my silence as confirmation. 'You're not the first young woman to try to bend the rules, my dear, and I don't think you need to ask what became of those who came before you.' He raises his glass to me. 'I do wish you luck, though. Sundays seem to be the best for begging. Unless, of course, you feel yourself above that.'

Numb, I stand without curtseying and walk to the door. He doesn't follow me. I get there before Jane and let myself out. Keeping my composure as I cross the square is easy, and even walking through the village with my head held high is manageable, but as I reach my house and put my hand on the doorknob, I find I can't bring myself to turn it. Mama is inside, waiting for me. Hoping, because I gave her hope.

And once again, I have to disappoint her.

My lip quivers, and suddenly I'm running blindly. I collapse to my knees in the bluebells, sobs taking over my body. Of course my feet brought me here. Where else can I cry without anyone hearing me and reporting back to that horrible man?

I weep until my face burns and my head pounds. How could I let myself believe that a glorified scarf and an afternoon with Roslyn would make the mayor change his mind about me? How could I have been so stupid?

Arms encircle me, pulling me close. I look up and see Mama, her own eyes wet.

Stroking my hair, she doesn't try to comfort me. She knows there's nothing to say.

But Mayor Jones isn't done with us yet.

I come home on Monday to find Mama bent over the table, our small store of money in front of her. She counts it, skewed fingers dragging each coin over the scuffed wood.

'What's happened?' I ask, a sinking feeling in my chest.

'Mayor Jones no longer requires my services,' Mama says unsteadily. 'Samuel will be married soon, and Jane will clean as well as cook until his new wife takes over.'

Disappointment and fury surge through me at once. I turn around and march straight back out the door.

Mama races after me, trying to keep up but struggling with her stiff joints. 'Emma!' she cries. 'Emma, stop.'

But I refuse, charging up the street. Mama manages to catch hold of me, fingers gripping my wrist. I see curtains twitch, eyes peeping out. Let them look, the leeches. Let them see how miserable we are.

'Emma, don't,' she says, clutching desperately at me. 'It's done.'

'He can't treat you like this,' I hiss. 'You've worked for him for years. He knows he's the only one who pays you properly. What does he expect you to do now? Starve?'

'I would have been dismissed when they were married anyway,' she says helplessly. 'It's the way it is.'

'It's the way it is because *he* makes the rules,' I insist. 'It isn't fair!'

'And what do you think screaming at him will achieve?' she asks. 'What do you think you can change?'

My fury dulls. She's right. 'This is all my fault,' I whisper, slowing to a stop. 'Mama, I'm so sorry.'

She puts an arm around me. 'You did nothing,' she says.

My voice sounds small and young. 'What are we going to do?'

'We'll live, Emma. Somehow.'

Returning to the house, we spot a thin figure dressed in blue standing at the top of the meadow. Louise holds a meagre bundle of white daisies, picked from the very verge. She stares fearfully down the hill. We must have walked past her on the way out, not even noticing her in my outburst.

'Louise?' I ask gently. 'What are you doing?'

'Mother liked the flowers I brought home that day from class. We're having people over for dinner and she wanted some white ones for the table, but…' she glances at Mama and whispers, 'I'm scared, Emma.'

'And rightly so,' Mama confirms her fears. 'The meadow is no place for young girls so late in the day. Best be getting home.'

'But mother wants the flowers for tonight,' Louise insists.

'She should have sent your father, then.'

'I'll get them,' I say. 'I'll find you some snowdrops and some yarrow.'

Louise looks at her thin bouquet. 'And more daisies?'

'So many daisies,' I promise.

Mama isn't impressed by my offer, but Louise looks relieved. Mama takes her hand. 'Shall we have some hot chocolate while we wait?' she asks Louise. As gruff as Mama has become, she'll still share what little she has. I smile sadly at her and step into the meadow.

Expecting the search and the familiar scent of the wildflowers to calm me down, I find myself imagining each snowdrop and daisy is the mayor. 'Arrogant, presumptuous pig,' I snarl to myself, ripping stalks violently from the ground. 'Pompous arse. *Bastard.*'

I return home and present Louise with an enormous bouquet, every white flower a symbol of somewhere I'd like to put the hard toe of my boot. Mama ties some leftover ribbon around the stems to hold them together. 'Make sure she puts them straight in some water,' she tells Louise. 'They wilt quickly.'

'I will,' Loise says, looking warily to the window.

'I'll walk you home,' I say, pulling on my cloak. The air has taken a chill as the sun goes down.

'Thank you,' she says gratefully. Mona's warning about the woods still has her thoroughly spooked, and I wouldn't be surprised if Nicole has been whispering horror stories to her.

'There's nothing to be afraid of,' I assure her softly as we pass the meadow. 'Nobody knows for sure if there's anything in the woods, apart from fireflies. Are you afraid of fireflies?'

A sheepish smile creeps over her face. 'No.'

We turn into the high street. Despite my assurance, Louise looks relieved to be away from the meadow. 'But what if I have bad dreams about them?' she asks. 'The woods, I mean. Not the fireflies.'

Mayor Jones emerges from the blacksmith, further down the street. He tips his hat politely at us, gracing me with a smile. My eyes drop to his neck, and I see he's wearing the embroidered cravat. My blood runs ice cold with anger, but we turn into Louise's lane before I can scream any or all of the things I want to.

'Emma?'

'They're just dreams, Louise,' I mutter wearily. 'Dreams can't hurt you.'

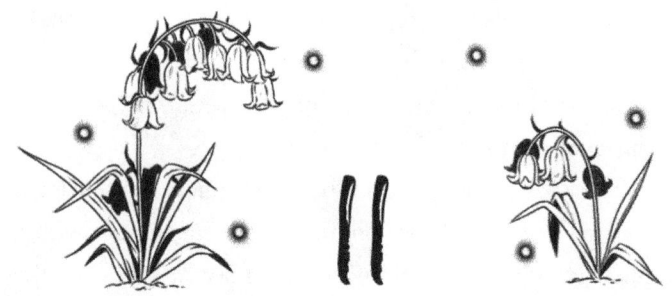

The long grass whips my bare legs as the wind sends the trees rustling. There's no other sound, no light but the narrow moon.

I stumble and put an arm around the white tree, stepping beside it to call Lonesome's name, but my voice echoes over the bluebells and fades into the pitch black of the woods.

'Lonesome!' I call again, and again, and again, until I sink to my knees in the nest of white roots. 'Please,' I call, my voice a horse whisper. 'I don't want to lose you, too.'

A hand touches my shoulder, emanating heat. Lonesome stands over me, fireflies clinging to his horns. It looks like he's wearing a crown of captured sunlight.

'You were right,' I whisper. 'I couldn't fix any of it. I just made everything worse.'

He kneels beside me and wraps his arms around my shoulders. 'I'm sorry,' he says. The heat of him rushes through me, clouding my mind, though I don't shrink away from it this time.

'I don't know what I'm going to do,' I say, raising my thumbnail to my teeth. My heart races. 'Mama lost her best paying job because of me. She thinks we can make up for it by offering laundry services, but she's only guessing, and if it doesn't work I'll have to start begging in the square. But barely anyone ever gives anything to beggars. Mama will starve and it'll be all my fault…' I yelp as I bite down too hard on my nail, ripping it down to the skin. Tears prick behind my eyes.

Lonesome takes my thumb away from my mouth, holding my hand tight. 'Stop. Breathe. Do you want to dance?'

'No,' I sniff, letting my head drop into the curve of his shoulder.

'Do you want to talk?'

'No.'

His voice trembles. 'Do you want to come with me?'

I open my mouth to decline again, but nothing comes. This is *my* dream, after all. Why shouldn't I go? 'Just for tonight?' I ask.

He releases me and gives a wide, crooked grin. The heat retreats from my body in an instant, leaving me cold and woozy. 'For as long as you like,' he says, standing and offering his hand to me.

I steady myself against the white tree and reach for his hand, but our fingertips only brush. He's standing further away than I thought. I stand and take a step out to meet him, letting his hand engulf mine. The heat returns, taking away the chill.

'Come,' he urges, and I realise my other hand is still on the white tree. Almost reluctantly, I let my hand fall away from the bark.

Lonesome's hands are on my waist in a second, lifting me as easily as if I were a child 'I knew it!' he whoops, spinning me in a giddy circle before returning my feet to the bluebells. 'Come. They're waiting.'

The night keeps spinning, even though I'm no longer moving. 'They?' I ask, wiping my burning forehead and finding no sweat.

'My people. I've been telling them about you forever.' He turns to the trees and pulls me along by the hand, walking faster than my legs can keep up.

The heat in my skin intensifies the closer we get to the woods. The trees loom before us, and then around us. How did we get here so quickly?

'Wait,' I say, my voice heavy and slow. 'Wait.'

'Don't worry,' he says. 'You'll forget all about those awful people. We'll dance and eat and drink and never think about them again.'

I swallow. My throat is thick. 'Mama…'

'Her too. All of them.'

I press my free hand to my head. I feel like I'm on fire, and yet my skin is cold to the touch. 'I don't want that,' I say, my words slurring together. Lonesome doesn't seem to hear me. 'Wait. *Wait.*' I wrench my hand away so hard that I stumble back and fall to the ground.

Lonesome turns back. 'What's wrong?'

Words from what feel like a lifetime ago come to me out of the fog in my head.

'You didn't go in, did you?'

'Where?'

'The woods, in your dream.'

I blink up at the trees, thin shafts of moonlight piercing the canopy. Looking back, I can just make out the spectre of the white tree.

'No, I was in the bluebells.'

'Try not to, if you dream about him again.'

'Emma?' Lonesome looms over me. For the first time, I appreciate just how tall he is. How much strength lies in those lean, bare muscles.

'You don't know what will happen.'

'I've changed my mind,' I say, forcing myself to sound firm. I slide myself backwards through the carpet of bluebells, wondering how far away from the tree line we've come. 'I don't want to go.'

The shadows paint a terrible mask over Lonesome's face. 'What do you mean? Why?'

'I don't want to go,' I repeat. The words come easier without him touching me, without the heat cooking my brain and choking my words. 'I want to go back to the meadow.'

'No, you don't,' he insists through gritted teeth. 'You're just scared again.' He reaches for me, but I flinch away from his touch. 'Let me help you.'

'I don't want your help. I want to go home.' I use a low, jutting branch to pull myself to my feet and turn my back on him. The edge of the woods is close. I can see the white tree standing like a beacon in the moonlight, equal distance between the woods and the bottom of the hill. I march towards it.

'Stop!' Lonesome calls, grabbing me roughly by the wrist. His nails pinch at my skin. Were they always this long?

'You're hurting me!' I cry out, trying to pull myself free.

'I wouldn't have to if you'd just listen,' he insists, pulling me close and wrapping his arms around me. 'I know you're afraid,' he says. 'But you'll understand once you see it. You'll never want to leave.'

He's too strong. I close my eyes, trying to ignore how uncomfortably hot I feel in his arms and focus on waking myself up. My feet leave the ground. He's carrying me.

I dig my nails deep into my palms, waiting for the pain to send me back into my bed.

Nothing.

This is a nightmare, and I'm stuck in it.

A firefly lands in his hair, illuminating his long, smooth neck. I sink my teeth into his searing hot skin, biting down as hard I can. Something wet blossoms across my tongue, though it lacks any of the sharpness of blood.

Lonesome lets out a howl of pain and drops me. The fireflies in his horns scatter at the sound. I spring to my feet, wiping my mouth as I dash through the bluebells.

His hand closes on my shoulder. He pulls me back hard. 'Why can't you trust me?' he asks, a growl in his voice.

'You're not real,' I shout, kicking hard behind me. I catch

him in the shin. His hand loosens, and I take the chance to wrench myself away. I run for the white tree, leaping over the roots and not stopping until I reach the top of the hill.

Panting hard, I look back.

Lonesome stands beside the white tree. Two fireflies circle him in slow, bobbing loops.

'Is that all?' he calls up, his voice cracking. 'Because you think I'm not real?'

The burst of energy that helped me escape wears off. I sag to my knees, head thick and hot. 'I want to wake up now,' I murmur. 'I don't want to dream like this anymore.'

'I'll prove it, then,' he calls. 'I'll prove it and then you'll see that I can help you. I'll make it so that they never hurt you again.'

'*You* hurt me,' I whisper, pushing myself to my feet and staggering wearily up the hill.

'Emma! Emma!'

I cover my ears and keep walking, hearing his voice long after it's been lost across the meadow. I stagger into the house and fall into bed, waiting to wake.

○

I open my eyes to Mama find standing over me. Her body shifts and blurs, but I can see that her face is pale. I hear something. Her voice, maybe, asking me something.

'Wha…' I murmur. 'Why are you already up?

Her voice swims and clarifies. 'It's morning.' She puts a cool hand to my forehead. 'Lord, Emma, you're burning up!'

'I'm not. I'm fine,' I say, trying to sit up. My arms give out. I fall back onto my pillow.

Mama pulls the blankets back up to my chin and strokes my hair. 'Stay still. You're not going anywhere today.'

'I'm all right,' I insist as the room warps around me. 'I just had a nightmare.'

'Hisht, Emma,' Mama says softly. Her hands on my hair soothe me almost back to sleep, but I battle against it, afraid I'll go back to the night meadow. But my head is pounding, and my body burns, and my eyes droop shut against my will.

○

I don't see Lonesome, but his song chases me from dream to dream: sharp and angry, screeching in my mind.

My eyes open to Roslyn and the doctor, to Mama, to heat, to darkness, to Mona, to an empty house, then close again to find the song waiting for me.

○

I wake up, finally, feeling cool and covered with sweat.

Dusk is falling outside the window, though there are no candles lit. I have to squint in the dimming light to make out Mama slumped over the table, unmoving.

'Mama?' I ask, my voice rasping. At the sound of my voice she jumps up and rushes to my side, feeling my forehead and then wrapping me up in a warm hug.

'Oh, Emma,' she breathes, kissing my cheeks. 'It's gone. The fever's gone.'

'I'm hungry, Mama,' I say, snuggling into her arms. I feel five years old again.

'Tea,' she decides. 'And then we'll see if you can stomach something stronger.'

I notice a jar of bluebells on the table. 'What are those?'

'I found them outside the door yesterday. There was a note.' She raises herself stiffly and fetches a small square of paper, neatly folded. Inside is thin, wobbly writing: *I wish I could be there to hold your hand.*

I smile weakly, clutching the note to my chest.

'You're playing a dangerous game, my girl,' she warns, and yet I don't feel that she entirely disapproves. 'If the mayor catches you…'

'What more can he do to us, Mama?' I ask.

She sighs, and runs a hand through my lank, sweaty hair. 'Chocolate, I think. Not tea.'

For all I don't have, I'm lucky to have her.

12

Mama insists on walking me to the schoolhouse before she heads to work. Only two widowers are left to employ her, and only one-half day a week each.

I catch sight of Mona across the square. Remembering her face at my bedside, I raise my arm, opening my mouth to call out to her, but I stop myself before I can. Being rejected by the mayor again doesn't negate anything she said to me in the meadow that day. She asked to be left alone, and even though I hate it, I have to respect it.

I turn back to Mama. A second later, I'm almost bowled over by the force of someone throwing their arms around me. 'Emma!' Mona shrieks straight into my ear. 'You're all right!'

I wince at the noise, but return the hug. I don't care if anyone is looking. I have my friend back, and that means everything.

Mona pulls away, wiping her eyes and taking my arm. 'I'll look after her,' she assures Mama.

Mama smiles. Not having to worry about our reputation

is a weight off her shoulders. 'Make sure you walk her home at lunch,' she orders. 'Don't let her rush herself.'

'Mama,' I protest. 'I'm fine.'

'Hisht,' Mama says, kissing my cheeks. 'I'll see you at home. Don't touch dinner. Don't touch anything. Get straight into bed and wait for me to look after you.'

I sigh and look to the sky. 'Yes, Mama.'

Mona leads me towards the schoolhouse. 'Be patient with your mother,' she says. 'She was scared for you.'

'It was only a fever,' I say.

'Don't be like that. People have died of a fever.'

I look at her. 'I know. I'm sorry.'

She sniffs, squeezing my arm. 'No, I'm sorry. I was scared for you as well.'

'If it means we're talking again, then it was worth it,' I tell her sincerely.

'I was so stupid to even suggest it,' she says, shaking her head. 'Nothing got easier. I was just miserable the whole time.' She pauses. 'I heard about what happened with the mayor. I'm sorry. I really thought he would change his mind about you if I stayed out of the way.'

'So did I.'

'What a bastard,' she announces, squeezing my arm again.

I smile. 'I missed you, too.'

○

My strength returns quickly. Once I'm well enough for Mama to stop fussing over, I go door to door in search of prospective laundry customers. The response is slow at first, but once Charlotte accepts our services the work comes in greater numbers.

I help her on the afternoons I'm not in school, and Mona joins us for dinner on the days I do. She brings pilfered fruit whenever she can, earning Mama's praise each time. We spend Sunday afternoons together again, and every lunchtime, and every other moment we can spare. She hasn't said anything about leaving again, and I don't ask her about it. It's selfish of me, but I hope it means she's decided to stay.

Despite my failure with the mayor, Roslyn insists on continuing our lessons twice a week. While my voice is nothing special on its own, something wonderful happens when we sing together. Her mother sits in to listen to us often, and sometimes even her father joins us, his ornate silver cane keeping time on the floorboards. Afterwards, she slips me little parcels of cake and biscuits to take home to Mama. In the course of things, despite both of us knowing she'll have to stop speaking to me the moment I come of age, we've become friends.

'Doesn't the mayor disapprove of you spending time with me?' I ask one afternoon, a note of bitterness creeping into my voice.

'He did,' she says with a sly smile. 'But Daddy told him how strongly I feel about charity work.'

'Damned fool of a man,' the doctor grumbles, overhearing us as he passes through the house. My jaw drops, but Roslyn only giggles and shushes him.

One day, walking me to the door, she presses a piece of paper into my hands with a glance back into the house. 'From a mutual friend,' she whispers, though there's nobody to overhear us. I've learned that Roslyn has a secret collection of adventure and romance novels – books totally frowned on by the mayor but peddled by various traders – and that she adores a good intrigue.

Raising my eyebrows, I open it and recognize the wobbly writing at once.

'This really doesn't bother you?' I ask at a normal volume.

'Oh, please,' she says, disappointed I won't play along. 'I hardly know him.'

'But you're getting married now,' I point out. It official. I've heard the tailor's already ordered pearls for Roslyn's wedding dress.

'So?' She asks with a shrug. 'I don't mind sharing him with the less fortunate.'

I chuckle at the jibe. She's right. I could use the charity.

'Anyway,' she continues. 'The more time he spends with you, the less he'll hover around me, trying to think of something to say. It works out for both of us.'

'Who *would* you marry, if you could choose?' I ask, curious. For all her books, she's never mentioned anyone. I haven't even caught her looking.

Roslyn hesitates. 'Out of anyone?' she asks.

'Go on,' I urge her. 'I won't tell. And in a few months, nobody will listen to anything I say, anyway.' It was supposed to sound light, like a joke, but we can both hear the edge to it.

'You won't judge me?'

'I promise.'

She bites her lip and steps close to me, looking at the ground. 'I think,' she says, her voice soft and shy, 'that if I could choose anyone, it would be a woman.'

I try to hide my surprise, but the disappointed look she gives me tells me I've failed. 'Who?' I ask, lowering my voice to match hers.

Her lips twist into a wry smile. 'That's one secret I think I should keep for myself.'

'You're *all* secrets,' I point out, accepting the rebuff with a smile. 'Half the village wouldn't even know you had a brain.'

'I should hope I've managed to fool more than that.' She curtseys perfectly, batting her lashes at me. 'See you at school. Bring a reply for our husband.'

Chuckling, I pause before the wooden gate to read the message again.

'Can I meet you?'

My cheeks heat up. I drop the note into my bag and step into the evening buzz of the square.

13

Aware I'm being noticed by practically everyone, I try not to walk too quickly down the high street. I touch a hand to my temple as if I'm in pain, managing a wan smile at the blacksmith's wife. By now, everyone knows about the fever.

Reaching my street, I cast my eyes around for anyone watching and step into the meadow, letting myself gather speed as I hit the plateau and jog on over the hill. The air fills my dress, ballooning it out behind me as I run down the hill so fast I can only stop myself by wrapping my arms around the white tree.

Breathless with the fun of the run and the thrill of breaking the rules, I stand with my cheek against the cool bark for a minute or two.

It's been weeks since my last meadow dream. The last one, the night before the fever hit, only comes to me in bits and pieces when I try to remember it: Lonesome holding me tight, and then too tight. The looming trees, Lonesome calling my name over and over as I ran away.

A shiver runs down my spine. I walk back to the base of the hill and lay down against it. The crisp smell of the bluebells clears my head as I stare up at the blue-grey sky. Waiting.

Footsteps tread clumsily down the hill above me, waking the butterflies in my stomach. I stay where I am, trying to seem casual as a broad shape settles in the flowers beside me.

'Hello,' Samuel says, wiping his palms on his trousers.

'Hello.'

'I got your note.' He fishes it out of his pocket, as if I need more proof than him being here.

'I can see that.' I nod to the woods. 'You're all right with meeting me here?'

'Well, I've been here before,' he reminds me shyly, tugging gently at one of the bluebell stalks. 'For the flowers.'

'That's right.' I glance at him. Our eyes meet. The butterflies turn into a herd of cattle, setting my stomach churning with nerves. I look away, settling my gaze on the white tree instead. That's better. Being alone together feels strange. Intimate. At the schoolhouse, or even behind it, there was always the chance of being caught. No one's coming here. We could do anything.

'Besides,' he says, not noticing my flaming cheeks. 'I think my grandfather or maybe his father made up all that rot about the woods.'

I look back at him. His cheeks are quite red, too. It looks good on him. Sweet. 'Why would they do that?' I ask.

He shrugs. 'Who knows? To keep people afraid, maybe. People always seem to pay more attention in Deference when they're scared.'

'And Mayor Jones just plays along and keeps it going?'

Samuel shakes his head. 'Father believes every word of it.'

A silence falls, my teeth grinding at the thought of Mayor Jones and everything he's done.

'About my father…' Samuel says reluctantly.

I scrape my lip with my thumbnail, trying not to chew on it in front of him. 'I don't want to talk about him.'

'All right.' Another brief silence falls. 'What are we going to do about this marriage situation?'

I smile ruefully. Our options are so limited and unappealing there doesn't feel like any point discussing it. Either we stop seeing each other or keep stealing moments like this for the rest of our lives. 'I don't want to talk about that either.'

He tugs at another bluebell stalk. 'Neither do I.'

But apparently neither of us can think of anything we do want to talk about.

'Is that your lunch?' he breaks the silence, pointing to the little sack sticking out of my bag.

I open it and pull out a stale cheese sandwich. 'Looks like it.'

'You should eat. I don't want you to have to go hungry just to see me.'

'Do you want some?' I unwrap my sandwich and hold it out to him. 'I'd feel strange eating for an audience.'

'Sure, thank you.' He wipes his hands on his trousers again and takes a half. We sit and eat, staring at the flowers, the woods, anything but each other.

'Do you ever get this feeling,' he asks after a while, putting down what's left of the sandwich, 'where you're so nervous your heart feels like it's trying to jump out of your chest?'

My stomach is still churning. 'You're nervous?' I ask, lips twitching with relief.

'My palms haven't stopped sweating since I gave Roslyn that note.' He holds out one hand. 'See?'

Taking a deep breath, I slide my hand into his, and it's warm and clammy. 'Yuck,' I joke, closing my fingers tight around his.

'I can't remember the last time I had a real conversation with a girl,' he says with a smile. 'I think it must have been before we started school, on the weekends. When we all used to play chase in the square. Do you remember that?'

I grin. 'The traders would give us sweets afterwards.'

'I used to catch you all the time. I always wondered if you were letting me.'

I roll my eyes. 'No. I was always tripping on my dress.'

We laugh, feeling much more comfortable together.

'Why do you think they do it?' I ask him. 'Make us get married?'

'Because their parents did it to them?' he supposes. 'Because it's always been like this? I don't know. I hate it, though.'

'Why don't you say something, then? You'll be mayor next, after all.'

He digs a hole in the dirt with the tip of his shoe. 'But Father's the mayor now.'

I'm a little disappointed. 'What about when you take over? Will you change anything?'

'I want to. There are lots of things I'd like to do. But

Father's too young to die of old age, and he won't step aside until he's sure I'll do everything the way he would. Once he heard me practicing a sermon and gave me a hiding.'

My eyes widen. 'Why?'

'Because I don't agree with him or Grandfather. I don't think our Lord wants us to huddle in fear of each other. I think He wants us to be kinder to each other, to not act as though unmarried women and Strangers have done something wrong just by existing.'

'That sounds like the kind of sermon I'd pay attention to,' I say with a smile, then shake my head. 'It's so strange. None of us actually wants to do what they're asking. Not me or you or Roslyn. Not even Andrew. I wonder if our parents felt the same at our age.'

'Probably,' Samuel says, thinking it over. 'I think people change as they get older. They get more comfortable, and then they become afraid of change. I worry it'll happen to me.'

'It won't,' I say.

'It happened to Father,' Samuel says. 'He never used to be so petty and angry. I swear, he's more like my grandfather every day.'

'Well if you start acting anything like him, I'll kick you until you stop.'

Samuel's grin is like a morning in spring. 'You'll be around that long, will you?' he asks.

I purse my lips and look at my knees.

'You know,' Samuel says slowly, touching my chin. I look

back at him and see a gleam in his eye. 'I think you might have had a thing for me all this time.'

I raise an eyebrow. 'Based on what?'

He holds up his free hand, counting off on his fingers. 'That night you flirted with me on the high street…'

'You mean the night I *spoke* to you on the high street?'

'That time I asked to borrow your pencil before class, and you said I could keep it…'

'That never happened.'

'It did. Two years ago. I kept the pencil.'

'I don't even remember that,' I say, laughing. 'So it doesn't count.'

'Fine. That time… well, all those times you let me catch you in chase.'

'I told you, it was the dress.' I stand up, determined. 'I'll prove it.' I tug his arm until he joins me. 'Race me to the white tree and back. You'll win.'

'Only because you'll let me again,' he protests, but drops my hand and crouches into a starting position. 'Who's saying go?'

'Me. Go!' I start running, looking behind me to see if he's following. He waves, staying a full foot behind me at a leisurely jog. 'You're not even trying!'

'Fine,' he shrugs, easily closing the distance and tapping me on the shoulder. 'You're it.' He speeds away, laughing.

Stumbling on the hem of my skirt, I yank it up and charge after him.

'Catching me just proves me right,' he calls back.

'Not if I'm not tripping over my skirt.'

He looks back over his shoulder, eyebrows shooting up at the sight of my skirt around my knees. 'Father would definitely not approve of that,' he chuckles.

I grin. 'Good.' I speed up, launching myself at him and punching him lightly in the back. 'You're it!' I call triumphantly.

He skids to a stop, letting me crash into him and sending us both sprawling into the bluebells. Breathless, we lie beside each other, unable to speak.

Eventually, he rolls onto his side to look at me, reaching out to poke my cheek. 'You're it.' It sends us into another fit of laughter.

I stretch out. I prefer the meadow like this to the one in my dreams, full of scent and colours and light. And now Samuel.

He picks a bluebell and hands it to me.

'You're getting predictable,' I tease, taking it anyway.

'Am I?' he asks. He leans down and kisses me lightly on the cheek. A feeling surges through my body, pleasant and warm. Almost tingly. Without thinking, I slide my arm around his neck and turn my lips towards his. They brush together uncertainly. He pulls back, surprised by my advance, but only for a moment. Our lips meet again, this time with more purpose, and he's soft and warm and tastes like sandwiches.

'Can we just stay here forever?' he whispers, barely moving his mouth away from mine.

'Yes,' I lie, and we kiss again and again. I wrap my arms

around him and feel his hand at my waist, the other running lightly through my hair. It's a perfect moment.

'I'm sorry about my father,' he murmurs.

Well, it was a perfect moment. 'It's all right,' I force myself to say. 'At least we tried.'

He's quiet for a second too long. 'True.'

I pull away, looking at him. 'You did talk to him, didn't you? You told him how you feel about me, and that I didn't do anything to encourage you?'

Samuel looks away, guilty.

'Because he thinks I only wanted you for his money.' I sit up, vaguely aware I've raised my voice. 'And he took away my mother's job because of it.'

'Emma, I told you, he doesn't listen to me,' he insists, sitting up beside me. 'If you couldn't change his mind, there's nothing I could have said to help.' He touches my hand, but I flinch away.

'You didn't even try,' I accuse him. 'Did you say anything when he dismissed Mama?'

'No,' he admits. At least he has the decency to look ashamed.

I shake my head, appalled. 'You promised me. We had a plan.'

'I'll hire your mother back,' he promises. 'Or I'll hire you. As soon as I'm married.'

'That's big of you,' I scoff. 'And then what? I get to serve you and your horrible father for the rest of my life? I'd rather beg.'

'Emma…' he says, but he has nothing to follow it up with.

'You're a coward,' I say, staring him down. He won't even meet my eyes. 'Maybe you are like him after all.'

He opens his mouth to say something, but whatever it is never comes out. I turn away, too hurt to look at him anymore. I thought he was better than this. Or maybe I'd only hoped that he was. 'Just go.'

He doesn't move for a full minute, but then I hear him sigh. 'I'm sorry, Emma.' His footsteps recede up the hill.

I brush a finger over my lips, wishing they'd stop tingling. Wishing my stomach would stop fluttering at the memory of the kiss.

I stare at the woods, but something's wrong. They're blurry, the edges of the trees bleed into each other. Something tickles my face, and my fingers come away wet.

I wipe my eyes, annoyed at myself for crying over him, and blink until the woods come back into focus. Something moves, drawing my eyes to it. A body, naked to the waist, long hair flowing over its shoulders. Horns.

My blood freezes.

Lonesome looks out at me from the tree line. I rub my eyes, feel at my forehead. The fever isn't back, and Lonesome doesn't disappear.

'What?' I hear myself whisper.

'Emma?' a small, scared voice calls from above. I tear my eyes away from the trees to look up the hill. Louise stands at the edge, hugging herself. 'Emma, what are you doing down there?'

I look back at the trees. Lonesome looks up at Louise, then back to me. He holds a hand up, not quite waving, and steps back into the shadows.

'Emma?'

My breath comes out in a long, trembling stream.

He's real. Lord help me, he's real.

'I'm coming,' I call, but it doesn't sound very loud. I don't even know if Loise heard me.

How can he be real?

A hand touches me, making me gasp and snatch my arm away. Louise stares at me with big, scared eyes. How did she get down here so fast?

'Emma? Are you all right?'

'I'm fine,' I tell her, looking back at the woods. Lonesome is gone. But I can't shake the feeling that he's still watching me. 'I was picking flowers and I slipped down the hill.' I frown, forcing my attention back to her. 'What are you doing here?'

'Teacher was worried when you didn't come back to class,' she explains, glancing fearfully at the woods. 'She sent me to see if you were all right.'

'Oh.'

Louise takes my hand. 'Emma, can we go back up?'

'Of course we can,' I squeeze her hand, forcing a smile. 'Come on.'

I lead her up the hill, looking over my shoulder.

The woods stare back at me.

○

I make my apologies to the tailor's wife as we return to class. Flushed and pale, I don't have to work hard to convince her that I'm not feeling well.

'But now that you're already back here,' she says with a cloying smile, putting me to work helping the smallest girls thread their needles. The class passes in a vague blur, and suddenly I'm standing outside with Mona.

'Sorry,' she says. 'I though Mary would let you go for the day. I didn't realise she'd send Louise after you. Did she catch you and Samuel together?'

'No.'

Mona frowns. 'Why not? He did show up, didn't he?'

'He did,' I say, trying not to think about Lonesome. 'We had an argument.'

'About what?' she asks, eyes flashing. Her voice turns to stone. 'Did he do something to you?'

'No.'

'Then why…'

'I have to go home,' I say, interrupting her. 'I'll see you tomorrow.'

'Emma,' she calls after me, but I can't turn back without telling her the truth. And how can I tell her that without terrifying her? How can I tell anyone?

I walk home briskly, head down until I reach my door. The top of the meadow lurks in my periphery, daring me to look down the hill.

My fingers tremble on the doorknob.

Is he there now? Waiting?

I step inside and close the door, leaning heavily against it.

Mama is home early, toasting some bread in our small stove. She pulls the toasting fork free at the sight of me, marching over to reach up and press her hand to my forehead. 'You feel fine,' she breathes, relieved. 'I heard you came home at lunch.'

'It was just a headache, Mama,' I assure her, batting her hand away and taking the toasting fork. 'Sit down.'

She regards me suspiciously, but eases herself down at the table. 'Why does your hair look like that?'

I touch the back of my head self-consciously. The braids at the back are loose, messy from Samuel's soft hands.

My heartbeat quickens at the memory of his fingers, his lips, his skin.

Biting my nail, I remind myself that I hate him.

'I had a lie down,' I tell Mama, plating her toast and passing it over. 'And then I fell asleep. Louise had to come get me.'

Mama tuts, but lets it go.

I stoke the fire, prodding at a thick stick until one end glows orange and ignites. A flurry of sparks shoot up, like burning fireflies.

'Mama,' I ask, trying to sound casual. 'When was the last time someone disappeared into the woods?'

She stops chewing, returning her toast to the plate. It takes a moment for her to speak. Maybe she's forcing herself to sound calm too. 'Why?'

'One of the girls asked me,' I say with a shrug, looking

back at the fire. 'The boys were spreading stories again, but it made me realise that I don't know the answer.'

'It's been a long time,' she says, nodding slowly. 'You were just a baby.'

'Who was it? Did you know her?'

'It was a Stranger girl, just a little older than you are now. It took a long time for the news to spread. Nobody saw her much. She didn't go to school. Some thought she'd just taken the road, but that Stone man said she'd been taken by the woods.'

'Did she say anything before she disappeared?'

'About what?'

'I don't know,' I stall. 'Did she see something? Maybe hear something?'

'I wouldn't know, Emma. Nobody ever spoke to her, except the other Strangers. Mister Stone...'

'Papa Stone.'

'...went to speak to the mayor, but nothing came of it. Someone said she'd been struggling to find work for herself. Someone else said she'd just had a baby, though she wasn't married. Nobody really knew, except the Strangers, and they weren't interested in sharing gossip.'

'What about the other girls?'

'Jemima went when I had just started morning classes,' Mama says reluctantly. 'She'd just been married. A few years before that was unmarried Claire. Before that, your grandmama said it was a girl who hadn't quite come of age yet. None of them ever came back.'

Gnawing at my nail, I leave the stove open for warmth and sit down beside her. Her toast is forgotten, and I can't even think of food. Mama shakes her head, her eyes narrowing. 'And nobody ever went after them. The mayor reminded us of the dangers of neglecting our Lord, and we all mourned. And then we all moved on, those of us who could.'

'Maybe they're happier where they are,' I say without thinking. A place without fear or anger, marriage or money. That's what Lonesome said.

If he's real, the place he's been telling me about must be real, too.

Mama frowns at me. I flash her a weak smile. 'Anywhere would be better than here,' I joke.

I expect her to tell me off, but she pulls my thumb from between my teeth and takes my hand. 'You don't know how often I've thought exactly that,' she says, staring out the window with unfocused eyes.

She's quiet for so long I think the conversation's over, shifting in my seat to reach for her plate.

The movement brings her back, and she squeezes my hand. 'You tell those girls to stay away from the woods,' she says gravely. 'Tell them to block their ears and cover their eyes if they see or hear anything strange. For the sake of their mothers, if not for them.'

'I will,' I tell her, standing.

But she doesn't let go of my hand, reaching up to remove a crushed bluebell from under my collar. 'Promise me, Emma,' she says. The look in her eyes is almost desperate. She knows I'm not telling her everything. Maybe she's too afraid to ask.

'I promise, Mama.'

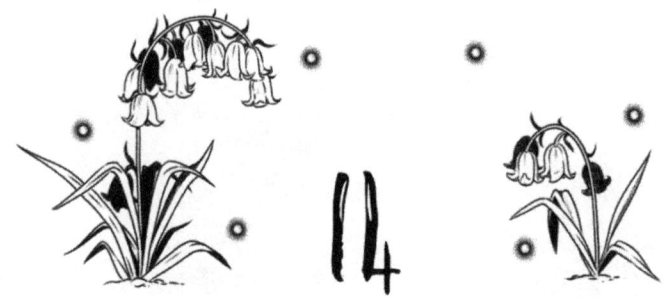

I stare at the ceiling, my eyes tracing the line of bunting Mama put up all those years ago. The coloured cloth triangles are faded now, but never dusty. It feels like I've been watching them for hours, waiting for Mama's snoring to rumble through the house.

She shifts in her bed. Out the corner of my eye I can see her lying on her side, watching me. Making sure I'm still here.

The minutes pass slowly. I tap my fingers nervously under the blankets, blinking hard and suppressing yawns.

The moon passes over to the other side of the house, leaving the room in deep, silent darkness.

My eyes droop shut.

The sky is the dull grey of early dawn when I open them again. Blinking, I sit up and look to Mama. She's sleeping soundly and loudly, though the shadows under her eyes tell me she stayed awake most of the night.

A pang of guilt hits me as I slip out of bed, but I squash it. I need answers.

He's waiting for me against the base of the white tree. The wooden flute is at his lips, playing so softly I can barely hear it. He looks up as soon as my feet sink into the wet bluebells, his skin, hair and horns leeched of all their colour by the cold light.

'I was just about to leave,' he says, pushing his hair away from his face. It catches in his horns.

'Do you turn to dust in the daylight?' I ask, only half joking.

He gives a crooked smile. 'You've seen me in the daylight,' he reminds me. 'I'm tired. I've been waiting for you since yesterday.' He pats the ground in front of me. 'Sit.'

He cocks his head as I sit just out of arms reach, keeping my distance in case he tries to grab me again. I don't think he can go past the white tree. There's a boundary there, a rule he can't break.

'So. You are a monster,' I say.

'Maybe,' he says. 'I don't know what a monster is.'

I look down, biting what's left of my thumbnail.

'What's wrong?'

'This is all too…' I stop, spreading my hands helplessly. 'You're real. How are you real? What are you? Were you sent to tempt me away from our Lord?'

'What's our Lord?'

'This isn't funny,' I say, crossing my arms. I sound upset. I think I am.

His smile fades.

'The first time I saw you, when I was a little girl,' I go on. 'Was that real too?'

He nods.

'But I woke up. I remember waking up.'

'You scared me,' he says. 'I came out to watch the sunrise over the hill and I fell asleep. It was day when I woke up. I'd never seen so much blue sky before. I didn't know anyone was near when I made a song for it.'

'But how…'

He holds up the flute. 'The music. It can reach out and call, and it can send you away. It's how I brought you to me again.'

'Why?'

'Why what?'

'Everything. Why did you bring me back here? Why didn't you tell me you were real?'

'I couldn't stop thinking about you. I'd never met anyone my age before. My kind are all old, and the humans they keep are old, too. I snuck back out to look at you again, but it took forever to find you. You were always so far away from the trees. But I kept coming back.'

'Why?'

He doesn't like questions. 'Because I liked it,' he says, tense. 'I like seeing you. It makes me feel… something.' Orange fingers begin to lick across the sky from the east. Lonesome gets more real by the second, lit by the sun rather than the moon or the fireflies. 'I hated it when you played with the others.'

'Why didn't you join us?'

He looks up at the white tree, confirming my suspicions. 'Can't leave.'

'Why not? What would happen?'

He shrugs. 'Who knows.'

Something doesn't feel right. 'Why weren't you honest with me in the first place? Why did you let me think you were a dream?'

He shrugs again.

'But you asked me to run away with you,' I say slowly. 'If I'd gone with you, would I have come back?'

He drags a hand through his hair, sending more of it into his horns. I fight a maddening urge to fix it. 'No.'

Fear and anger compete in my chest. 'Why did you even bother asking, then?' I ask. 'Why didn't you lure me all the way in?'

'The music can only call people to the edge,' Lonesome explains. 'It can't make anyone cross. They have to choose it. And they all do.'

'Only because you trick them,' I say furiously, clambering to my feet. 'Of course they feel safe disappearing into the woods with some gorgeous boy who tells them everything's going to be all right. They think they can wake up afterwards!'

'No, because they were unhappy,' Lonesome insists, standing to match me. 'They would have left either way.'

I shake my head. 'Why me?' I ask bitterly.

'What?'

'Why did you call me?'

'Because you were miserable,' he says with a frown, as though the answer was obvious. 'You used to laugh louder than anybody. I could hear it all the way from the trees. They made you quiet and sad and scared. That night I saw you crying, I knew I couldn't just watch anymore.' He reaches out, tracing his thumb down my cheek so lightly I barely feel the heat from his skin. 'You almost came to me once. Why did you stop?'

The night comes back to me vividly. The crushing hopelessness, my gaunt, blank face in the mirror. If I'd known then that Lonesome was real and waiting to take me away, I'd have kept running down the hill and into his arms. I know it.

'Because you weren't real,' I admit softly.

'But I am.' He glances at the sky. The roosters will crow any minute. 'Come with me now. You'll never think about this place again, I promise.'

I shake my head slowly. 'How could you have watched me all that time and think I'd ever leave Mama?'

He frowns. 'She makes you sad.'

'Mama and I fight, but I love her. She loves me.'

'*I* love you,' he insists.

I step back. 'Don't say that. You don't know what it means.'

He reaches out, but I'm too far away for him to touch. 'Where are you going?'

'Home. I came for answers, and I got them. Thank you.'

'Emma!'

'You scared me last time,' I snap. 'You tricked me, you wouldn't let me leave, and *you* hurt me. Why would I go anywhere with you? How can I trust you?'

His bright eyes flash. 'Because you know me.'

'I don't! I haven't had the benefit of creeping after you my whole life.'

'You named me.'

I turn away. 'It doesn't mean anything.'

'Will you come back?' he calls, a note of desperation creeping into his voice. 'Emma?'

Turning back, I see him gripping the tree with one hand, leaning after me as far as he can. 'Will you come to me?' I ask. 'Up there, at the top of the hill? If you love me so much, will you do what you're asking me to do and leave everything you know behind?'

His lips part, but he can't answer me.

'I live here. In the real world, with the people *I* love. If you want to be one of them, come join us.'

'I can't!'

The rooster crows.

'Then this is goodbye,' I say firmly, turning my back on him and racing back up the hill. I only have a few minutes before Mama is fully awake.

'You'll change your mind!' he shouts after me, voice strained with anger, or maybe with hurt. 'You'll come back. You'll look for me. I know it!'

His voice fades as I reach the plateau. I bend down to swipe up handfuls of buttercups and poppies. I'm breathless when I open the door. Mama jumps up at the sound.

'What are you doing?' she gasps, hand to her chest.

I kiss her cheek, pressing the hasty bouquet into her hand. 'Good morning, Mama.'

The corners of her eyes crinkle in delight as she breathes them in. 'What's this for? What have you done?'

'Nothing, Mama. I love you, that's all.'

Her face lights up with such a slow, sweet smile the years melt away. 'Oh, Emma.' She kisses my cheeks and wraps me in a warm hug. 'I love you, too.'

Lonesome can watch me as much as he likes.

I'm not going anywhere.

○

The days creep by. I sleep under the covers with my hands pressed against my ears, but though I feel the creeping sensation of being watched, I don't see Lonesome again.

Weeks pass, and the sensation ebbs as autumn draws near. Eventually, I forget to worry about him looking at me, and then I forget him completely.

Samuel tries to deliver notes to me through Roslyn, but I return every one of them unopened and unread. Mona and I spend more time with Roslyn and Nicole, though Nicole only just tolerates our presence. We eat lunch together every day, gossiping and laughing. Between them, Roslyn and Nicole know everything that happens in the village. At night, I report all the news back to Mama and she laughs and sneers and tells me exactly what she thinks of every last person we talk about. Most of them don't come out well.

I try to make the most of teaching the younger children.

Mary asks me to cover for her several more times, and though I don't take the girls outside again I let them sit on the floor as we read and act out scenes from their books, then create our own, and whenever we read from the book of the Lord, I redirect them to the passages that encourage kindness, which Mayor Jones somehow always omits at Deference.

It's not much, but I do what I can.

While I can.

●

'Emma,' Mary snaps her fingers at me, getting my attention. 'Did you see Louise at lunch?'

The room is full of alert young faces, with only one chair in the middle empty. The bell clanged a while ago. 'No,' I say, shaking my head. 'Nicole wasn't here this morning, either. Maybe they're sick?'

'Go and check on them, then. See if they need anything. If both girls have it, Sarah probably does too.'

'Yes, Teacher,' I half curtsey.

The air outside is cool and crackling with the promise of rain. I bow my head and walk quickly, wishing I'd thought to bring my cloak.

I knock on Nicole and Louise's door and wait.

Nobody comes to the door.

I knock again, louder. 'Sarah?' I call through the door. 'Nicole? It's Emma. Are you feeling all right? Mary sent me to check on you.'

Footsteps approach. The door swings open to reveal

Nicole, face pale and empty.

'Lord,' I swear. 'You look awful. Is Louise the same? Is there anything I can do?'

Nicole struggles to look at me, her eyes darting everywhere until they finally make contact with mine.

'Nicole?' I ask, speaking slowly. She looks like she's having trouble understanding me. 'Do you need me to get the doctor?'

She shakes her head.

'Where's your mother? Where's Louise? Are they all right?'

Something in the house clatters to the floor and breaks. And then, another sound. Crying.

'Is that Sarah?' I ask. 'Nicole, what's wrong?'

It takes Nicole a long time to form the words. 'It's Louise,' she manages.

My blood runs cold. 'What? What's happened?'

'She's gone.'

15

Nicole's been staring at the same spot on the wall for hours. Her eyes are rimmed red, but her cheeks are long dry.

Sarah won't stop crying. Her sobs fill the house, the sound spilling into the lane outside. Word hasn't spread yet, but it's only a matter of time.

I pour two more cups of tea, letting them steam on the table as I remove the untouched cups and tip them into the garden outside. Nicole's neighbour, another labourer's wife, is in her own garden, peering through the open door.

'Good evening,' she wishes me, clearly putting her feelers out for some juicy gossip.

'No,' I say flatly. 'It isn't.' I go back inside, closing the door and windows. The workers will be making their way home soon. Nicole and Sarah don't need an audience.

I touch Nicole's shoulder gently, putting the fresh cup of tea beside her. She looks up at me, blinking, then returns her attention to the wall. I do the same with Sarah, who at least is capable of speech.

'You don't have to stay,' she manages through heaving gasps.

'I do,' I assure her, wrapping her hands around the teacup. It begins to rattle against the table as a fresh wave overtakes her. 'At least until your husband is home.'

'Thank you.'

There's a feeling in my chest, gathering weight with every one of Sarah's tears and words of gratitude.

Guilt.

I stand in the kitchen for another hour or so, making six more cups of tea that never get drunk and a simple dinner that goes untouched. There's nothing more for me to do, but how can I leave?

Sarah's husband arrives shortly after nightfall with Mayor Jones and Samuel in tow. Richard has always been a severe looking man, but tonight I'm afraid to even speak in his presence. Underneath his beard his face is contorted with rage and grief, his eyes as red as the rest of his family's.

'No one has ever come out of those woods alive,' Mayor Jones says in a voice almost as frightening as Richard's face. 'Anyone we send in after her may be lost as well.'

'The woodsmen are in there every other week,' Samuel says.

Neither men seem to hear him, though I see an annoyed twitch in the mayor's moustache. 'I'm not suggesting we send anyone, Mayor,' Richard thunders. 'I'm going after her, whether anyone joins me or not. I'll be hanged if I leave my little girl to fend for herself in there.'

'And what about your wife?' Mayor Jones counters, as if she isn't in the room with them. 'Your other daughter. Will you leave them to fend for themselves? You've seen what happened to the old tailor's wife and daughter, would you wish that on them when you don't return?'

I grit my teeth and bang a pot loudly enough to let them know I'm here. Samuel's eyes widen at the sight of me, but Mayor Jones doesn't even have the nerve to look embarrassed.

'Miss Emma,' Mayor Jones says. 'What are you doing here?'

'I came to collect Louise for class,' I say stiffly. 'When I heard the news, I stayed to keep Nicole and Sarah company until Richard returned.' Richard looks at me, eyes softening momentarily in thanks. It throws another dagger of guilt into my heart.

'He's here now,' Mayor Jones says, not missing a beat. 'And Nicole's quite capable of looking after her own mother. Aren't you?' He gives her the briefest of glances.

Nicole manages a nod, standing up and silently taking my place by the kettle.

'I'm sure your mother will be wondering where you are,' the mayor dismisses me, turning back to Richard.

I curtsey, collecting my bag and looking to Richard as I reach the door. 'I'm sorry,' I tell him, though he has no idea how responsible I am for this. 'I'll pray for Louise.'

He gives me the look again and moves to stand beside weeping Sarah.

'I should walk Emma home,' Samuel tells his father.

'We *will* act, Richard,' he says, ignoring Samuel again.

'But the manner in which we do…'

Samuel steps out after me and pulls the door closed.

'He really doesn't listen to you, does he,' I say, not really asking.

Samuel shakes his head and offers an arm. I take it, and we walk in silence.

My skin prickles as we walk past the meadow. Unthinking, I squeeze Samuel's arm.

He looks at me, frowning with concern. 'What's wrong?'

My throat feels thick. 'Everything.'

We stop outside my house, the windows glowing with candlelight. Samuel drops his arm and bows. 'Stay safe, Emma,' he says, turning to leave.

'Wait,' I call. He turns back, but I can't see his expression in the dark. 'Don't go near the trees again. Not for anything. Not even in your dreams.'

He looks out at the meadow, the black ocean of leaves stretching out into the darkness. 'You don't think she ran away?'

'No.'

He turns back to me, reaching out, then thinking better of it. I hear him sigh. 'I won't if you won't.' He bows again.

I watch him walk away, worried Lonesome will spring out of the shadows at the edge of the meadow and snatch him away.

Is this how it's going to be from now on? Waiting for everyone Lonesome's ever seen me with to be stolen in the night?

I look back at the house. The warm glow beckons me with its safety. Swallowing hard, I turn to the dark meadow and plunge down, sliding down the hill to the bluebells.

I don't see Lonesome, but that doesn't mean he's not there.

'Lonesome!' I shout, hugging myself tight. 'Lonesome, bring her back! She's just a child!'

There's no answer. The trees are dark and silent.

Trembling, I walk to the white tree and keep a firm grip on the trunk. 'Lonesome!'

He doesn't come. I know what he's waiting for.

Heart racing, palms wet with fear, I take a tentative step. And then another, until only my fingertips are touching the smooth bark. 'Lonesome!'

Something twitches in the flowers beside me. I gasp and throw myself backwards, landing on the safe side of the tree with a heavy crash. A cricket hops past me, twitching from bluebell stalk to bluebell stalk.

Shame grips me. 'You coward!' I scream, though I'm not sure if I'm yelling at him or me.

○

Mama is on me before I can close the door, wrapping me in a fierce hug. 'Mama,' I say, pulling her gently away. 'Mama, I'm all right.'

She steps back and turns away, wiping her eyes.

'Mama?'

She takes a moment before turning back, composing herself. 'Tell me what happened. There are rumours.'

My voice is paper thin, throat thick from the guilt swelling inside me and from screaming at the trees. 'Louise was taken. She disappeared last night.'

Mama sinks into a chair. 'But she's so young.'

'The mayor won't send anyone after her,' I whisper. 'He talked Richard out of going. Do you think they're going to just leave her in there?'

'They usually do,' Mama says sadly. 'She's just one girl. Not worth losing men over.'

The dam inside me bursts. I gasp for breath, hot tears dripping down my nose. Mama steers me to my bed and sits down beside me. She pats her lap, and I ease my head onto it. She strokes my hair as I sob and sob.

'I know,' she whispers. 'I know. It's a terrible thing.'

'It's my fault,' I hiccup.

Her eyes widen in fear, hands stopping. But she steels herself. 'What do you mean? Tell me everything.'

The words tumble clumsily out of me, starting with my fifth birthday. Mama listens quietly, fingers unbinding my braids and smoothing my hair out as I speak.

'I should never have taken you into that meadow,' she says, shaking her head.

I sniff. 'I'm sorry I didn't tell you sooner.'

'I'm sorry I didn't notice you were gone.'

'I'm sorry I didn't listen to you. I'm sorry I ruined everything with Samuel. I'm sorry I'm such a terrible daughter.'

'Hisht,' she shushes me, bending down to put her arms around me. 'Thank you,' she whispers.

'For what?'

'Staying.

○

I stare at the ceiling for hours, ears stuffed with scraps of fabric. I begged Mama to wear them in case he tries to call her, and she demanded I wear them as well. Knowing I've been leaving in the middle of the night without her noticing – unwillingly or otherwise – has deeply unsettled her.

But though Mama is safe, I can't relax.

Where is he, if he isn't lurking at the bottom of the hill? What's he doing to Louise? He's lied too many times for me to believe him about his wonderful retreat. The stories about the woods creep back into my head, dark and insidious.

What did he really want with me? What does he want with her?

Is she even alive?

I squeeze my eyes shut, trying to block out the thought.

But it won't leave.

○

A faint, dull clanking wakes me. I sit and blink in the pale morning light, eyes sandy from a night spent tossing and turning.

'Emma, get dressed,' Mama orders, pulling the scrap from my ear. The clanking gets louder. 'There's a meeting.' Already dressed, the shadows under Mama's eyes tell me she barely slept either.

'But I have class,' I yawn, rubbing my eyes.

'Not today.'

The morning has dawned dark and moody. I dress quickly in red stockings and a grey dress. The clanking continues long and loud, urging us on. I begin to braid my hair, but Mama slaps my hand away and puts it in a rough, simple bun. 'Come.'

We hurry up the almost empty streets towards the town hall and are among the last to arrive. There's only one seat free, in the back row, and I give it to Mama. Standing behind her with my hand on her shoulder, I scour the crowd for Mona and find her beside Papa Stone on the other side of the hall. Even Strangers are required to attend town meetings. Relieved to see her, I hold up a hand in greeting. She returns it, worried lines etched deep in her forehead.

Mayor Jones stands at the podium. Samuel stands with him, though a little way behind. His face is solemn, but then, so is everyone else's. Unlike Deference, nobody chats as they wait. Apart from the sound of shuffling, settling bodies and the quiet weeping of Sarah somewhere towards the front, the hall is quiet.

The clanging outside stops. Kevin the blacksmith enters a few moments later with a big brass bell tucked into his belt. He approaches the front of the hall, footsteps echoing loudly, and squeezes into a seat beside his wife and sixteen-year-old son.

Thunder rumbles outside. Rain patters over the roof in a rolling wave.

Finally, Mayor Jones speaks. 'A terrible thing has happened,' he says, voice booming easily over the rain. 'A young girl has been taken. Younger than ever before.'

There are gasps here and there throughout the congregation. I see shaking heads, mothers grabbing the hands of their daughters.

'It's been seventeen years since the last time a girl was lured into the woods, stolen by demons sent to tempt us away from our Lord. We have grown lazy, we have lapsed, and we have allowed this to happen.'

The entire village holds its breath, hanging on the mayor's every word.

I glance at Samuel. Although he wears his passive mask, I think I see him clench his jaw.

'We must take steps. The demons prey on the weak, the unfaithful, the wicked. We must protect our women where they cannot protect themselves.'

My hand tightens on Mama's shoulder. Throughout the hall, I see signs of silent agitation in many of the women. But the men are nodding. Almost all of them.

'We must strengthen our souls,' Mayor Jones continues. 'We must renew our efforts and give deference to our Lord in the schoolhouse, in our homes, and here, together. We will hold Deference on Saturdays, as well as Sundays, and there will be penalties for any who do not attend and attend with fervour.'

The Strangers in the hall look to each other with alarm. There's a faint hum of confusion, the word 'penalty' whispered between them in concerned tones. But among the villagers, there's a scattered murmur of agreement, with only a few grimaces from the shopkeepers.

'To protect the very weakest of us from temptation, we will build a wall to shield the village from the sight of the trees.'

More agreement, this time with much enthusiasm. But again, the Strangers look worried. Papa Stone shakes his head angrily.

'And finally, no woman may walk without a man after dark – if indeed she has any reason to be walking anywhere at that time.'

'This is ridiculous!' The words are out of my mouth before I can stop them, and I find I can make my voice louder than the rain, too.

The village turns to look at me in one perfectly synchronized movement. It's so intimidating I take a small step backwards, but Mama's hand clamps on top of mine, her fingers digging in. Her message couldn't be clearer: *apologise and be quiet.*

'I beg your pardon?' Mayor Jones asked, and for the first time in my life I see him look rattled, as if he can't believe my audacity.

Neither can I.

'What are you doing to help Louise?' I demand. 'None of this will bring her back.'

'This will protect other girls from making her mistakes,' he says.

'What mistakes? She's twelve! She's never done anything wrong, even by *your* standards.' Several people look back to the mayor, waiting to hear his answer. I can see I've struck a chord in everyone who knew Louise.

'That's enough,' the mayor says sharply.

'He's right, Emma,' Mama says quietly, but I've gone too far to stop now.

'Louise was in her own house with her family when she was taken, not wandering the streets alone or skiving off Deference. Nothing you've proposed would have saved her, and it won't save the next girl.'

'Then you're suggesting we do nothing?' he asks, as if he thinks he's cornered me. 'You're saying we should let the demons take who they want?'

'No. I'm saying we should go in there and bring her home.'

'Nobody has ever come out of the woods.'

'No woman, you mean,' I shout, angry at him for being so ready to abandon her, angry at myself for everything else. 'The woodsmen are in and out of there all the time. Did your father ever try sending them after the lost girls with axes and torches? Or have the mayors of this village always shrugged their shoulders at our Lord and thanked Him for only taking another weak, useless girl.'

'*Enough!*' the mayor shouts, and I know I'm right. The people looking at me wear a rainbow of disparaging looks: disgust, anger, pity. But here and there I see concerned and thoughtful faces too.

Behind the mayor, Samuel's eyes beg me to stop.

'You can't just abandon her!' I look for Richard in the crowd, but he won't meet my stare. The mayor's talked him out of looking for his own daughter. 'Why won't *any* of you do the right thing? Are you all so afraid?'

'Louise is gone.' The mayor's voice is cold and low. 'And you embarrass yourself and all the village with your nonsense. Leave now, before I throw you out.'

'Don't I need a man to chaperone me?' I retort icily.

'*Out!*' he roars.

I feel invincible. There's nothing more he can take from me, nothing more he can do to me. And the troubled look in his eyes tell me he knows it, too.

Mama tries to stand and join me, but I squeeze her shoulder and gently push her back down. Across the room, I see Papa Stone doing the same to Mona.

I walk to the door of the hall with my head held high, turning back to curtsey sarcastically at the mayor. His face turns a brilliant shade of burgundy, and I leave before he can say anything else.

Walking home in the rain, my hair drops out of its bun and slops down my back. I slam the door behind me and prepare to make a fire, knowing Mama will be sore and cold from walking home in the wet.

Stoking the wood with our rusting iron poker, a fresh wave of anger surges through me. How *dare* he stand at the front of the village and talk about wicked women and walls, convincing a family to give up a child for dead.

Sarah's quiet weeping haunts me, playing on a loop in the back of my mind.

But how am I any better than the mayor? Hiding in my

house, blaming him when I'm the reason she's gone. Sleeping with fabric-stuffed ears when I know exactly where she is.

My hand shakes. I know what I have to do.

Pinning my old cloak around my throat and pulling the hood up, I swing the poker over my shoulder and step back into the rain.

Gathering speed down the hill, I cross the plateau in seconds and plunge down. My feet slide on the steep slope, but I keep myself upright and stomp through the bluebells, boots crunching through their soft stalks.

Heart racing with adrenaline, I march past the white tree without hesitating, not letting myself slow as I approach the edge of the woods.

'I'm here, Lonesome!' I shout the challenge, fingers tight around the iron poker as the trees close in around me. 'Come and get me!'

16

The rain spatters through the thick canopy, sending cold, heavy drops down to burst against my cloak.

There's no sign of Lonesome. Or anything else. There are no birds, no animals. Not even an insect. Strange.

I glance back at the meadow, still visible through the thickening trees. My resolve wavers. I thought he would have come for me by now. Surely he was just waiting for me to cross into his territory.

Shivering, I shout his name again, and then Louise's, and then every foul word I can think of.

Damn.

Taking a last look at the meadow, I send a silent apology to Mama and Mona and walk on. They'll know what I've done when they find the house empty. They know I'll be back when I can.

If I can.

The bluebells eventually disappear, giving way to thick green clover and rich brown soil. The trees are enormous, their roots slithering in and out of the earth like giant, static snakes. I trip over some and stub my toes on too many more.

'Louise!' I yell. 'Lonesome!' My words don't echo. It's as though the woods simply swallow them whole.

I walk on and on for what feels like hours, shifting the poker to use as a walking stick. The slow, seeping rain has turned the soil into a thick mud, and my thighs complain at the effort it takes to get through it. My stomach rumbles, reminding me I didn't eat breakfast and I start to curse myself for not breaking off some of the bread in the kitchen cupboard, or better yet stopping in the bakery to take some of the soft white rolls I always see but can never afford. It's not like anyone would have been there to see me.

Squinting as the light grows dim, I look up to see the tiny patches of sky turning dark grey. Nightfall. I exhale with relief. Night brings the fireflies, and the fireflies will lead me to Lonesome.

I stop in the hollow of a tree so big it would take four of me to reach all the way around it and rub at my arms. I'm wet through from my sopping cloak to my underwear, but I don't dare strip off and try to get dry. Not here.

Teeth chattering, I search the darkening woods for the familiar golden sparks.

They don't come.

Terror grips me. I curl up into a ball, clinging to the poker. 'Louise!' I try to call, but my voice comes out small and scared. I suddenly imagine Lonesome watching me in the dark, closing in on me with Lord knows what behind him.

My body shakes, and not from the damp seeping into my bones.

○

My head lurches. The poker lies in the mud beside me, glinting in the dull sunlight.

I don't remember falling asleep.

Rubbing my bleary eyes with mud caked hands, I use the poker and smooth inside of the tree to push myself up. My aching legs groan with the movement. Now I know how Mama feels.

I trudge on. The rain stopped sometime during the night, and despite the clouds I glimpse through the leaves, the weather stays dry. My clothes slowly lose their moisture, the mud covering them drying to a hard shell.

Stomach churning and mouth dry, I stop to drink from one of the receding puddles, but it's so full of mud and silt I gag and spit it back up.

This isn't the rescue I'd imagined.

I keep walking. The trees begin to thin out after a few hours, and a carpet of bluebells springs up beneath my feet. I blink at them, disbelieving. I can't have turned myself around. Can I?

Stumbling into a run, I make for the edge of the woods. Blinded by the sudden, unfiltered daylight, I can just see a meadow of red, yellow and white.

My eyes well with frustration. I'm back to where I started.

Wiping my eyes, though, I realise I'm not looking at a hill, but a long, flat plain scattered with ranunculus and black eyed Susans. Three white trees stand in a line, and beyond them is a walled town, much bigger than our village. Rooftops peep over the stone wall, chimneys smoking merrily.

Swallowing hard, I step forward, almost mesmerized by the promise of food and water. Maybe even some fresh clothes and a real weapon.

'Stay back, witch,' a sharp voice cracks across the meadow. A man rises from the flowers, a drawn arrow pointed straight at me.

I gasp and stumble back, putting my free hand up. 'Please, I'm not what you think! I'm trying to find someone.' He releases the arrow and it hums past my head to bury itself in a tree. My heart pounds.

The man mutters something to himself, putting another arrow to his bow and drawing it back.

'Please,' I try again, backing up slowly. 'I just want some food. I've been in here since yesterday, I–'

'We've got nothing for you,' he says, closing one eye and adjusting his aim.

I hitch my filthy skirt and run. Again, the arrow buzzes past me. Too close. I scream and drop to my knees clutching my left shoulder. I'm cut. Not deeply, but I'm bleeding a little. I grit my teeth and get back on my feet, running back into the trees before he can send any more after me.

❂

The day passes slowly. The skin around my wound itches, and my stomach knots in pain. The rumbles turn into roars, drowning out my croaking calls for Lonesome and Louise.

The light fades, and once again I curl up in the roots of a tree and wait for fireflies that never come. I sleep a little and dream of throwing myself face first into a stream of cold, clean water. I wake with the sun and walk.

I try to think of home, wondering what Mama and Mona, and even Roslyn and Samuel are doing now. But it makes me too sad, so I focus on my path instead, counting my footsteps in groups of a thousand. Anything to keep my mind off food and water, or the fact that I'm failing Louise, or the new, creeping thought that I'll die here.

I collapse in what must be the late afternoon. The trees spin around me, then fade into nothing.

Instead of food or water or home, I dream of music weaving through the darkness. Then of a firefly, drifting lonely and lost through the trees. I reach out as it meanders towards me, smiling as it makes lazy circles around my hand.

I sit up so quickly my head reels. I'm not dreaming, I'm awake. I poke my wound to be sure and grimace triumphantly at the pain. The music really is playing, though it's muffled and distant.

'Lonesome,' I breathe, looking towards the music. Far away, another speck of light bobs from tree to tree. *Finally.*

I clamber to my feet and use the poker as a guide, checking for roots and dips as I make my way slowly towards the firefly. Two more reveal themselves as I approach, dancing further ahead. And beyond them, a group of four or five.

This is it! I stumble after them, following the glowing path through the gloom. The music gets louder as I go, and for one glorious moment, I allow myself to feel hopeful again.

The music stops.

'No!' I rasp, but the fireflies flicker and, one by one, they disappear. 'Come back! Louise! *Louise!*'

I walk on, the heavy poker guiding my way, but neither the music nor the fireflies return. Did he hear me? Is he taunting me? Teasing me?

I blink. I can see my hands gripping the poker for dear life. Slowly, the trees around me emerge from the darkness. It must be dawn.

Refusing to let my last spark of hope be snuffed out, I sit in the nook of a tree and push the poker into the earth beside me. When the sun sets again, I'm going to be ready.

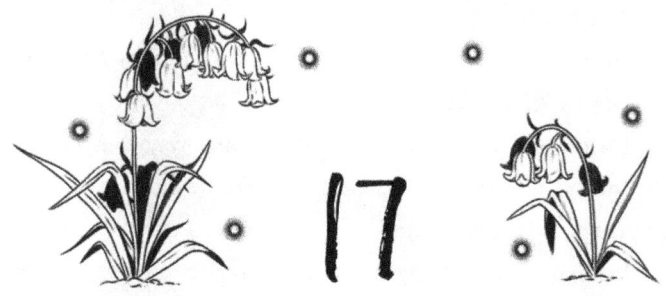

17

I stare up at the canopy, my exhausted mind rambling from one subject to the next in quick succession: Mama, water, Lonesome, Mayor Jones, Mona, food, Mama, Louise, Nicole, Andrew, water, Roslyn, Samuel, Lonesome, water, Samuel, Mona, water,

Water,

Water.

The woods darken and disappear. I hear myself wonder if I've died and am answered with a spark of light bursting to life above me. I reach for the fire poker and wrap my fingers around the comfortingly hard metal as the woods ripple with golden light. Not dead. Ready.

My head spins as I stand, feeling lighter than the time Mona stole a cup's worth of fermented cider and we took turns sipping it behind my house.

I heft the poker over my shoulder, ready to swing at a moment's notice, and walk slowly, steadily, up the firefly road. Ahead, far but distant, a drum beats time with my heart.

Delicate strings join them, urging my shaking legs onwards.

Fireflies ignite in the air by the hundreds, bouncing and drifting to the melody. A flute joins the symphony, playing a mocking little counter melody. My feet itch, sending me to my knees as they try to ignore the commands of my mind and join the dance.

I reach down. The ground beneath me is soft and spongey. I dig my fingers into it, pulling out two chunks of what must be moss and cramming them in my ears. The music dulls, and with it my feet's urge to mutiny.

I force myself back to standing and plod on, step after step, until a bright glow appears ahead, as though the sun has set in the middle of the woods. I don't need to pull the barricade from my ears to know this is where Louise and Lonesome and Lord knows what else will be.

Heart pounding in my ears, I drop to my belly and crawl towards the light. The music is so loud I can feel it in my ribcage, even if I can't hear its siren call.

My hands shake as the glow clarifies itself into a wide expanse filled with shapes. I stop behind the high, thick root of a tree that must be as old as the world itself. Gripping the poker and uttering a silent prayer, I peep over the edge.

The expanse is a clearing, vast and perfectly circular. Trees reach high above it, sheltering it with loving, branching arms to create a domed ceiling filled with fireflies by the thousands.

I swallow and tighten my grip on the poker. I don't know what I expected, but it wasn't this. The clearing is filled with figures. Dozens, maybe more than a hundred of the loveliest creatures I've ever seen. At a glance, they look human, but even from here, I can tell that they're more than a head taller than the tallest man in the village. Some wear draped robes and shawls, some wear loose trousers, and some wear nothing but their long, loose hair. Here and there I see horns protruding from the temples of the males and females alike, some ram-like and curling, others branching like Lonesome's do. It should be frightening, but every one of them looks so serene.

Only after I recover from the shock of so much beauty and tranquility do I see the humans. They're dotted amongst the creatures, looking so small and plain beside their towering guardians. Some recline with the creatures in lazy piles, others wander, still more dance in a high-spirited circle. Most of them are women, ranging from a little older than me to positively ancient.

And there, dancing in the circle, a brown-haired human girl in a white nightgown, the smallest and youngest by far.

Louise. She's so far away, but it must be her.

I watch the white-clad figure as she skips and twirls with a grace I didn't know Louise possessed, straining to see her better. At last, she reaches the other side of the circle and I see her face clearly.

She's smiling.

No, she's *laughing*. She looks happy. They all do. Everywhere I look, I see a blissful human. A bowed woman who must be eighty, at least, cackles from between two gorgeous horned males. A woman Mama's age dances barefooted in a barely-there shawl. Even a young woman, bent double in a coughing fit, looks perfectly content once the fit passes.

I don't understand. Lonesome's song could call me to the woods and it could make me dance, but it couldn't make me *feel*.

Was he telling the truth about this place? Did all of these women *want* to come? Did Louise?

I find Lonesome in a group of musicians not far from the circle, his wooden flute to his lips. He smiles with the other musicians as they play, all of them joking and laughing on the spot. It all looks so… fun?

My spine stiffens as a new smell reaches my nose, a change to the rich earth and leaf litter.

Roast chicken.

My stomach roars. I forget Lonesome and Louise, searching for the chicken. I have to move, crawling out from the colossal root to another tree until I see it. A long table absolutely laden with food. A middle-aged man stands beside it, demolishing a leg of chicken. Not far from him, a woman kneels beside a narrow spring, barely more than a bubbling puddle, and fills a wooden cup.

I lick my cracked lips. I know I should be studying Louise and the others, formulating a way to grab her without anyone seeing and lead her away, but I can't take my eyes off the spring. I'm so thirsty. So hungry.

I shut my eyes and hold my nose, trying to forget the smell, but it's already in my head and in my gut, calling me louder than any song ever could.

Giving up, I open my eyes and let go of my nose, studying the table. It's close to the edge of the clearing, one end of it hard up against a tree. I could get there, if I was careful. None of the creatures are paying the slightest bit of attention to it. I could reach around the tree and grab the first thing my hand fell on. And then I can think. One bite and I'll be able to concentrate again.

Glancing at the creatures, I make my unsteady way around the clearing until I'm close to the table and the tree. I can do it. I can make it.

But a small, sensible part of my mind not yet addled with hunger makes me hesitate. Despite the protests of my gurgling stomach, I tear my gaze away from the table and to the spring. There, running from the edge of the clearing and safely away through the trees, is a stream.

I smile, lips stinging as they stretch wide for the first time in days. I retreat from the clearing and scramble to the slick, mossy bank. Casting a look over my shoulder to make sure I'm still hidden, I drop my poker and dip my hands into the water. It's cold and crystal clear. I shudder with relief as I splash it over my face and raise handful after handful to my lips.

A hand touches my shoulder, squeezing through layers of mud and wool. I grasp for the poker, but it's somewhere behind me. How could I have been so senseless?

I look over my shoulder and see Lonesome kneeling behind me, a lopsided smile on that wonderful, terrible face.

18

I dream of bluebells.

A boy with warm eyes and a constellation of freckles leans down to kiss me. His lips are soft, his hands are gentle. They tremble against my skin.

'Can we stay here forever?' he breathes.

○

My eyes open, bleary and blinking. There's something heavy around my waist, something warm at my back. I look down. My dress is gone. My boots and stockings, too. I've been stripped down to my thin white petticoats and my sleeveless undershirt. An arm hangs over my hip.

My blood runs cold. Swallowing the urge to shriek, I wait for my vision to clear and look carefully around without disturbing the owner of the arm. I'm lying in the clearing. All around me are sleeping bodies, creatures and humans curled around each other like cats. The sky beyond the ceiling of branches is bruised with purple. Dusk. They'll be awake soon. And then what?

I hold my breath and try to roll out from beneath the arm, but it tightens in response. I hear a soft breath and a murmur from behind me. The moss in my ears is gone. The hand moves again. I clench my teeth and close my eyes, resisting the urge to slap it away. Just in time. The creature behind me sits, shifting its hand to rest on my hip as it leans over me. The gesture is too familiar, too intimate.

'Emma?' Lonesome asks. I feel his hair brush my bare arm. 'Emma, are you there?'

I don't dare ask what he means by that. I keep my eyes shut and force myself to take the long, slow breaths of sleep. Something's happened that I don't quite understand. I have to be patient until I understand what it is. I have to be clever.

He sighs and lets go of me. A few moments later, I hear movement. The sounds of waking and stretching. Of intimate, sleepy whispers.

Lonesome touches my shoulder and squeezes.

I cautiously open my eyes. Lonesome sits behind me, his long legs stretched out as he untangles his hair from his horns. His attention occupied, I search the clearing for Louise. I don't see her, but I spot several of the other humans. They look dazed and groggy, still half-asleep.

I follow suit and feign a hard yawn as Lonesome smooths his hair and arranges himself to kneel beside me. I blink, avoiding his eyes as I rub clumsily at my face. He sighs again and takes my elbow, pulling me haphazardly to my feet. Without speaking, he leads me to the table of food. Around us, creatures do the same with their humans.

Their humans?

I balk from the thought and glance at the others. They don't look so happy now. Their faces are blank, their footing clumsy. They mindlessly reach out to take something from the table, cramming it into their mouths like messy children.

Lonesome's hand leaves my shoulder. I look back and see him retreat across the clearing without so much as a backwards glance.

What in our Lord's name is going on?

'You.' My shoulder's tense at the sound of an unfamiliar voice, sweeter than music. I look back to the table. A creature on the other side of it watches me closely, her arms wrapped possessively around a wrinkled man. Her face is a vision beneath her curled horns. She smiles as our eyes connect. 'Are you not hungry?'

I look down and realise I'm the only human not eating. Trying to look as sluggish as the others, I reach for a perfect green apple and take a bite. The creature's smile stretches wider, splitting her face. My apple sticks in my throat as her lovely face becomes something nightmarish for a fraction of a second, and then she looks away, satisfied.

My hand trembles. Swallowing hard, I look down the table. There, at last, I see Louise. One of her hands is held tightly by another female creature, the other is wrapped around a bread roll. I try to catch her eye, but she doesn't look up.

I drop my apple and step towards her.

❂

I dream of a road.

A girl sits beside me, her wild hair tickling my cheek as she leans her head against my shoulder. 'What would you be,' she asks, 'if you could be anything you wanted?'

'Rich,' I say, without skipping a beat.

She laughs. 'Everybody wants that. Go on, tell me something true.'

'All right, then. I'd be a teacher. But I'd do a better job than any of ours. And I wouldn't read those speeches about the Lord.'

The girl clicks her tongue. 'You're going to do that anyway. Dream bigger. There are no restrictions.'

'No restrictions?' I ask. 'That's easy, then. I'd have to be the mayor.'

The girl grins. 'Mayor Emma. I can almost see it.'

'Almost?'

'Your sermons would be terrible. You'd have to get someone to be the voice of the Lord for you.'

'You mean you're not volunteering?'

She snorts. 'Don't be stupid.'

'What would you be, then? If you could be anything?'

'I think I'd like to be a trader,' she says, staring dreamily at the horizon.

○

I wake with a start, face down in the thick blanket of moss. My heart begins to race. What's happening to me?

Lonesome shakes me, helps me stand. My face feels slack, my arms and legs so heavy it's an effort to make them move. Lonesome barely looks at me, pushing me back towards the table.

The coughing girl from the first night stands beside me, her skin sallow. Her body racks with loud, wet hacking. She doesn't even seem to notice, reaching for a round, red tart and pushing it into her mouth between gasps and splutters.

Lonesome hands me a cup of water. It takes two tries for my hand to close around it. I'm ready to scream at him, to demand to know what they're doing to me. But he's already walking away, joining a group of creatures on the moss.

I spin, looking for Louise. I find her in the lap of a horned female, with two more smooth-headed females on either side. They take turns feeding her fruit and cups of water.

I try to call out to her, but the word comes as a thin whisper. '*Louise.*'

She looks at me, her eyes meeting mine for just a moment. And then they slide away.

I take an unsteady step towards her and see Lonesome's head snap up. He looks from her, and then to me. 'Emma?' His voice is urgent, hopeful.

Another creature, hovering behind one of the other humans, steps in and puts his hand over mine, raising the cup to my lips.

○

I dream of a wooden floor.

A pair of oval spectacles fall, the glass in the right eye cracking in three places as they bounce to a halt.

A woman is bent over a bed, clasping the hand of a man lying completely still, open eyes staring blindly at the wall behind my head. Her shoulders convulse, but she makes no sound. Another man cleans his hands in a bowl of water staining red, wiping them on a towel. He covers the face of the staring man with a clean white cloth and puts a hand on her shoulder.

'I'm sorry, Grace,' he says. His voice is kind. 'Take Emma home. I'll take care of the rest.' The woman doesn't move. He looks to me, beckoning me close. 'Emma. Your mother needs you.'

I walk to the woman on short legs and putt a chubby arm around her. 'Mama?'

She lets go of the hand and wraps her arms around me, tears dribbling down the back of my neck.

The man nods at me, whispering some advice.

'I love you, Mama,' I repeat dutifully.

Her arms tighten around me, and she kisses both of my cheeks. 'I love you, Emma.'

○

Sunlight streams through the branches as tears run down my cheeks, trickling into my ears.

I want to go home.

Wiping my face, I realise I'm not being touched. I sit up and look around. Lonesome lies some way away with his back to me.

Is this a test?

I flex my jaw, trying to bring my face back to life. Lifting my heavy arms, I knead my cheeks and wriggle my toes. My body slowly wakes up, letting me feel in control again.

Clambering to my feet, I take a moment to survey the clearing. Louise is near the centre, sleeping in a nest of giant, beautiful women. I tiptoe closer, giving every sleeping creature a wide berth.

Louise looks different. I've never seen her with her hair loose before or dressed in anything other than her sensible school dress or second-hand Deference clothes. Now, in her nightdress, with her long hair tumbling over one shoulder, she seems older that she was, but still so very, very young.

I can't get to her. Not without leaping over the creatures or navigating the maze of tangled limbs and horns and fanning hair. And then what? From the look of the sun, it's already past noon. Night will come too quickly.

My shadow creeps across the moss with the sun as I struggle to come up with even the broadest plan. At last, I make a decision and return to where I woke up.

I close my eyes, determined to rest now, while I can.

○

I dream of a room.

An older woman with a hard face and kind eyes takes me by both hands and cheers, pulling me into a funny, skipping dance devoid of any rhythm. I laugh, swept up in the mood and duck down so she can spin me around. She laughs with me, and her face transforms into something beautiful.

○

I'm woken by the sound of hushed arguing. The other humans are already crowded around the table like pigs around a trough. Lonesome sits against a tree on the edge of the clearing, spinning his wooden flute between his fingers. Another creature crouches beside him, angrily whispering. He points at me, and I flutter my eyes like I'm still half-asleep.

Lonesome sighs and nods. He walks over and nudges my shoulder with his foot. I open my eyes, doing my best to pretend to feel how I did the last time he woke me. 'Up,' he says.

I purposely stumble on my way to the table and take up a powdered white bun, just like the baker makes, and just like I can never afford. My stomach rumbles lightly at the promise of it. I take a bite, savouring the taste on my tongue. Lonesome looks over my shoulder at something, or someone, and gives a nod. He walks away, leaving me alone again. It's a shame he didn't discover that compulsion months ago.

Glancing at the other creatures around the table, I make sure that none of them are paying attention to me and spit the soft, sweet mouthful into my hand and toss it under the table. Whatever they're doing to me, it's in the food and the water. It must be.

One of the creatures takes up a wooden drum and plays a cheerful beat. Lonesome puts his flute to his lips and joins in, contradicting the tone with a moody little trill.

The other humans break out in slow, wide smiles. Several creatures begin to dance, beckoning them to join in. Louise is the first to join the circle, flanked by two of her female creatures. Others take seats on the moss and watch. An older man continues to eat.

All of them look content again.

Wanting to stay close to Louise, I paste a grin on my face and give in to the familiar itch in my feet. I skip into the circle, using every bit of my will to keep my mind clear as I watch her.

Even now, skipping and laughing, I don't recognize her as the sweet, shy girl I see every other day in class. Her eyes are vacant, glazed over and unchanging despite her unwavering smile. It's as if Louise isn't even in there anymore.

The other humans are the same. They move on their own, smiling at each other and the creatures who hover beside them. They laugh when the creatures laugh, wander back and forth from the table when they're hungry. But none of them ever speak. None of them wears any expression other than pure, mindless bliss.

Is this how I've been acting the past few days?

I shudder, shooting Lonesome a sharp glare. He glances at me, catching my eye and faltering. I force myself to smile again and spin away.

Louise dances for hours. My breathing is ragged by the time she finally steps away. Her guardians follow her, leading her to sit in the centre of a group of females. They turn all of their attention on her. One combs Louise's hair with her fingertips, another strokes her hand, another coos at her, another holds a cup to her lips and laughs in delight when it spills down the sides of her mouth and seeps into the front of her nightgown. My lip curls in disgust. They're treating her like a baby. No, like a pet.

The flute disappears from the song. I look to the musicians just in time to see Lonesome charging towards me. I throw my hands up to defend myself, but he bends low, looping his arm around my thighs and throwing me over his shoulder.

The sudden impact of my stomach against him winds me, stopping me from fighting back. It's just as well. If I resist, the creatures will know I'm not dead-minded like the other humans and shove food down my throat. But Lord knows what Lonesome thinks he's going to do to me when he has me alone.

I hang limply from his shoulder as we reach the trees, waiting until we're a safe distance from the clearing to dig my nails into his lower back. He recoils and grunts in pain, but doesn't release his grip.

'Let me go!' I hiss.

He looks back. The clearing is only a dim glow behind us, but still he steps behind a tree before he puts me down. A few stray fireflies follow us, settling in the branches above.

'You're back,' he breathes, cupping my face. 'I knew it.'

I slap his hands away and punch him in the chest as hard as I can. 'You stole a twelve-year-old girl!' I punch him again. 'Her family is broken because of you!' And again. 'My mother is all alone now!' And again.

'I'm sorry,' he says.

Breathing hard, I lower my fist. 'What?' I wasn't expecting that.

He rubs at his chest, but I don't believe for a second that I've hurt him. 'It was the only way I could think of to get you here.'

'That is *not* an apology,' I hiss.

Lonesome frowns. 'Yes, it is.'

'You told me that everyone was happy here,' I say, raising my fist again, but he catches it before it can make impact.

'They were,' he insists, then stops himself. He lowers his voice and looks guiltily back to the clearing. 'At least, I thought they were.'

I scoff. 'You thought *that* was happiness? None of the humans here talk! They don't do anything but eat and dance and let your kind do Lord knows what to them.'

'I know that now.'

'You should have known it before!'

'How?' Lonesome asks, dragging his hands through his hair. He stops at his horns, gripping them in both fists. 'I'm not like you! I never met any of those humans before they came here! I didn't know they were being any different than they were before.'

It takes everything in me not to hit him again. 'But you'd seen me and Mama. You knew we weren't silent, grinning goons.'

'No,' he says, struggling to explain himself. 'But I thought they liked being here. You smile when you're happy. I've seen it.'

'Not like that.'

He swallows and nods, releasing his horns. 'That's how I knew. I was so glad to see you that first night. I thought if I could just get you here, let you see how it could be, you'd want to stay. But you went strange after you drank the water. You were smiling, but you couldn't hear anything I was saying. You were there, but you weren't. That's not what I wanted.'

A chill creeps through me. The idea of my body being awake without me makes me feel sick. 'How disappointing for you,' I whisper angrily.

'I tried to get you back, but the others wouldn't let me,' he says, as if that changes anything. 'So I left you alone instead.'

'Why didn't you take me home? Why is Louise still here if you got what you wanted?'

'Nobody leaves the woods. If you go home the other humans won't be afraid of us anymore. They'll get brave and come in further with their iron axes and cut down more trees. They'll find us.'

'So you were planning to leave me here and ignore me until I grow old and die?'

'Not now that you're you again,' he says, reaching for my hand. I cross my arms, clamping my hands beneath my armpits. It doesn't seem to dissuade him. 'We can go somewhere else. Just you and me. As long as we stay inside the trees the others will leave us alone.'

'Have you not heard me?' I ask, voice cracking. 'I don't want to be with you. Not here, not anywhere else in these damn woods.'

He scoffs. 'You'd rather stay here and be like the others?'

'No. I'm taking Louise home.'

'You'll never make it. They'll catch you.'

'And do what? Drag us back here?'

'They might hurt you.'

'They're already hurting us!' I say, glaring at him. 'How do you not understand that?'

He frowns and looks back to the clearing. 'You could die,' he says. 'They could kill you.'

'I'm willing to take that chance,' I say, my voice flat.

A look of hurt distorts his face as he finally hears me. He looks away, ducking his chin to let his hair shield his face from me. He stands that way for so long I start to wonder if I should walk away. But then he holds his hand out to me, palm up. 'Come, then,' he says.

I look at his hand, unsure. 'What's happening?'

'They'll notice if we come back separately.'

I hesitate, but what choice do I have? I put my hand in his, bracing myself for the heat of his skin. We walk in silence until we're almost at the clearing.

'Smile,' he mutters, not looking at me.

He spends the rest of the night at my side as we sit in the moss near Louise and her doting creatures. Several of them give Lonesome approving looks as he strokes my hair. I make myself smile up at him, but he doesn't return it. When the others aren't looking, he drops his hand and sits quietly, tapping his flute against his chin.

My cheeks are aching by the time the night recedes and the fireflies put themselves out. My stomach groans with hunger, but I ignore it, keeping an eye on Louise as she lies down with the creatures around her.

Lonesome tugs on my arm, and I lie beside him, close, but

not touching. I hear whispering and snatches of laughter all around me.

I close my eyes and wait.

19

The air is filled with a soft symphony of breathing.

My fingers clench nervously, digging into the moss. I open my eyes. The sky above the canopy is brushed with the gold of sunrise. Lord, I've missed the sun.

I turn my head tentatively, looking at Lonesome. He lies on his stomach, using his arm as a pillow. His face is turned towards me, but hidden beneath his thick hair.

Without thinking, I brush the hair aside and look at him. His eyes are closed, his crooked mouth in repose. Sleep has softened the sharp lines of his face, making him look more like the little boy I met in the meadow.

I run my hand through his soft hair, watching him closely. He doesn't react. Letting out a breath of relief, I let his hair slip through my fingers and cautiously stand. My feet make no sound in the moss as I run to the spring, following the narrow stream back into the trees to the place where Lonesome and the others first caught me.

The fire poker is gone.

Damn it. I kick at the ground in frustration, but instead of kicking up a clump of slimy moss, my toes strike something hard. Gritting my teeth against the pain, I drop to my knees and dig my fingers into the moss. They brush something cool and hard and long.

I frown, pulling chunks of dirt and moss aside until I can ease my hand around it, ripping it from the earth with an uncomfortably loud *sucking* sound. I stare at the muddy poker, and then the deep hole it's left behind in confusion. *How…*

A ray of sunlight breaks through the canopy, reminding me of how little time I have to enact my haphazard plan.

I set the poker against my shoulder and return to the clearing, carefully picking my way through the sleeping bodies to Louise and her protective nest of beautiful creatures. There's only one way I can get her out, and it's a gamble. An enormous one. If I fail, it'll be the end of both of us.

An awful thought creeps up on me as I weigh up my odds of success. *It would be so easy to leave now.* To run home to Mama and tell the rest of the village that I couldn't find her. To tell Mayor Jones that he was right all along if it meant I could live…

No. I push the thought away, furious with myself for letting it in. Either Louise goes home, or neither of us do.

Sticking the poker into the ground, I step gingerly over an arm and into the nest. My petticoat is already short, sitting just below my knees, but I hitch at the hem as I navigate my way through between the sleeping creatures anyway.

It's the most stressful game of hopscotch I've ever played.

Louise lies flat on her back in the centre of the creatures, her legs straight and her hands folded peacefully over her stomach. She looks like she's been laid out for a funeral. I shiver and plant my feet on either side of her waist, taking a moment to centre myself.

This is the hard part.

Squatting down, I inch my fingers under Louise's waist. Her eyes fly open, scaring me so badly that I have to put my elbow down to stop myself from falling.

We stare at each other. I can't tell if she knows who I am, but she doesn't move or make a sound. Willing my heartbeat to slow, I recover my position and snake my arms around her. She doesn't resist, hanging limp as I strain to lift her.

A groan escapes my lips. I drop her and cover my mouth, looking for any movement amongst the sleeping creatures.

They lie still.

Bending down again, I try gripping Louise by the armpits, but this only pulls her up into a sitting position.

She's too heavy for me.

Failure washes over me, bitter and crushing. How naïve was I, to think I could just throw a twelve-year-old over my shoulder and run out of here?

Lip trembling, I swallow hard and give Louise a gentle shake. I have no other plan. There'll be no other opportunities to escape. 'Please,' I whisper, as if will alone can move her. 'Please get up.'

Blank eyed and slack jawed, Louise does what I ask. I stare at her, stunned, as she stares back.

'Louise,' I try quietly. 'Turn around.'

She does.

I give a breathy little laugh. The humans are so malleable they'll follow anyone's orders, not just the creatures.

Hopping back through the sleeping figures, I collect the poker and turn to Louise. 'Louise,' I whisper, too afraid to raise my voice any higher. 'Without touching anyone, step forward.' She moves right over one of the women. 'Jump to that patch of moss,' I point to a gap in the nest. 'Watch out for your skirt.'

Slowly, anxiously, I puppet Louise through the labyrinth of limbs, hair and horns. Finally, she reaches the female creature on the outer edge. 'Now jump to me.'

She leaps forward, but not high enough. Her toe catches on the creature's chest and it sends her sprawling to the ground. She doesn't take any precaution to shield herself from the fall, landing heavily on her side, eyes open and unblinking. If it wasn't for the strand of hair dancing on her breath, I'd think she was dead.

The creature sits up. A bewildered frown mars her gorgeous face. She looks at me, eyes widening, lips parting.

My heart pounds. Without thinking, I swing the poker hard at the side of her head. She crumples immediately, falling back into unconsciousness. But for how long, I don't know.

'Louise, stand up!' I whisper. She rises clumsily to her feet. 'Take my hand.' Her hand slides into mine, clammy and warm.

Gripping my poker tight, I scan the trees, trying to determine which direction will lead us home.

'Follow me.'

Louise trots beside me as I circle around the edge of the clearing, terrified of making the wrong decision, of leading Louise deeper into the trees.

A twig snaps. I freeze, looking down to see a broken stick underneath my foot. None of the creatures stir. I exhale, relieved. If I'm waiting for a sign, this will have to be it.

'Louise, *run.*'

○

Louise lags behind me. She runs like someone who has forgotten how legs work, tripping and stumbling on everything, but I don't stop. I don't dare. We have to cover as much ground as possible before nightfall. Even if we come out of the woods a hundred miles away from the village, it'll be all right. I can get her home from there. We just need to make it to where they can't follow.

Flinching at every rustle, every sound, we go on for hours.

At what must be midday, my leg gives out beneath me, sending me crashing to my knees. I try to climb back to my feet, but my trembling muscles refuse to support me.

Letting go of Louise's hand, I see she's still in the same blank state. She waits patiently, staring at me. The only indication she's a real person are her quick, short breaths. She exhausted too, even if she lacks the ability to show it.

'Louise?' I take her hand again, pulling her down to kneel

beside me. 'Louise, it's me. It's Emma.'

She stares at me with a mindless smile. No, not at me. Through me.

I shake her. 'Louise, you've got to wake up. We have to go home.'

She keeps staring. It's heartbreaking. I feel like I'm talking to a doll.

'Wake up!' I order. 'Wake up, we have to run! We have to get out of the woods before they come after us!'

But it's one order she can't seem to follow.

Massaging my rubbery legs, I begin to panic. What if she never wakes up? None of the other humans seemed to.

What made me so special?

The dreams flash back into my head, one after the other. Samuel, Mona, Mama. All of my reasons to stay.

I grab Louise again. 'Louise, your mother is waiting for you. Do you remember her? She's chubby and kind, and she has brown hair and brown eyes just like you do. Her name is Sarah and she loves white flowers. I helped you pick them for her once. Do you remember? Yarrow and daisies.'

Louise blinks.

'Your mother cried when she found out you were gone. I sat with her for hours, in the kitchen. Remember your kitchen? All made of wood with your black stove and a yellow cloth on the table.'

Louise's smile falters.

'Nicole was there too, your big sister. She's got a scary face, just like your father does. She acts tough, but she loves you.

She misses you. Your father does, too. He even tried to stand up to Mayor Jones for you. I was there. He yelled through his big black beard right into the mayor's smug face.'

'Father?' Louise whispers, frowning. It sounds more like she's testing the word than recognising it.

'Yes. You live with him in a cottage with a green door. Nicole walks you home from school, and on Sundays you walk to Deference with your whole family, all dressed in white. You sit between Nicole and your mother in the middle of the hall. Sometimes you turn around and wave to me. You know me from the schoolhouse. I help the teacher when Nicole and Roslyn aren't there.'

Louise's eyes finally focus on me. She blinks, with effort this time. 'Emma?'

'Oh, thank our Lord,' I cry, pulling her into a crushing hug.

Her voice is soft, scratchy with disuse. 'Where are we?'

'In the woods.'

She stiffens. 'That tall boy. I had a dream…'

'It was real, he tricked you.' I pull back, looking at her. 'I'm so sorry, Louise. It's all my fault.'

'Where is he?' she asks, eyes wide.

'Sleeping. But he'll wake up at nighttime, and more like him. They'll come after us and drag us back. This is our only chance, Louise. Can you stand up?'

She rises slowly, using my shoulder to steady herself. She looks down at me with a confused, sad frown. 'Nobody else came with you?'

'Your father wanted to, but Mayor Jones made him too afraid to leave your mother and Nicole alone. We have to get you back, to show them he was wrong.'

Louise takes a moment to process what I'm saying. She swallows hard and offers me her hand. 'Then we should go,' she says, determined.

'Yes,' I agree, taking her hand and leaning on the poker to stand up. Louise loops an arm through mine for comfort. We walk, gathering speed as our aches and pains recede.

'How long have I been here?' she asks after a while. She sounds troubled, and I can't blame her.

I try to count the days I spent wandering the woods, the nights I spent fighting the influence of the food and water. 'A little over a week,' I say.

Louise's frown deepens. 'I don't remember anything,' she confesses. 'I went to bed, and I had a dream about the boy. I'd dreamed about him before. Most nights, he scared me. But that night he played a flute and told me about a party. He said he knew I liked to dance. The music he played was so pretty I agreed to go with him. And now I'm here.' She shakes her head. 'How can it have been a whole week? What was I doing?'

'You have been dancing,' I assure her. 'The boy and his friends didn't hurt you.'

'What about you?'

'They didn't hurt me either. I was lucky.'

'If they catch us, will we go back to not remembering anything?'

'Probably.'

'Then it'll be like we're dead, won't it? If we can't remember being alive?'

I nod. 'Yes.'

She's quiet for a moment. 'I think we should run,' she says finally.

○

We alternate between running and walking until the light wanes and we're left feeling our way blindly in the darkness.

'Emma,' Louise says, voice trembling. She feels for my hand and clings to it. I raise the poker, heart pounding, warning myself not to hesitate in using it.

Louise looks back every few seconds, but I focus on the way ahead. We trip and stumble again and again, but we stay upright, we keep moving.

We make it further than I thought we would before she tugs on my arm. 'Emma!'

Turning back, I see a golden glow rushing towards us. Fireflies. They surround us in an instant, but I only increase my speed, using their light to our advantage. Dragging Louise behind me, I jump over a root and dash over the soft earth.

Just get home, I urge myself, though I can't be sure if I think it or say it out loud. *Just get home, just get home.*

The creatures don't appear.

I should be relieved, but something doesn't feel right. They're planning something.

I keep running, breath loud and wheezing in my ears. And underneath it, something else. Music.

Louise slows, her hand slipping out of mine. I turn back to her, clamping my hands over her ears. 'Don't listen!' I cry, hoping she gets the idea. My own feet itch. How could I have forgotten about the damned music?

Louise shakes her head to pull herself out of it and raises her hands to replace mine.

I can't cover my ears without dropping the poker, so instead I picture Mama. The last dream, the memory of us dancing together after Mona gave us the raspberries comes to my mind as clear as if it had only just happened. The itch recedes.

'Where are you?' I yell at the night, brandishing the poker.

The music gets louder. I turn in a circle, searching for any sign of them.

'Up there!' Louise shouts, looking up. I follow her gaze to the trees. The creatures perch in the branches all around us, barely more than shadows above the golden glow.

'I won't let you touch her,' I shout, brandishing the poker. 'You'll have to kill me first!'

The music stops abruptly. The creature nearest to us crouches down. His muscles are coiled, ready to pounce. My palms are so sweaty I worry the poker will slip right out of them.

Hearing a low growl, I turn in time to see a creature charging for me. I throw myself out of the way, dragging Louise after me and cursing myself for not meeting him head on with the poker.

More creatures leap down from the trees, their faces contorted with rage. Louise lowers her hands, clinging to my free arm. 'If you get the chance,' I tell her, 'run.'

They surround us, forming a ring. They look at the poker warily, and I hear the word 'iron' whispered between them. None of them have weapons, but I don't doubt for a second they could overpower me easily. Turning in a circle, trying to keep an eye on all of them, I not that Lonesome isn't among them. Far fewer creatures have come after us than I'd anticipated. The musicians and the females who adopted Louise seem to make up the bulk of the ring.

'What are you waiting for?' I shout.

One of the females pounces. I thrust my poker out, but not before her long nails, no, *claws* reach my face and open four straight lines across my cheek. It hurts more than anything I've ever felt before. Crying out, I put all of my weight behind the poker as the point makes contact with her chest. I brace myself for the impact, but she gasps and shatters into a thousand golden fireflies.

I recoil as they surround me, flying at my eyes to distract me from the others. Another creature pummels into me from the side, tackling me to the ground. I look up and see that his lovely features have warped and distorted into something monstrous. His long, bare back is hunched and ridged, his brow protruding beneath horns that seem to curl and grow. He bares his teeth, canines long enough now to tear flesh.

'Emma, help!' Louse shrieks.

The creature's claws cut into my arm as he pins me to the ground. My head spins from the pain, the blood, the heat of his skin.

Louise cries out again, her voice sounding further away. I struggle against the creature above me. He's so strong, but he doesn't seem to want to kill me. Just keep me away from Louise.

Well, too bad.

I bite his neck as hard as I can, ripping his skin as I pull away. The creature howls and recoils as his strangely sweet blood gushes over me. I creep my legs beneath his chest and kick him away. Not far, but enough raise my poker and banish him in another wave of gold.

'Louise!' I scream, wiping my mouth and battling my way through the angry fireflies. She's in the arms of one of the women, kicking hard against her.

'Let go of me!' she yells in reply to something I can't quite hear. 'I already have a mother!'

I run at them, but the other creatures turn on me, angrier than ever. Their faces are unrecognisable, their claws and teeth bared to meet me. I raise the poker, daring them to come at me even as I say a silent goodbye to Mama and Mona and Samuel.

The creatures race at me. My poker finds one of them as two of them find me, claws and teeth biting deeply into my arm and thigh. I hear myself scream as pain sears through me, but I lash out with the poker again and again. The fireflies are so thick around me I have no choice but to aim blindly.

Another claw finds me, raking me across the back. The pain is so intense I almost black out.

Gritting my teeth, I wait for the next blow. The poker is

slippery with sweat and something else, but I cling to it, raising it for what might be the last time. I'm almost out of energy to draw on. My head is spinning so badly it would take only the smallest nudge to push me over.

But nothing comes for me.

I hear a loud snarl, a scream of pain. Guttural, inhuman. The fireflies around me flock to the source, illuminating a new, disfigured creature dragging his claws across the neck of the female creature holding Louise. But there's no new wave of fireflies. The female's neck blooms with darkness before she slumps in his arms, dropping Louise.

His bright eyes meet mine. I recognise him, this monster with hair caught in his immense, branching horns.

Lonesome points a long, yellowed claw behind me and lets go of the female. She falls to the earth with a thud, unmoving. He runs in the opposite direction, moving so quickly it almost looks like he steps into thin air. The other creatures screech with fury, disappearing behind him with the fireflies swirling in pursuit.

My legs buckle. Louise runs to catch me as I fall, her face wet with tears. She eases me to the ground and hands me a fistful of captured fireflies, the only light left in this dark hell. I trap them in my fingers. They glow red with blood.

'You're going to be all right,' she tells me resolutely, ripping wide strips from the bottom of her nightdress. 'We're going to get home.' She tightly bandages my wounded arm and leg, even attempting to wrap up my face. She looks so serious as she ties a knot over my cheek, but the fabric blocks my mouth and nose.

I almost want to laugh. My head is so woozy I barely feel the pain anymore.

'Leave it,' I say, pulling the bandage over my head and dropping it. It's already soaked through with red. 'It's not that bad.'

She takes my uninjured arm and helps me up, pulling it around her shoulders. The trapped fireflies bob angrily beside her ear, lighting our way. I drag the poker behind us. It's hard to hold on to, but I refuse to let it go.

'Nicole's not allowed to say anything mean about you again,' Louise tells me as we start to move.

I laugh at that, the sound echoing madly through the trees.

20

Day breaks. The world blurs. My feet feel light, and then heavy.

Everything hurts.

My mind skitters from thought to thought, memory to memory. My life replays itself out of sequence.

Something soft and damp cushions my face. Did I fall or have we stopped to rest? I'm not sure anymore.

I feel Louise shake me, rolling me over. Her lips are moving. Her voice sounds strange, far away.

'Emma, you have to get up. We're almost there.' She waves something in my face. 'See? Bluebells! And just up ahead you can see where the trees stop. Please, you just need to go a little further.'

'I'm coming,' I promise her. My voice sounds even further away than hers. I try push myself up, but my arms are like jelly. I can't even feel my legs. 'I'm coming.'

Louise's eyes well with fresh tears, but she wipes them away and hooks her arms under my armpits. I feel the poker slip out of my hand, and I don't have the energy to ask her to stop and pick it up.

She drags me, slow and halting all the way to the tree line. The early morning sunlight blinds me as it rises over the hill. *My hill.* Louise slips on the dewy flowers, falling onto her backside. Panting with exertion, she crawls beside me and curls up over my chest. 'Emma, please,' she begs, clutching the front of my undershirt. 'You have to get up.'

'I don't think I can.'

'Then we'll wait until you're strong enough.' She's a sweet girl. She always was.

'But I won't be,' I force myself to say. It's hard, being so close to home and knowing I won't get any closer. But as long as Louise makes it back, it's worth it. I put an unsteady hand on her shoulder and push. 'Go on. Your mother's waiting for you.'

She doesn't move. 'So is yours.'

I don't know how long we lie there, Louise crying quietly into my chest, before something makes her stiffen. A sound I can't hear, or someone I can't see. She stands over me protectively. 'Go away!' she shouts.

'No.'

Lonesome kneels beside me. The monster in his face is gone. Shreds of velvet hang from his horns, and his body is marked all over with weeping claw marks. His bright eyes are so sad.

'I'm not going to say thank you,' I whisper.

He scoops me up. 'I know.'

'Don't you dare take her!' Louise screams, taking my leg

and pulling. 'We're not going back!' But Lonesome carries me out of the trees, taking me into the open air.

The breeze feels wonderful on my raw skin.

'It's all right, Louise,' I promise, trying to give her a reassuring smile. It hurts my cheek, reopening the cuts.

'I'll get help!' she promises, glaring at Lonesome. 'Just hold on. I'll bring everyone!' She races away, nightdress hitched up around her knees.

'I'm sorry,' Lonesome says, looking down at me.

'You should have told *her* that.' It's an effort to talk. My vision swims and refocuses on his torn chest. 'Are they angry at you?'

He gives his crooked smile. He sets me down at the white tree. My feet fail somewhere beneath me, sending me stumbling back against the bark. Lonesome catches me by the shoulders, holding me in place. 'Could be worse,' he says. He's better at lying than I am, but then, it seems just about everyone is.

'What will they do to you?'

'I can't go back. They won't come near me while I'm with you and your iron stick, but as soon as you go…' he looks back.

'Would they really kill one of their own?'

'You killed four of them.'

'Me, not you.'

'I helped you. Now you'll tell your people about the iron and the men with the axes will be braver. Word will spread between your villages. My kind will have to move further in, away from the people.'

'Only if I live,' I remind him.

'You will,' he cups my cheek, the unmarked one. It sounds more hopeful than certain. 'You have to.'

I close my eyes and immediately feel better. Was keeping them open really that much effort? 'Why?'

'I can't be the reason you die.'

'Why?'

'Because I made a mistake. I wanted to make you happy. I really thought…' His voice cracks. 'I should have listened to you. I should have come to you, instead of forcing you to come to me. I should have told you the truth in the beginning. I should have left the woods that first day, when we were still children.'

My mind swims back to that first day, the music, the fireflies. I remember dancing.

'Emma?' His voice is urgent. His grip on me tightens. I'd forgotten he was holding me up. 'Emma, wake up!'

My eyelids flutter. The world spins. 'Put me down,' I whisper. 'Please.'

Lonesome scoops me up and sets me down in the bluebells. They bob over me, the smell overpowering the blood. I touch the tip of my finger to one and smile. I still love them. I'm glad.

'Emma?'

I try to look at Lonesome as he leans over me, but his features blur into his skin, his eyes two smudges framed by tangled locks and looming horns. I set my hand against the side of his face and feel the sharp plane of his jaw. Concentrating on my hand, the rest of him slowly becomes clearer. 'What?'

'What can I do?'

'About what?'

'Everything. Everything I've done. I need to make it up to you.'

I almost laugh, though it isn't funny. 'I don't think you can.'

His eyes are pleading. 'Don't say that. I'll leave the woods, even if it kills me. And if it doesn't, I'll live like you in your awful little village. I'll spend the rest of my life looking after you.'

I let my hand fall back to my side. 'No.'

He slumps. 'Do you hate me that much?' he asks.

Yes, I want to say, out of spite more than anything. But what would it gain now? One cheap point before I die? 'No.'

He looks through his hair, tentative.

'You were my friend when I had nobody else,' I concede, my voice so thin he has to lean in to hear me. His hair tickles, but I have no energy left to laugh. 'Whatever else you did, that was real. It mattered.'

'What do you want me to do?' he asks again.

'Leave,' I say with a sigh. 'Be better. Make it up to me somewhere else, with other people.'

He leans back, running a hand through his hair. His eyes meet mine, uncertain and afraid. 'And then you'll forgive me?'

It's too big a question, and I'm too tired to give a real answer. 'Yes.'

He swallows, but nods. 'All right.'

There's nothing left to say, but he doesn't want to leave

me yet. I could tell him to go, but I'm afraid too. I don't want to die alone.

I stretch out my fingers. For once, he knows what I want. He takes my hand between both of his, wrapping it in heat.

We sit in silence for what feels like hours, but must only be minutes. He glances up, cocking his head. 'Your people are coming,' he says.

A smile creeps across my face, painful but real. 'Really?'

'I hear them. There must be twenty of them.'

'You should go.'

Lonesome nods again, but lingers. 'Can I kiss you?' he asks. 'Just once? As a friend?' He looks so nervous. It reminds me of the little boy.

Maybe that's why I don't say no.

He leans down, letting his lips hover over my skin before brushing them against my forehead. They're as light as firefly wings. 'Goodbye, Emma,' he whispers. 'Be happy.'

'Goodbye, Lonesome.'

And then he's gone.

The bluebells sway gently in the breeze. The clouds drift slowly across the blue-gold sky. I pick a flower with trembling fingers, holding it to my chest.

Far away, or maybe just at the top of the hill, I hear the sound of voices and footsteps crunching through the wildflowers. Someone shouts my name.

'I'm here,' I murmur, closing my eyes. 'I'm here.'

21

Something cold and wet nudges at my cheek.

I open my eyes to a big black dog. It rests its head on the bed, tongue lolling out the side of its mouth.

Blinking, I take in the room behind it. Small, wooden. Faded bunting hanging from the ceiling. Light peeping in through a gap in the wall outside the window.

Wall?

'Stranger, come away,' a woman's voice says.

Stranger? Stranger's a puppy. A small, clumsy thing. This dog must be as tall as my thigh.

'Wait,' says another woman. 'Do you hear that?'

There's a silence while the first woman listens. I don't hear anything. 'No,' she says.

My eyes focus on the table behind the dog. Mama sits with her shoulders bowed over a mug of tea. Mona is beside her, her curls pulled back from her face in a half braid and a slow smile creeping over her face. Her voice is a little deeper, her face a little longer.

How long have I been asleep?

They turn as one and stare at me for a long moment, as if they're not sure I'm really here.

I part my dry, cracked lips. 'Mama?' I croak, reaching for her.

The spell is broken. Mona flies to my side, Mama taking a few seconds longer. When she arrives, she takes my face in her hands and kisses every inch of it. 'Emma,' she cries between kisses. 'You're awake. You came back to us!'

'The doctor didn't know if you would,' Mona says, squeezing my hand.

I try to smile up at them, but something stiff covers my cheek. I raise my fingers to it, feeling something hard. Mama captures my hand and pulls it away.

'It's just clay. You've been hurt.'

I remember the claws. 'Louise?'

'She's fine,' Mona assures me. 'Nobody could believe it when she ran into the square, screaming that you needed help. They thought she was a ghost. Almost everyone had given you both up for dead.'

'Did anyone try to follow us?' I ask.

'Samuel and Richard were ready to march into the woods with half the woodsmen after Grace came home and found you missing,' Mona says. 'But Mayor Jones talked them out of it, of course.'

'Of course,' I echo.

'Still, a lot of people were on your side after that performance at the town meeting. So many people thought you'd make it back. But you were gone so long…' her voice fades, her eyes shining. She slides her hand out of mine and scratches Stranger's neck. I look back at the full-grown dog.

'How long?' I ask.

Mona blinks. 'What?'

'Pardon,' Mama corrects her absently.

'How long was I gone?' I ask, trying to sit up.

'You don't know?' she asks.

I can't take my eyes off Stranger. I remember the poker buried beneath the layers of moss. How different Louise looked laying amongst the creatures. 'It felt like days,' I whisper. 'Weeks, maybe.'

Mona's face fills with anguish. I look to Mama, knowing she'd never lie to me. 'Mama?' I ask.

She touches my face, and I notice all the new lines etched in hers, the strands of silver in her dark hair. 'It's your birthday next week, my darling,' she says. 'Nineteen.'

I take a sharp breath. Cold blossoms in my chest. I was gone for the better part of two years?

'How long have I been asleep?' I ask faintly.

'I'll make some tea,' Mona says. 'Come on, Stranger.' The big dog follows her obediently to the stove and lies beside it.

'Two weeks,' Mama says.

I raise my thumbnail to my lips. It's longer than it's ever been before, clean and neatly cut. 'I thought I was going to die,' I say, my voice thick as my teeth close around the nail.

Mama catches my hand and pulls it away from my mouth. 'So did I,' she says gravely. 'You had a fever when they found you. You'd lost so much blood. You were still covered in it when I saw you. Head to toe.' She brushes a strand of hair from my face. 'You looked like nothing I'd ever seen before.'

'A monster?' I ask.

She smiles. 'A miracle.'

A damp patch blossoms against my pillow. 'You brought me home,' I tell her. 'You're the reason I made it back.'

Tears slip down her cheeks, following the contours of her skin. 'Then I did my job,' she says.

'Louise has been telling everyone what you did,' Mona says from the stove. 'She says you took on an army of monsters armed with a fire poker.'

'There were only about a dozen,' I say wearily.

'A dozen *is* an army,' Mama says.

'The mayor's not happy about it,' Mona says.

'Which part?'

'Any of it. You've made him look like a coward.'

'Good.' I want to ask what happened in all the time I was gone, but I can't make the words. I still don't quite believe it, despite the evidence before me. For now, it's enough to know that I'm home, and that Louise is safe, and that the people I love most are here with me. 'What did you hear before?' I ask, holding my hand out to Stranger. She leaps to her feet and pads over, sniffing my hand eagerly. Tail wagging, she gives my knuckles a cold lick.

'When?' Mama asks.

'When I woke up,' I say, scratching Stranger between the ears. 'You said you heard something.'

Mona and Mama exchange an amused look as Mona brings me a steaming mug of tea.

'Oh,' Mama says. 'That.'

'What?' I ask. 'Tell me.'

'You snore, Emma,' Mona laughs. 'Like a pig in a thunderstorm.'

'*Pardon?*'

'I've never had the heart to tell you,' Mama admits.

I stare at her, then burst out laughing.

○

The doctor knocks on the door in the early afternoon and is pleasantly surprised to see me sitting up in bed. Mama and Mona keep to the table, giving him space to work.

'How's the patient feeling?' he asks, smiling kindly.

'Better,' I tell him honestly. The dull throbbing around my injuries is nothing compared to how I felt in the woods when they were fresh, or the pain of when I was starving and cold.

He leans his silver cane against the wall and kneels beside the bed. 'May I?' he asks, gesturing to my bandages. I nod. He systematically removes the clay from my cheek, the bandages from my arm and thigh and, finally, the square piece of cloth covering my back.

'They're healing very nicely,' the doctors says when he's done. 'No inflammation or infection. You're very lucky.'

'Will they heal?' I ask, staring at the vivid red stripes on my thigh, stitched together with black thread. They're ugly, angry. I can only imagine what my face looks like.

'In time,' he says. 'Though perhaps not fully. The wounds on your leg were deep.'

My voice trembles. 'Can I walk?'

'Would you like to see?' He stands and offers his hand. I take it, throwing the covers aside and swinging my legs over the side of the bed with a wince. At least they respond to commands.

Easing myself up, I find I can put a little pressure on my leg, though it buckles beneath me when I try to take a step. The doctor catches me before I can fall.

'Maybe it's too soon,' Mama worries. She and Mona are on their feet, tea spilled across the table.

'Try this,' the doctor suggests, fetching his silver walking stick. The ornate handle fits my palm perfectly. I take a step, though it's more of a hop.

'Let the stick take your weight instead of your leg,' the doctor says. 'Trust it.'

I lean on it, arm wobbling as I take a step. It feels strange, uneven. I take another step. I tremor, but I don't fall.

'How does it feel?'

'Different,' I say, taking another step and overbalancing. I land on my knee, tears stinging my eyes at the pain.

The doctor kneels beside me. 'You'll get better at it,' he says. 'It'll take practice.'

'I'll find you a stick,' Mona promises.

'No need,' the doctor says with a wave of his hand. He smiles at me. He has the same light, kind eyes as Roslyn.

'Keep it,' he says, setting my hand back on the top of the stick and helping me to my feet.

'I can't,' I say, gaping at him. The etched silver stick must have cost more than Mama's earned in her whole life.

'It's too much,' Mama says firmly. 'A wooden one will do for Emma.'

'On the contrary,' the doctor says. 'It's the least I can do. Consider it a gift on the behalf of the village.'

I swallow. 'But… won't you need it?'

'It's just a bit of vanity,' he admits. 'You need it for something much more worthy.'

I look to Mama, unsure what to say.

'Say thank you, Emma,' she urges me.

I run my hand over the stick, fingers tracing the leafy patterns running down the shaft. 'Thank you.'

'You're very welcome,' the doctor says. 'Now. Shall we get those stitches out?'

Mama and Mona try to distract me from the sound of snipping and the burning sensation of the thread being pulled out of my skin.

'The wall went up a few weeks after you left,' Mona explains, brewing a fresh batch of tea. 'It took months to finish it. The farms are all outside the wall now, and there's only one gate out, which closes at sunset and opens at sunrise. Everyone who works on the farms hates it.'

'What about the Green?' I ask, frowning.

'Outside, of course,' she rolls her eyes. 'Papa Stone protested, and the mayor had him locked up for weeks.'

'Locked up? Where?'

'Jones had the pub converted into a penitence building,' the doctor says with a scowl. 'For those who don't follow our Lord's will.'

'Strangers and women,' I guess.

The doctor and Mona nod.

'Women caught outside after dark without their father, husband, or older brother go straight in for the night,' Mama says. She strokes my hand as the doctor moves from my leg to my back. I wince as he pulls at a row of stitches. 'As well as anyone who misses Deference, anyone caught going near the woods, or even talking about it.'

'Why is everyone putting up with it?' I ask.

'Because he's the mayor,' Mama says with a shrug. 'It's the way it is.'

'It's the way it was,' the doctor corrects her. 'People are talking.'

Mama looks away.

'About what?' I ask.

'You,' Mona says. 'You stood up to the mayor, all that time ago, and it was fine when everyone thought you'd marched off to your death…'

'Thank you,' I interrupt with a snort.

'But you lived. And you brought Louise home. You proved him wrong. Which means he could be wrong about other things, too.'

'You've done something very important for this village, Emma,' the doctor says. 'Don't let them forget it.'

The doctor finishes some time later and bids us good afternoon. 'I'll check on you again,' he promises. 'The day after tomorrow, after Deference. But if you feel any unusual pain, send for me at once.'

'Could you…' I begin, then hesitate.

'Yes?'

'Could you give my best to Roslyn?'

He gives me a sympathetic look. 'She doesn't live with us any longer,' he says. 'But I'll tell her the next time I see her.'

I close my eyes, reminding myself that everything is different. 'Of course,' I say. 'She must be married by now.'

'Yes,' the doctor says. 'But she'll be very glad to hear from you, even if she can't visit you herself.'

That's right. I'm officially an unmarried woman now. The mayor's daughter-in-law couldn't possibly come see me.

I give a terse smile. 'Thank you again.'

He tips his hat and closes the door.

○

Mona stays to help me wash and braid my hair. Stranger wrestles herself between my legs and presents her belly, silently demanding scratches, and Mama hovers at my side as if she's afraid to let me out of her sight. We talk about the past and ignore the difficult subjects of the present and the future until the light through the window dims with the promise of evening.

'We'd best be going soon,' she says to Mona.

'We?' I ask.

'Curfew,' Mona says, rolling her eyes. 'Your mother walks me home.'

'Who walks Mama home?' I ask.

'One of the guard sees me back,' Mama says.

Sounds efficient. 'Can I come with you?'

'No,' Mama says firmly. 'It's too far. You need rest.'

'I need fresh air,' I insist. 'And practice using the stick.'

'We could help her,' Mona says. 'The exercise might do her leg good.'

'Or make it fall off,' Mama mutters, but it's as good as a yes.

They help me dress, easing my grey stockings up my legs and over the puckered, healing claw marks. I bat them away as they try to button up my grey blouse, wanting to achieve something on my own. I reach for my mustard dress and sigh as Mama hands me a brown one instead. Unmarried women don't wear cheerful colours.

I limp to the mirror and brace myself before I look, preparing myself to see a face I might not recognise.

'Emma?' Mona asks when I hesitate too long. 'You don't have to do this now.'

I look at her, biting my lip. 'Does it look awful?'

'No,' she says with a smile. 'You look fierce.'

'You look like you,' Mama says.

They're both right. The face that stares out of the mirror is my own, though older. A woman's face. Four brown scars rend my cheek, starting beside my eye and ear and curling around to the corner of my mouth. It's not pretty, but it tells a story. I meet my own eyes, and they shine back at me defiantly.

Mona stands on tiptoes to rest her chin on my shoulder, smiling at our reflections. 'I'm glad you're home,' she whispers.

I meet her eyes in the mirror. 'Me too.'

'Come,' Mama says from the door. 'We'll lose the light.'

Mona offers me her elbow. I loop my arm through it, the beautiful silver stick in the other. Stranger lopes behind us, tail wagging.

'No speaking,' Mama instructs me, brusque. 'You won't recover any faster from inside a prison cell.'

'Yes, Mama.' It's actually nice to be lectured by her again.

'And if you get tired, let me know.'

'How? I can't speak.'

'Hisht.'

It's strange, stepping out my front door to see a wall rather than the vista of the meadow and the woods below, though I'm heartened to see a lone poppy snaking through the wooden boards, its red head leaning haphazardly over the cobblestones.

We walk slowly, my stick tapping loudly on the street. People look at us, as always, but now their eyes widen at the sight of me. I return their stares unflinchingly, and they turn away.

The high street is busy at this time of day, the last rush before the shops close up for the night. The hum of voices fills the air, but one by one the people on the street fall silent as they notice me.

Everyone is still as I pass by, slow as a snail and unsteady as a colt. The shopkeepers come to stand in their doorways, among them the baker and the tailor. I keep my head high, letting them see my scars, refusing to let them feel sorry for me as my arm trembles over the stick.

The silence follows us into the square. Across the way, I see Andrew knocking on the door of the mayor's house. He's marked with dirt, wearing the overalls of a labourer. Jane answers, and a moment later Nicole steps out. She takes his arm stiffly, neither of them exchanging a single word.

Just like the others, she freezes as she sees me. Andrew follows her gaze, his mouth setting in a line. He tugs at her arm, but instead of following him she pulls her arm free and walks towards me.

'Nicole, stop,' he orders.

She ignores him, quickening her pace to intercept us. She plants her feet in the square ahead of me, arms crossed. She takes in my scars, my stick.

'Nicole, damnit,' Andrew swears, coming after her. 'You can't speak to her.'

Nicole looks back at Andrew, her face set with deep dislike. 'She saved my sister,' she shoots back, loud enough for everyone in the square to hear.

'She's unmarried!'

Nicole snorts. 'Lucky her,' she says, and turns her back on her husband. She looks different. Both harder and softer. Strands of white thread through her brown hair, though she's months younger than I am.

'Thank you,' she says fervently, putting her hands on my shoulders and kissing my wounded cheek. Andrew shakes his head and walks away, leaving her behind. All around us, the people watching begin to whisper.

Nicole doesn't seem to hear them. 'Mother cried every day,' she tells me quietly, 'and Father drank himself stupid. I don't know what would have happened to them if you hadn't brought Louise back. If there's anything I can do for you...'

I don't know what to say, which is just as well.

'Get home, Nicole,' Mona urges, gently pushing Nicole away from me. I look over and see Mayor Jones standing in the doorway of his house, watching us. He's the only one who looks the same as when I left him. 'Before he calls the watch.'

The mayor nods to someone I recognise as a labourer, now dressed all in black. He marches towards us.

'I don't care about the watch,' Nicole says, resolute. 'I mean it, Emma. Anything you want. My home, my food, my husband. You deserve everything.' The man in black takes her arm firmly. She raises her voice again. 'You deserve more than this.'

'Let's go quietly, shall we?' he asks in a clipped voice. He doesn't even look at me.

'None of you even offered to go,' she accuses everyone watching as the man steers her towards what used to be the pub. 'None of you did anything!'

I take a step after her, but Mama and Mona restrain me.

'Don't,' Mama says sternly. 'You won't help.'

I look back at the mayor's house just in time to see him glance at my walking stick before he shuts the door.

○

The streets are abandoned by the time Mama and I return home. I ache, leaning on her shoulder to make it the last few steps to the door. She bundles me inside and helps me strip, smoothing a herbal clay paste over my aching scars and putting me straight to bed.

'Mama?' I ask, struggling to keep my eyes open.

'Mm?'

'You snore too, you know.'

She smiles. 'I do. Your father used to tease me about it.'

'I missed it.'

She strokes my hair. 'So did I,' she says. 'I can't sleep without you thundering beside me.'

I chuckle and close my eyes, feeling safe and warm, and slip into a dreamless sleep.

22

Mama wakes me late in the morning.

'Don't get up,' she instructs, setting a plate of toasted bread and cheese beside me. 'I'll be at the doctors until this afternoon. Mona will be here after she's finished in the orchard. Stay in bed until then.'

'Yes, Mama,' I say meekly. The doctor hired her to clean his surgery while I was in the woods – a job I intend to take over the second I master the use of my walking stick.

She squints at me suspiciously, but kisses me on both cheeks and takes a lingering look at me.

'Go, Mama. I'll be fine.'

She kisses me again and leaves.

Wolfing down the toast, I count to one hundred just to be safe, then climb out of bed. My stick in hand, I manage to walk ten laps of the house before someone knocks at the door.

'Who is it?' I call, looking down at my nightdress. The fabric isn't thin enough to see through, but it's not exactly appropriate for company.

'Your mayor.' Mayor Jones' voice sends a chill down my spine. 'I'm not decent.'

'I'll give you a moment to make yourself more presentable.' His tone tells me he's not going anywhere.

I weigh up the likelihood of my being able to get dressed on my own. Coming up with nothing but the image of Mayor Jones opening the door to find me on the floor with my dress over my head, I limp back to bed. Sitting up against the headboard, I pull the covers up to my chest and cross my arms.

'You can come in,' I call out grudgingly.

The door swings open. Mayor Jones looks instantly out of place in our tiny house with his fine suit and tall hat. He surveys the room, moustache twitching with distaste.

'What do you want?' I ask. There's no reason to pretend I respect him. Not while we're alone, anyway.

He pulls one of the kitchen chairs beside my bed, making a show of dusting it before he sits down. 'There is talk,' he says, 'among the people. They seem to think you've done this village a great service.'

'Didn't I?'

'You disobeyed your mayor and our Lord.'

I raise my eyebrows. 'And saved a girl you'd already given up for dead.'

'A true hero doesn't claim his achievements or seek reward,' Mayor Jones recites. 'He only does his duty.'

'Finding Louise *was* my duty.'

'Was it?' he asks, crossing his legs and leaning in. 'How? How is it that you cared so much more about her safe return than her own family?'

'I didn't,' I say, meeting his eye. 'You scared them.'

'Their fear saved them from rushing blindly into the woods. I don't think you were quite so impaired.'

'Louise was my student,' I say, avoiding the accusation. 'I liked her.'

His moustache twitches. 'One does not march into hell for someone they *like*, Miss Emma. They either do it for love or because they feel responsible.' I look away. He smirks. He knows he has me. 'I thought so. Tell me about them.'

'Why?' I ask warily.

'*My* duty is to protect this village. I can do that better if I know what I'm protecting it against.'

I open my mouth to argue, but however much I don't like his methods, he hasn't said anything I can argue with. Instead, I reluctantly tell him about Lonesome, leaving out everything personal and reducing our encounters to one. I describe the music, the way they can call people to the trees, the illusion of the dreams. I describe the creatures and the clearing, the way they change when they're angry, their vulnerability to iron.

The mayor listens with his fingertips pressed together, head bowed over them. He's quiet after I finish speaking.

'Was there anything else you needed?' I ask.

'Yes,' he says. He leans back in his chair, removing his hat. 'I came to bring you some happy news.'

That catches me off guard. 'What news?'

'That of your engagement.'

I raise my eyebrows. 'My what?'

'As I said, there's been talk. Much of it about your so-called sad situation. You retrieved the girl Louise, yet you're to live the life of an unmarried woman.'

'But there's no one left to marry,' I point out. 'Andrew and Samuel…'

'Are *happily* married, yes. But the blacksmith has offered his son and I have accepted on your behalf.'

'The blacksmith's son?' I think back to the schoolhouse. He's younger than I am, but the only thing I can remember about him is overhearing him saying something awful to Samuel once. 'Dominick?'

'He's apprenticed to his father. They make a very respectable income and you'll get to live in a house with more than one room. Some might say it's more than you deserve.'

I don't know what to say. Suddenly I have the chance to give Mama a home and rest. But at what cost? Why is he offering this to me so freely?

'What if I say no?'

The mayor snorts. 'Why would you? There'll be no other offers. This communal interest in your wellbeing is merely a thing of the moment, and I suggest you seize it before everyone forgets you again.'

Footsteps crunch up to the door. 'Emma,' I hear Mona's voice. The door swings open. 'If you're out of bed, so help me…' she freezes as her eyes land on the mayor.

He glances at her but doesn't acknowledge her. 'You and your mother will accept the proposal formally tomorrow, after Deference,' he says, standing and putting on his hat. 'The wedding will be held on your nineteenth birthday. I shall, of course, officiate.'

I open my mouth, but I can't think of a thing to say.

He tips his hat, cold eyes gleaming. 'Good day.'

○

'He's trying to keep you in line, you know,' Mona says. We sit outside my house, our backs to the new wall. Stranger lays in the middle of the empty lane, enjoying the sun. 'Look at what Nicole did yesterday. People aren't talking about you being unmarried, they're talking about you standing up to the mayor. The women are talking about how you've proven they can be more than wives and mothers.'

'They?' I nudge her. 'You're not a woman now?'

'I'm a Stranger,' she reminds me. 'We're not talking about anything. We know we won't get away with it.'

'What does he think marrying me off is going to do about it?' I ask. 'How will that keep me in line?'

'Think, Emma. As an unmarried woman, what do you have to lose?'

'Nothing.'

'And if you get married and realise how much nicer it is to be able to eat until you're full? When Grace has nothing to do but read in armchair and help you keep your children in check?'

I let my head rest against the wall. 'Everything.'

'Exactly. As an unmarried woman, you can cause trouble.

None of them have before, because they didn't think they could get away with it. You *know* you can, but he can't throw you in prison while everyone thinks you're a hero.'

'Damn him,' I mutter, closing my eyes. 'What do I do?'

Mona sounds surprised. 'Is it really that hard of a decision?'

'Of course it is,' I say, opening my eyes. 'You said it yourself. Mama wouldn't have to do anything but what she wants. She could have a real bed, and a room of her own. How can I say no to that, after everything I've put her though?'

'She doesn't mind the work, Emma. Especially now the doctor's taken her on.'

'But how much longer is she going to be able to do it?' I ask. 'And how can I do anything but beg on this useless leg? I'm an adult now, I should be taking care of her.'

'So you're going to say yes, then?'

'I don't know. Will you hate me if I do?'

She puts her arm through mine, resting her head on my shoulder. 'No. I'll just hate him even more for making you do it.'

I sigh. 'I can't believe I got through everything that happened in the woods just to be bullied by a skinny man with an ugly moustache.'

She looks at me, sidelong. 'Do you want to talk about him?'

'Who? The mayor?'

'The boy in the woods. Lonesome. Your mother told me about him while you were gone.'

'There's not much to say.' I bite down on my nail too hard, tearing it down to the skin.

'Did you care about him?'

'For a while. Maybe still, a little. It's confusing. I won't miss him, though.'

'Did you kill him?'

'No.'

'I wish *I* could,' she says, the fire in her voice taking me aback.

I squeeze her arm. 'He's not worth becoming a killer for.'

She hears something in my voice. 'Do you want to talk about *that?*'

The memory of my poker plunging into a creature's chest comes back to me. Of a terrible face tearing into a thousand points of golden light. 'Not really,' I say.

'You should have told me what you were going to do. I would have gone with you.'

'I didn't know I was going to do it until I did.'

Mona picks up a pebble and tosses it down the lane. Stranger lazily raises her head as it bounces from cobblestone to cobblestone, then skitters to a rest outside our neighbour's house. 'Still.'

I drop my thumb from my mouth, watching as Mona feels for another pebble and sends it skipping after the first. Stranger wags her tail.

'You didn't leave,' I say, trying to sound casual.

'No.'

'Why not? You're of age. It's even worse here for you now than it was before.'

She tugs at one of her curls. 'You know why.'

'Everyone thought I was dead.'

'Your mother didn't. And even if she did, how could I have left her all alone? You went into the woods to look for someone else's daughter, the least I could do was look after her for you.'

I rest my head on top of hers. 'Thank you.'

She squeezes my arm.

'You know,' I say, the memory coming back to me. 'I walked in the wrong direction when I first went into the woods. I came out somewhere else, near another town.'

She sits up, eyes sparkling. 'Really? What was it like?'

'They shot me.'

'They *shot* you?'

I point at the wall, in the direction the town might have been. 'If you do take the road one day, don't go right.'

'South, Emma,' she says with a laugh. 'But noted. Left turns, only.'

○

We walk to the square in the late afternoon, collecting Mama from the doctor's surgery and leaving Mona at the great wooden gate separating the village from the Stranger's Green.

More people meet my eyes today, some going so far as to give me a smile or a nod. It's not much, but it's more than they'd have ever extended to an unmarried woman before. Enough to anger the mayor.

Leaving the square, I look back at his house. Samuel

stands at one of the upper windows, leaning his head against the glass. My stomach flutters as he raises a hand in greeting, and my walking stick slips on the cobblestones. Mama grabs me before I can fall, the baker's wife stooping to pick up the stick for me on her way home from the schoolhouse.

She hands it back, holding my hand for a second too long before moving on.

'Thank you,' I say after her, unsure if she can hear me.

Mama gives me a look, but doesn't tell me off. Taking my elbow, she hurries us on.

I glance back to the square, but the window is empty.

'I heard talk today,' Mama says as she closes our door behind us. 'The mayor was here?'

'Some things don't change,' I say, dropping onto the bed and rubbing at my aching arm. Somehow using the stick makes everything *but* my injured leg hurt.

'What did he want?'

I force a smile. 'I'm engaged. To the blacksmith's son. We have to formally accept tomorrow after Deference. I'm guessing in front of the entire village.'

Mama takes a moment to absorb the information, then goes to her bed and pulls the trunk out from under it. 'When's the wedding?'

'My birthday,' I say, frowning. 'Mama, what are you doing?'

She pulls the blue-grey cloth from the trunk and flaps it out, laying it over her bed. 'You'll need a dress, unless they're offering to buy you one.'

'So you think I should do it?'

Mama sighs. 'You might have done something brave and wonderful, but you still need to eat.'

'Mona thinks the mayor is trying to keep me from causing trouble.'

'Of course he is. What does that matter? You've done enough. You deserve a good life, Emma.'

And so does she. After all this time, I have the chance to make things right for her. I stand up, leaning on the silver stick, and hold my other arm out. 'I think I lost weight in the woods,' I say.

She nods, fishing out her tape measure and looping it around my waist.

23

We walk to Deference in matching grey, leaving early to allow time for my slower pace. Even so, we're overtaken by half the village. The blacksmith, his wife and three children pass us in blinding white. He meets my eye and nods politely. I've never had much reason to go to his shop, but he doesn't seem like a bad man. He's certainly not the worst prospective father-in-law I've had.

Dominick glances at me curiously, eyes lingering on my scarred cheek. He's not bad looking, but I know almost nothing about him. Still, I suppose that doesn't really matter. He'll either be unpleasant, in which case we'll avoid each other, or we'll get along.

Lord, I'm starting to feel like Roslyn.

'Emma!' I hear my name as soon as we reach the hall. Louise stands with her parents, restrained by her mother. Sarah shoots me an apologetic look, but after what happened to Nicole it's understandable. I don't see her anywhere.

I smile at Louise, holding my hand up to tell her to stay.

She scowls but stops struggling against her mother. Richard, however, walks past them and holds his hand out to me. I don't want to cause trouble for him with so many people looking, but to leave him hanging would only embarrass him. So I take it. He shakes my hand sternly and without words, and returns to his seat.

We sit down in the middle of the hall, crammed between the money lender and a labourer. Up ahead, I see Roslyn and Samuel sitting in the front row with the doctor and Charlotte behind them. Roslyn turns around to speak to her parents and, catching sight of me, offers me a brief but bright smile. She turns back and whispers something to Samuel, but he doesn't look.

I feel a pang of disappointment.

Mayor Jones takes the podium, but the hum of voices doesn't die down. His moustache twitches, and he clears his throat loudly.

The hum dies down, but only a little. This would never have happened before.

He clears his throat again, and silence eventually comes to the hall.

'Our Lord has blessed us with wonderful news,' he begins. 'As many of you have seen or heard by now, Emma, the old tailor's daughter, has woken from her long and, dare I say, well-deserved slumber.'

My eyebrows shoot up of their own accord. I wasn't expecting this. And from the surprised whispers around me, neither was anyone else.

The mayor looks at me with a smile that looks frighteningly convincing. 'It gives me great pleasure to announce her engagement to Dominick, the blacksmith's son.' So much for my formal acceptance. He must have been afraid I'd defy him again. In a way, I'm glad that he's taken the choice out of my hands. Now he'll never know for sure that he beat me.

The hall bursts into spontaneous applause. I look around, surprised. Everyone is looking at me, their faces lit by smiles. It feels strange, and more than humbling, to see how many of them look genuinely happy for me.

My eyes meet Mona's. She stands at the back of the hall beside Papa Stone. She gives me a sad, forced smile. I turn back to the front of the hall. I know what she wants me to do. But I can't. Lord help me, I can't do it this time.

'The wedding will take place here, on Emma's nineteenth birthday,' the mayor continues. 'It is unprecedented, I know, but as Emma missed her coming of age in the performance of our Lord's work, we will allow this rare break in tradition.'

There isn't a hint of shame on his face as he blatantly contradicts everything he said to me in my house. In fact, he's just hitting his stride, his voice taking on a trembling passion. 'For our Lord does work in mysterious ways. He sent Emma into the woods, armed with Lord given iron, to bring back Richard and Sarah's poor, innocent daughter. And in acting as the Lord's vessel, she succeeded where an army of us couldn't have.'

I roll my eyes as he absolves himself of all inaction. Nobody sees it but him. His eyes gleam at me. He raises his hands, his voice reaching a tremulous crescendo.

'And she has brought us back such a gift, greater even than the return of two precious young women. Emma has told me of the horrors she saw in the woods. At last, we know the faces of these demons who live to tempt us away from the light of our Lord and into the shadow.'

The hall is dead silent now. Other than Mama and Mona, and perhaps Richard and Sarah, nobody has heard more than rumours about what happened to us.

'And a deceptively beautiful face it is, hiding horns, teeth and claws until they have us in their grasp. Using music and food and drink to cloud our senses, doing whatever they will with our living but lifeless bodies, keeping us for their playthings to mock us and defile our standing with our Lord.'

The hall is captivated. Mothers unconsciously draw their children closer. Men put their hands on their wives' shoulders.

'But are we safe here?' he asks. 'Behind our wall, with the watch protecting us?'

'Yes!' the money lender's wife calls out from nearby, swept up in his words. The Mayor isn't angry with the interruption. He was counting on it.

'I say we are *not*, good madam,' he cries, slapping his hand on the podium. 'For the demons can reach us even here, appealing to our lustful urges and turning the weak-minded against themselves. What we have done is not enough, and now that we have brought the demons' ire upon the village, we must do more.'

I shift in my seat, uncomfortable. Where is he going with this? Knowing about the creatures should make us less afraid, not more.

'The demons can take us even in our sleep. Drawn to the most fragile of us, the most susceptible to temptation, they can invade our dreams at will.'

I frown as everyone around me gasps.

Mayor Jones looks at me, daring me to contradict him. 'Our curfew is not enough. Our wall is not enough. We must increase the watch, tighten the curfew. No woman is to be out of doors after dark, period. Any woman found or reputed to be doing so will be taken to the penitence building for her own good, until such time as we know she is not in the demons' grip.'

There's a low murmur of support. Mama puts her hand on my knee. *Stay silent*, the hand says.

'We must be vigilant. We must watch our children, watch our neighbours. Anyone afflicted by these dreams may not be willing to speak up and report themselves, so it is up to the rest of us to look for any strange behaviour and report it to the watch.'

'What about the Strangers?' Mona's voice rings out indignantly. 'How often will we be *reported* for suspicious behaviour?'

'As often as you exhibit it,' the Mayor returns coolly. 'If you don't like our way of life, you are welcome to leave.'

My fists clench. Mona's right. How many ways will this new rule be abused?

Forcing myself to look away from the Mayor, I focus instead on my walking stick. I remind myself how much better mine and Mama's lives will be if I do what the mayor wants.

I think of the blacksmith's house, a street back from the square. I've never been inside, but I know it has a small garden with a wrought iron bench beneath a dainty silver-barked tree. In the spring, it blooms with pink blossoms. It's pretty. I could be happy sitting beneath it.

If I could live with myself.

'Emma has proven to us that the demons cannot suffer the Lord's iron. In the weeks to come, the blacksmith will issue our women with iron bracelets to be worn at all times, for their own good,' the mayor continues. 'Though any man afraid for his safety may acquire one as well.' The way his moustache curls as he says *man* makes sure none will ever ask for one. Protection is for the weak, that sneer says. For women.

I close my eyes and picture myself and Mama, sitting on the bench. Mama is sewing, I'm reading a book.

Heavy iron shackles hang from our wrists.

I open my eyes, gaze returning to the handle of the walking stick. Intricate flowers and leaves are carved in the cool silver. The doctor spent so much to own it, and yet he gave it to me freely. Why?

'You've done something very important for this village,' he'd said. *'Don't let them forget it.'*

But they are forgetting. The mayor has them in the palm of his hand. Women around the hall are nodding in support of being bound in iron. And he's using me to do it.

Yes, mine and Mama's lives will be better if I marry the blacksmith's son, but I know the cost, and I'm not willing to pay it.

'I'm sorry, Mama,' I whisper. Her eyes widen in alarm as I wrap my hand around the silver handle and push myself to my feet, but she doesn't stop me.

'I think you're mistaken, Mayor Jones,' I say.

His jaw clenches. He thought he had me, this man who thought I cared about his son's money. As though that was the only thing of Samuel's that anyone would see any worth in. 'Please sit down, Miss Emma,' he says tightly. 'You're still recovering from your ordeal.'

'I'm quite well, actually,' I return evenly, raising my voice over the smattering of confused whispers rising from the crowd. 'And I never said the creatures – or demons, as you call them – could appear in our dreams. I said they could make it appear as a dream.' I turn away from him to speak to the others. 'They can call you to the edge of the woods, but they can't force you to cross it. They'll offer you whatever you want, and because you think it's only a dream you won't see the harm in saying no. But that's all you have to do. They can't come out, and so they can't do anything to hurt you. Our woodsmen already carry iron axes. We don't need iron bracelets.' I look back to the mayor. 'We don't even need to be afraid. Just aware.'

The whispers swell into a buzz.

The mayor clears his throat before he speaks, buying

himself some time to think. 'You gave me what information you had. As mayor, it is up to me to consult with our Lord and decide what course we will take.'

'Then make a better decision,' I throw back. 'Stop punishing women for something they haven't done.'

'Women are the most susceptible to these demons—'

'Why do you think that is?' I shout, frustrated. He tries to interrupt, but I keep talking, our voices duelling until mine drowns him out. 'You force us to compete against each other to marry men we barely know and punish us when the numbers don't work out. You make us rely on our husbands and shame us if we have to work to support ourselves. Why do you think we're so willing to follow someone who promises us happiness and freedom? If you want to fix the problem and stop women disappearing, fix the way we're treated. Make us *want* to stay.'

There's a smattering of enthusiastic applause. Caroline, Sarah, Louise, Mona and even Jane are on their feet, cheering me on. Roslyn turns to look back, giving me an encouraging nod. The doctor is smiling.

'I do as much work in the bakery as my husband,' Caroline calls. The baker's eyes widen, but he concedes a moment later with a nod.

'We all knew that Grace made most of Stephen's clothes,' Charlotte stands up in defense of Mama. It takes me a second to realise who she means by Stephen.

'It's true,' Matthew chimes in. Mary tugs at his arm, trying to get him to be quiet. 'Grace taught me how to draw a pattern.

Stephen was so sick I spent most of my apprenticeship under her. And the moment he died, you threw her out.'

I look down at Mama. She sits a little taller, a fiercely proud look in her eye.

'What does any of this matter?' the mayor asks, face reddening with anger. 'Our Lord has different roles for us for a *reason*.'

'I've read the book as many times as you have, father, maybe more,' Samuel says quietly, but somehow we all hear him and hush to let him speak. 'And your Lord looks nothing like mine. Stop hiding behind Him.'

Mayor Jones' face turns blotchy with shock, and for a full second he's silent, mouth flapping with nothing behind it but air. 'You,' he gapes, shaking with rage.

'So, you can hear me.'

The village is gaining confidence. Mayor Jones, so unreachable before, has been brought crashing to the ground. 'Business has suffered with these two-day Deferences,' someone calls. 'We can't get enough done.'

'The traders have been coming less and less since the wall went up,' another shouts. 'We're losing supplies over nothing.'

'My daughter is in a cell,' Richard roars.

'My people can't take another winter in those shacks and rags, and we can't afford to leave,' Papa Stone booms. 'Pay us for our work and pay us fair.'

The rabble goes on for some time, more and more people standing to air their grievances. Mayor Jones flounders. The tide has turned against him and he doesn't know how to stop it.

Mama stands up beside me, taking my hand.

'I'm sorry,' I tell her again.

She shakes her head. 'No. This is long overdue.'

The doctor looks to me, and mimes something. I imitate him, banging my walking stick on the ground three times. The sound echoes around the hall, causing the village to simmer down until only the mayor is left, shouting himself hoarse behind the podium.

'This is not done. I am the mayor!' he shouts. 'I speak for our Lord, as my father did before me, and as my traitorous son will after me.'

'Then perhaps it's time for a new mayor,' the doctor suggests calmly.

'How *dare* you,' Mayor Jones splutters.

'Quite easily. The people have spoken. None of us want to see you run this village into the ground any longer.'

'You think I don't know what you're up to? Replacing me with Samuel so you and your daughter can manipulate him?'

Samuel shakes his head. 'I won't be mayor.'

'Damn straight, you won't,' Mayor Jones bangs his hand on the podium. 'This is a ridiculous notion. Sit *down*, all of you.'

'The doctor should be Mayor,' the baker calls out.

The doctor shrugs. 'If there is no one else willing, though I suspect there are far more suitable candidates.'

He looks at me. I raise my thumb to my lips, glancing at

Mona. She raises her eyebrows, waiting. I frown back at her.

What do they want?

'It should be Emma!' Louise shouts, leaping onto her seat. Her voice sounds even younger in the wide hall. I laugh, shaking my head at her.

'Control your daughter, Richard,' the mayor snaps.

But Richard stands, eyeing him coolly. 'My daughter doesn't need to be controlled. I think it's a fine idea.' He looks to me, a hint of a smile softening that fearsome face. 'Why shouldn't it be Emma?'

My own smile fades. 'Pardon?' I ask, but my voice is so quiet I'm not sure I even hear it.

'My family and I have been blessed with Emma's presence in a crisis,' Richard continues. 'She's clever, courageous and compassionate, and it sounds like she has some ideas. I'd much rather my daughters live in her world than ours.'

The hall is silent, every eye on me.

'Aye,' the doctor nods. 'I agree. I vote for Emma.'

'This is ridiculous,' Mayor Jones stutters. 'What right does she have?'

'She has every right,' the doctor says. 'As much of a right as your great-grandfather had, and more right than you. What do you say, Emma?'

My mouth is dry, hanging open like a stunned fish. Me, as mayor? What is he thinking?

But then... who would *I* choose, if I could? Who would I want in charge of our lives? The doctor, maybe, or Papa Stone. Samuel, Charlotte, Mona, Jane, those are all people I'd listen to. But would they be right for everyone? How can just one person speak for so many?

'Emma?' the doctor prompts me. I'm running out of time.

'This is preposterous,' the mayor shouts. 'She can't even think without you putting words in her head.'

I swallow. 'There should be a council,' I say, raising my voice. I'm uncertain at first, but the idea appeals so much to me I gain confidence. 'With representatives from every group in the village.'

The mayor scoffs. 'And you would head this council?'

'If…' I begin, but my voice falters. I'm nervous about putting myself forward for something so important. After all, he's right. What right do I have? What qualifies me? I'm just someone who wants things to be better.

But maybe that's all I need to be.

Looking around the hall, I see so many people nodding back at me. Mona smiles, urging me on. 'Yes,' I say, channeling the iron in my blood into my voice. 'I'll head the council, if the village agrees. I do have ideas, and I'd like to hear everyone else's, too. I want to make our village better for everyone.' I look to Papa Stone. 'Including Strangers.'

He meets my eye. 'Do we have your word on that?'

'Yes,' I promise. 'You'll have every right we have. You'll work for money, at whatever job you like. We'll build new houses, expand the village. Any problem you have, I'll hear it. And I won't head any council that you're not a part of.'

'Aye, then,' he nods. 'My vote is for you, and this council.'

'Aye!' Mona shouts from beside him.

Louise follows a split second later, Sarah and Richard adding their voices to hers.

'You cannot be serious,' Mayor Jones shouts.

Samuel looks at me, a smile creeping over his face. I can't help but return it. 'Aye. My vote goes to Emma.'

Roslyn, Charlotte, Jane, Matthew, Caroline, one by one they stand and give me their support. The rest of the village joins in, even Mary and Andrew and the blacksmith's family.

Mama squeezes my hand. 'Aye,' she whispers, her eyes brimming.

'You'd all turn your backs on our Lord for *her*?' the Mayor Jones screams. 'She's just a woman!'

'Yes, Jones,' I say coldly. 'And you're just one man.'

Samuel indicates his head to two men dressed in black, the watch, and they move to the front and take Jones by the arms. 'Take him to the cells,' Samuel orders, a note of satisfaction in his voice. For the first time in years, his father is listening to his every word. But then Samuel remembers himself and looks back at me. 'If you say so, that is.'

I shake my head. 'He hasn't done anything wrong. Take him outside and let him go.' I meet the former mayor's eyes and give him a sickly-sweet smile. 'If he doesn't agree with how we do things here, he's welcome to leave.'

His mouth opens in outrage. His perfect moustache is dotted with flecks of spit. 'You!' he splutters as the watch glance at each other and escort him out. He struggles against them, unused to being handled. 'You'll all fall into shadow,' he shouts. 'When this village is ruined and forgotten by everything decent, you'll beg me to save you!'

His voice, once so compelling, has a manic edge. It fades with him as the watch removes him from the building.

Samuel walks up the aisle to my seat and offers me his elbow. 'Mayor Emma.'

I loop my arm through his, heart pounding. My walking stick makes a rhythm of my progress, and with a fluttering stomach I let go of Samuel and ascend to the podium.

This is it. My chance to make a better life not just for Mama, or me, or Mona, but for all of us.

Standing here, in front of them all, our tiny village looks so big. A sea of faces, some hopeful, some afraid, some glowing with pride.

I take a deep breath, and my nerves scatter like fireflies in the dawn.

'Well,' I say with a laugh. 'Let's get started.

24

The footsteps are almost entirely eaten up by the thick carpet, the opening of the well-oiled door only audible by the breath of air behind it. The silence of this house is deafening. Even Mama's snores are muffled by the thick walls.

I can't get used to it.

The footsteps tiptoe closer, a cloak swishing against the duvet. I squeeze my eyes shut, dreading what comes next.

A hand closes on my shoulder. 'Emma.'

I've been awake for so long that my eyes have adjusted to the darkness. Rolling over, I look up at the dark shape wrapped in a cloak, curls spilling out of the hood. 'It's time?' I ask uselessly.

'Yes.'

Reaching for my walking stick, I try to slide out of bed without disturbing the sleeping figure next to me. It doesn't work. He rolls over, the covers settling down around his waist.

'G'bye Mona,' he yawns. 'Take care.'

'Goodbye, Samuel.' I can hear the cheeky smile in her

voice. A lump settles in my throat.

I follow her out of the bedroom and into the hall. A lit candle sits on one of the many decorative end tables littering the mayor's house. Stranger sits obediently beside it, tail sweeping from side to side on the busy floral rug.

'It's raining,' Mona whispers, taking up the candle and patting her leg for Stranger to follow us. 'You don't have to come all the way out to the road.'

'Yes, I do,' I say, voice soft but firm. I don't want to wake anyone up. The mayor's house is also home to Jane and a number of Stranger families while they wait for their new homes to be built. As soon as they're done, and the improvements on our own little house are made, the enormous house will be remade into a school.

We hear giggles behind Jane's door. Mona and I glance at each other and grin as we move past. Roslyn and Samuel were among the first couples to part when the council decided that all unwanted marriages could be dissolved, though they've remained close friends. Roslyn can now be found, more often than not, in Jane's company. And now, it seems, in Jane's bedroom.

I couldn't be happier for them.

Mona takes my elbow and helps me down the stairs, then fetches my boots. I sit on the bottom step and pull them over my bed socks. 'Will your leg be all right in the rain?' she asks.

'It'll be fine,' I say. 'Stop fussing.'

'Never.'

My leg hasn't improved in the eight months since I woke

up from the woods, though I've become much more adept with the stick. The doctor – Thomas, now that we spend so much time together in council meetings – thinks it'll never be able to bear my weight again.

I wave Mona away and use the stick and the stair railing to get myself standing again.

The smell of wet cobblestones and chamomile fill the air as Mona opens the door. When Mama and I first moved into the house, I asked some of the labourers to help me rip out the mayor's cloying carnations. The next day, I woke to them replanting the garden beds with herb seeds and bluebell bulbs under the guidance of Samuel. Sleeves rolled up and dirt covering his trousers, he just nodded at me and kept working.

It was another week before he asked me to eat lunch with him behind the town hall, where he serves as our new voice of the Lord. His sermons are much easier to listen to than his father's. Although Deference is optional again, the seats are filled every Sunday. During the week, he invites anyone who feels lonely or unhappy to speak with him confidentially. His idea.

It wasn't hard to forgive him, in the end.

'Wait,' I say as Stranger races out into the drizzle. 'I have something for you.'

Mona raises an eyebrow. 'Is it money? Because I accept.'

I laugh and nod to a long object wrapped in green cloth on another end table. She picks it up, weighing it. 'It doesn't feel like money.'

'It's better than money,' I promise.

She pulls the cloth away to reveal the iron poker from one

of the mayor's fireplaces. It's more ornate than mine, which one of the woodsmen retrieved for me, but still curves to a wicked point.

'To keep you safe,' I say, choking up. 'It works on people just as well as monsters, if you swing hard enough.'

Mona pulls me close, wrapping her arms around me so tight I can barely breathe. But I don't care. I return it twice as hard.

'Do you have to go?' I ask, even though I'd promised myself I wouldn't. 'Things are different now, aren't they?'

'Emma, please.'

'I'm sorry. But they are. You don't have to leave to be a real person.'

'I know.' She pulls back, her eyes wet. 'Things *have* changed. I can leave and know you'll be fine. Better than fine. But I still want to see the world. I want to see a city, and that spindly tower, and whatever else is out there. I still want to meet new people and find something to do with my life.'

I nod, sniffing.

She wipes a tear from my cheek. 'Emma, you know this isn't goodbye forever. You've given me somewhere to come home to.'

'Write to me,' I insist, forcing a smile. 'Send letters with the traders. Tell me everything.'

'I will.'

'Promise me.'

'I promise. I'll draw terrible pictures and everything.' She looks out into the rain, taking a deep breath. 'Ready?'

'Ready,' I lie.

The sky is lightening to a deep, steely grey. We pass a shape sleeping under the awning of the inn – formerly the penitence building, formerly the pub. We ignore him, knowing full well Jones would never accept our help anyway. He'll be awake soon and start preaching at and damning whoever walks too close. But nobody listens. Jones may as well be invisible to everyone but Samuel, who only sits with him long enough to give him food.

We walk against the wind with our hoods up and heads bowed. There's so much I want to say to her: how much her friendship means to me, how much I'll miss her, how happy I am that she's doing this for herself, how afraid I am that she'll never come back. But all I can do is find her hand and hold on tightly as we walk, tears mingling with raindrops.

Aaron the spice trader waits on the road with his horse and wagon. Papa Stone stands beside him, arms folded. 'It's in good condition,' he allows, nodding at the wagon. Aaron raises his eyes to the sky. 'You should make it to the nearest town in one piece.'

'How far is that?' I ask curiously, making a note to ask one of the traders to talk me through it sometime soon. We've been too isolated for too long.

'We'll be there by mid-afternoon, if we make good time.' Aaron says.

'Which direction is it?'

'North.'

'Left, Emma,' Mona says with a smile. 'You see? I'll be fine.'

I nod, swallowing hard. Aaron climbs onto the wagon as Papa Stone embraces Mona. I don't eavesdrop as they say their goodbyes. He steps back, giving Stranger's head a scratch before folding his arms again.

Mona flies into my arms. We're both getting drenched, but neither of us care.

'I love you,' I say through the dripping mess of her hair.

'I love you too, Mayor Emma.'

She pulls away reluctantly, and through her tears I can see a brightness in her eyes that wasn't there before. She's finally taking the road, past the horizon and onwards. Who am I to try and stop her?

I step back as she climbs onto the wagon and pats the seat beside her. Stranger bounds up and snuggles close, licking Mona's cheek. With a nod of goodbye, Aaron snaps the reins. Mona turns back once to wave and blow a kiss. Then she looks ahead. Papa Stone and I watch silently as they disappear past the farms, where the road meets the trees.

Papa Stone offers me his elbow, and together we walk back to the village.

'Do you have time to talk through some of the expansion plans before the council meeting?' he asks, breaking the soft quiet of the morning. 'I have some thoughts I'd like to run past you before we take it to the others.'

'Stone, I'm still in my nightdress,' I point out.

'True,' he concedes.

Somewhere in the distance, the roosters begin to crow.

'Give me ten minutes to change,' I laugh, shaking my

head. 'We can talk over breakfast.'

Something lands on my shoulder, little legs scratching at my cloak. I catch the soft, pulsing glow out the corner of my eye. A firefly.

I flick it away without a second thought.

A Special Note

One of the things I was looking forward to most about publishing my first novel was sharing it with my parents. I've never been good at saying 'I love you' or 'thank you,' but in our family of bookworms a book seemed like the next best thing. Unfortunately, my dad passed away a few weeks before it could happen.

Dad was a born storyteller, poetry lover and proud Welshman. His was the kind of voice you couldn't help listening to, and his stories of his youth in Wales and travelling the world in the Merchant Navy were exciting, compelling, funny, and usually inappropriate.

Although Dad didn't always understand why I would choose to go into a profession with no job security, barely any money and no real career progression, he was always behind me 100%. He rejoiced in my every achievement – however small – and commiserated my every defeat. I'd often come home to find stacks of newspapers saved for me with tiny articles on local writers making good or writing classes. Anything he thought might cheer me on. He was thrilled when I started writing this book, and his face would light up whenever I updated him on my progress. Here, at the very last stop, it feels like something's missing.

Dad was a kind and loving man, a passionate man, and a man of deep principle. We didn't always see eye to eye, but I hope I can be half the person he was and, more importantly, half the storyteller.

I love you, Dad.

Ceinwen Langley, May 2014

Acknowledgements

Mum, there aren't enough thank you's in the world to cover all the love and support you've shown me on this long, bumpy, occasionally unemployed road of a writing career. You've always been my biggest cheerleader, and I couldn't have done any of this without you. I love you.

Jack, my best writing buddy, thanks for keeping me company.

A big thanks to Caroline at Bubblecow for being a wonderfully encouraging editor and for patiently dealing with all of my Superfluous Capital.

Amy and Mindy, thank you for reading this book in advance and giving me such lovely (and useful!) feedback. Ames, we've come a long way since Harry Potter. Well… we're older, anyway.

To Carly, for putting up with my constant (and unasked for) word counts and updates, for politely listening to me babble about story issues and characters, and for the final proofread. I owe you a beer. Or five. Let's say six; I think I still owe you for that one I knocked all over your bag. Thank you for putting up with me.

To all of my amazing support network: my brothers and

their families, the No Scrubs Book Club, friends and mentors who've stuck with me from high school, university, Neighbours, my day jobs, my travels and online, thank you for everything. There are too many of you to name individually, and that in itself is beyond humbling.

And finally, thanks to you. Whether you're one of the above, or someone I've never met, thank you for spending a little of your time and money on me.

About The Author

Ceinwen Langley is an Australian television scriptwriter, game writer and author. She lives in Perth, Western Australia with her partner, her puppy and very reasonable number of plants.

When she's not chasing a deadline, she can usually be found in her garden, or curled up on the couch with a book, a television series she's already seen eight times in its entirety, a cross stitch project, or a video game.

You can find her on twitter and Instagram @feedthewriter or keep up with her latest releases and projects at www.ceinwenlangley.com.

Printed in the USA
CPSIA information can be obtained
at www.ICGtesting.com
LVHW092255140724
785501LV00021B/358